Breath

Breath

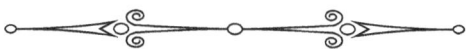

Jackson Creed

White Cat Publications

Published by White Cat Publications, LLC.
2750 Oakwood Blvd.
Melvindale, MI 48122
www.whitecatpublications.com

For Benzaiten Umi, my constant reader.

Acknowledgements

I would like to thank Rani Graff and Lavie Tidhar for Tel Aviv, Sylvia for the return to Istanbul, Gabriela Epuras for Bucharest, and life itself for Paris and other places.

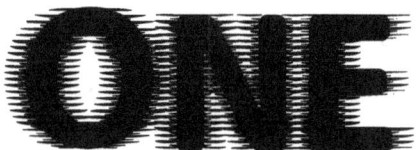

ONE

"... its mother is unclean by reason of the birth, for it is a child but it has wings."

—Babylonian Talmud on Tractate Nidda 24b

Breath

The child reached up and grasped three of his fingers; it was all that her tiny hand could encompass. She looked up at him, the long dark hair falling around her face echoing the color of her eyes, and in those eyes, there was trust. No, not trust, but something else…

"Come with me," she said.

Avram looked down, first at her tiny pale hand and then beyond her to the wide set of sand-colored stone steps that spiralled into the depths of the deep circular stone chamber. It was cold, the pale stone blocks all around them seeming to breathe their chillness into the air. Below, he knew, there was little more than a circular space, a flat stone floor. There was nothing down there. It has been empty for years, as far as he knew. The smooth, shiny steps bore the marks of many treads, worn into shallow depressions towards their centers over the centuries.

"I can't come with you, child," he said.

"Please. I cannot go there alone. I need you to come." Her voice was imploring. Something about her accent …

Avram glanced back over his shoulder. Outside, the dirigible lay tethered, awaiting their departure, the next stop on the grand tour, arc lights illuminating its grey, leathery skin, the others all there, still waiting, indulging him in his request for one final diversion. They would be growing impatient, eager to be off. He pictured them leaning forward at the viewing ports, wondering where he was.

Avram crouched before the child, putting his face level with hers.

"What is it you want?" he said. "I really don't know how I can help you."

He didn't need this complication. He'd simply desired one last look at this place before they took off. There was something about the history, about the weight of ages that hovered in suspension in the atmosphere within that attracted him. He cleared his throat, the sound echoing in the spaces of the domed roof above, eager to be on.

"Where are your parents, young lady?"

1

"I have to find them. Please. Come with me. They went down there. I need to find them. I'm afraid."

As he straightened she kept her grip firmly on his fingers, her gaze fixed on his face.

"What's your name, child?"

"Lilith. Please come." Her voice was imploring now, and she tugged at his fingers.

Avram sighed. "All right. But not for very long. You understand?"

The child turned, dragging his arm forward in her eagerness. She had on a dark dress, patterned with flowers, a broad white collar at the neck. White stockings and dark brown shoes completed the ensemble. There was something not quite right about the style, as if it were a little anachronistic, but perhaps it was just a local thing. Avram took a couple of hesitant steps after her and then matched her pace, taking one broad step after another. He was a little nervous about heights, and there was no railing at the edge of the spiral stairs, but he didn't have much time to think about this as the child hurried him downwards.

He cleared his throat again. "Where are they?" he asked, looking down at her. Hanging from her neck, on a simply woven, dark string lay some sort of amulet or pendant. He wasn't quite sure how he should refer to it. Small, set with a round stone that alternatively reflected the light with flashes of violet and green, it swung back and forth as she took each step. The clothes, the necklace, the condition of her hair, all meant that she didn't look anything like one of the street kids that habitually frequented these parts, hands outstretched, tugging at the hems of your clothing and pointing towards their mouths. No, this child was different. He was more inclined to trust what this little girl was saying, and he was normally a pretty good judge, or at least he thought so.

"What's that around your neck, Lilith?" he asked.

"A stone."

"Ah," he said. A wealth of information there.

They had made one and a half circuits of the inverted tower by now, and he risked the edge to peer down towards the bottom. Nothing; the place still seemed empty. Why didn't the child call out? Was he imagining it, or was the air somewhat cooler? They were further down, close to the base now, so the drop in temperature made sense. Still, he could see no evidence of anyone else in the place.

"Where are they?" asked Avram, again, starting to frown.

The child stopped her descent, still keeping her grasp on his fingers and pointed. He'd not noticed it in his previous visits, but across the other side of the circular chamber sat a small dark archway. Even the lighting in the place appeared not to reach into its blackness. His frown grew. He should have noticed that. How could he have missed it on his previous visit?

The child continued her downward path, dragging him forward by the fingers, forestalling any other thought about what he should or should not have noticed. He was becoming more and more conscious of the time, of his companions above.

They reached the end of the slowly winding staircase and stepped out onto the floor. Large slabs of smooth gray stone, the surface made irregular over time, stretched from end to end of the chamber, featureless, apart from the occasional pocked indentation in the stone surfaces. No furnishing, nothing built into the stonework to give any real indication of the original purpose of the place. Down here, high up on the wall, dark metal rings hung from thick iron pegs, brown-black with age, driven directly into the stone. What had hung from them? Chains? Something else? He had no idea, even dreaded to think. He conjured desiccated corpses, skeletal remains.

"Hello?" he called.

There was no response, nothing more than his own voice echoing distorted from the chamber walls. He looked around the empty space and then back over at the small darkened archway that seemed to swallow all light. Again, he cleared his throat, the noise sounding unnaturally loud in the confined space.

The child drew him to the chamber's center.

"Please help me," she said.

"What?" he said looking down at her face. "I am helping you."

"No," said the girl. "Please take this off." She indicated the small pendant around her neck.

"I don't understand. Can't you do it?"

"I'm not allowed. I cannot wear it in there." She gestured at the darkened hole that sucked away the illumination.

Avram shook his head and reached for the necklace. This child was certainly becoming more and more strange. He sighed. Whatever he had to do to get this over with now. He didn't want to offend the child. It was as if the weight of ages contained in the chamber stilled any protest. He lifted the thin cord past her hair and over her head, letting the tiny stone dangle between his outstretched hands.

"Haaaah," the child said with a gentle exhalation of breath.

And in the next instant she was gone.

"What?" he said. He shook his head. She wasn't there anymore. The child had simply vanished. Letting the necklace dangle from one fist. "What the hell …?" He looked round the chamber, but there was no sign of her. He crouched down and tried to peer through the impenetrable blackness beyond the small archway.

There was movement, a stirring of the air as if a light wind moved across the chamber floor. It was cold. Involuntarily, he shivered.

Something touched his shoulder, small fingers in his hair. Something was at his neck, a vague pressure. The necklace dropped from his grasp and the pendant hit the floor with the high click of stone on stone. He tried to stand upright, but suddenly, it was impossible. He was fixed, incapable of movement.

And then came pain, sweet and sharp and then dull, coursing

Breath

through him. His neck, his throat, and then something, and yet nothing. Without really comprehending it, Avram stepped into another place.

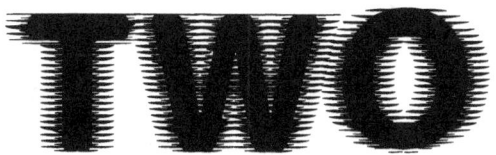

Six things are said respecting demons: In three ways they are like angels, and in three they resemble men. They have wings like angels, and like angels they fly from one end of the world to the other, and they know the future as angels do.

—The Talmud

Breath

Avram found himself crouching in the empty chamber. "Found himself" was a good description, for he seemed to have little recollection of what he had been doing mere moments before. He knew he had been … what? Absent-mindedly, he scraped up the stone pendant from the floor in front of him and pushed it into his pocket as he got to his feet. Right now, his confusion was taking precedence. He'd been here too long; he knew that, but he had no idea why. Outside this deep echoing space, a city moved and breathed its exhalations into the heavy night air. Outside, somewhere, his companions waited.

He rubbed his neck and grimaced. He was not going to be popular at all. He walked across to the bottom step and started the long climb back up to the surface, taking the stairs carefully, one by one, his head bowed, lost in thoughts of nothingness. Still he had no understanding of the brief lapse he had experienced. He hoped that it was not the sign of something gravely wrong. So lost in his thoughts was he, that he even forgot to be fearful of the unprotected drop lying open to his right as he ascended. He reached the vast metal door, dark, slightly dented and dully shining with the reflected arc lights of the landing space. Their brightness cut starkly delineated shadows across the courtyard, stretching palms and building tops over the stone paved flatness, the outline of a single streetlamp stretching like an accusing finger at the doorway. You, Avram Davis, are late.

He sighed and then looked up towards their vast conveyance, a bloated sack against the dark night sky. There'd be hell to pay as soon as he climbed the gantry and entered the gondola, shining white in the strong lights and then made his way into the passenger quarters proper. He paused, despite his lateness, thinking about his fellow passengers, his companions on their grand adventure. They had all the time in the world, really, all of them, and there was no reason for them to begrudge him a few extra minutes to absorb the sights and sensations that were so much a reason for them all being here. All the time in the world, except perhaps for the children. But, this expedition, this adventure was such a thing for a formative mind, he thought. How could you deny an experience such as this? Samantha and Alfred Green would be benefitting from this rich tapestry for years to come, regardless of the time taken from schooling. This was education in and of itself.

Avram's reason for being here was something else. The divorce, the acrimony, the angst and pain were all things that he wanted to get away from, excise from his mind. To absorb himself in the experiences, the sights and the sensations, the differences, was like a tonic. The different chased away the day to day, and that was definitely what he needed. Not sage advice from a medic nor headshrinker, the need had come from within, and deep within his bones, he knew it was right. He simply needed to forget what he had been through in the last few months.

A gentle breeze stirred across the wide, paved courtyard like a warm breath, almost a sigh on its own, echoing his feelings. Forget. That was the word, and yet...he didn't want spaces in his memories, voids filled with darkness that were impossible to touch. That particular thought stirred something within him, as if there was something that he was already missing, a gap, a well of unknowing. He frowned and shook it from him. He had to get inside.

Captain Prinsloo was standing at the top of the gantry, leaning a little forward, his slightly battered white uniform standing out clearly against the dark gray bulk of the ship above him. It was hard to tell from down here, but it looked as if he might be scowling, but at this distance, his face, the mane of steel gray hair and the moustache, made the expression unreadable. Avram shook his head once more and took the first step up to the gangplank, the metal echoing across the courtyard. Before he had reached the top, Prinsloo had already disappeared inside. The Captain was, after all, a man of few words at the best of times, and he supposed this was not one of those.

As he crossed the small walkway, ducking a little for stability—it was the whole heights thing again—Selena's head popped out from the oval entry port.

"Avram, where have you been?" She was clearly annoyed. Avram lowered his head and looked at his feet. "Well, you know ...." he said.

"No I don't know. I never quite know with you. Well, you are here now. Come on. You had better come inside. They are waiting for you. We all are waiting for you, Avram. We were wondering if you had become lost."

She moved back inside the gondola to allow him to pass. Selena Green, wife of Max and solid, blonde, organized to the point of intimidation—he should have expected that she would be the one to stand in ambush to admonish him. He met her green eyes as he ducked inside.

"Well I'm here now, aren't I?"

"Yes, I suppose you are," she said and crossed her arms.

If there was anyone aboard this voyage that Avram had a little bit of a problem with, it was Selena. Her husband, Max, a tall thin rangy sort of man, was far more easy going, but then Selena more than made up for it and her demeanour of overall efficiency was only compounded by her slight accent.

"Where are the others?" Avram asked. He already thought that he knew the answer, but the question was a way of forestalling any more scoldings from her ladyship.

"They are up in the Observation Lounge, of course. They are waiting for us to depart, so we can all get the view of the city at night."

"Yes, of course," he said.

The dirigible's gondola served mainly as an entry and loading area. Fixed to the sides were half a dozen simple, and frankly not very comfortable, bench seats with smaller windows set above them. The Observation Lounge, with its wide open space and the grand windows, almost floor to ceiling and angled slightly to give a downward-looking view, was far more practical, not to mention agreeable for viewing their progress or just generally sitting and relaxing over a drink or two when they were either in transit, or when they were moored and had had enough of the exploratory ventures into whatever city they might be visiting at the time.

Selena was still standing there, her arms folded, fixing him with a level gaze.

"Well?" she said.

Avram shook himself. "Yes, yes." He didn't know what came over him, but he felt like he was moving through some sort of ethereal, invisible soup. His thoughts were slow, disconnected. "I'm going, okay?" he said.

To get to the Observation Lounge, he had to mount two separate circular staircases inside the craft's main body. The lowest deck was simply utilitarian. There was machinery of various forms, the pilot's area and storage. The middle level contained the Observation Lounge, dining area, kitchen, and above, connected by yet another spiral, lay their quarters. Individual and double cabins, narrow, cramped, but perfectly sufficient for their needs during the months long voyage they were undertaking. No different from being at sea really. The walls were sufficiently insulated and the noise of the rotors when they were en route afforded a good level of privacy between accommodations as well.

As he mounted the stairs, the thrumming of the engines vibrated through the ship, felt through his feet and as a sensation, just below true perception. They were about to get underway, it seemed. He could feel as well as hear Selena climbing the stairs behind him, as if guarding against any last minute escape he might contemplate. Below them drifted up the noise of the other single other crewman, apart from the cook and general hand who prepared their meals, as he sealed tight the doorways to the gondola.

At the top of the staircase, Avram turned and walked down the carpeted corridor, heading for the Observation Lounge, Selena following close behind. The deep thrum was intensifying, forming a strange harmony with the latent buzzing sitting annoyingly in the back of his head. He clenched his teeth against the sensation and wandered distractedly into the windowed space.

"Yes, about time!" said Max, his long lanky frame, draped on one of the four couches that sat strategically placed around the room. His clear blue eyes fixed Avram with disapproval and narrowed slightly before he looked away.

"Okay, yes I'm sorry," Avram muttered almost below his breath, his jaw still tight against the feeling in his head.

The children, Max and Selena's offspring, were up against the viewing ports, their faces pressed against the glass, hands on either side, palms flat watching Avram knew not what. The preparations for departure, people below? In any case, they'd be fully absorbed for the next while caught up in the excitement of the freeing of tethers, the drift and slow climb from the city into the night sky. Normally, he'd share their enthusiasm, but in his current state, he just couldn't summon the interest. The rest of their travelling party had arranged themselves in various positions around the area, the Bartkos with drinks in hand staring through a nearby port, seemingly lost in their own thoughts, Marcus Wall, tall, prematurely gray and severely good looking sitting close to his partner Joseph on individual chairs rather than a couch, currently heads together in some private conversation.

Joseph glanced over at Avram and for almost an instant, he thought there was something in the look, something...but no. As soon as he had noticed it, Joseph had looked away, turning back to his conversation with Marcus. Normally, when he looked at this little group, Avram felt warmth, a sense of well-being. They were, after all, his extended family, his little group of close companions who understood him, understood the things that made Avram Davis tick, but now, looking around, he felt detached, somehow removed from them. And god knows, he was a little bit the odd man out here, the only one without a partner, the solitary voyager, not only on this trip, but right now, in life itself. The separation and eventual divorce had seen to that.

"We are about to depart," came Prinsloo's voice over the intercom, cutting short Avram's impending bout of self-pity.

"Ladies and gentleman, will you please take your seats."

From experience, Avram knew the kids would likely ignore the request and Selena and Max in the Green's usual inimitable style would say absolutely nothing to alter it. As the gentle thrumming of the deck increased in pitch, he rapidly decided to take his place on one of the unoccupied couches and turned to watch with the others as the ship began to move. Gradually, the vast vehicle started its gentle drift upwards, the movement almost imperceptible at first, and then becoming more noticeable, bringing with it a slight feeling of instability and vertigo, an awareness in his body that something was not quite as it should be. The ground beneath one's feet was not supposed to move, so, even though consciously, he knew what was happening, the primal part of him felt a vague unease and coupled with the already present feeling of something already awry within himself, it made Avram feel even more uncomfortable. It was as if the bottom of his stomach had deserted him entirely. He glanced around the others, nervously checking if they may have noticed his discomfort, but everyone's attention was on the outside, the gradual shifting of the lights and shadows. Selena had reached for Max's hand and was holding it in front of them; the children were still pressed up against the glass.

Pavel Bartko had placed down his drink and sat with his hands steepled beneath his narrow face, observing with a detached scientific curiosity, while his wife, Aggie peered out through her thick glasses, a rapt expression on her face. The other two, Marcus and Joe had barely shifted from their former position, except now they were silent. Avram gave a little sigh and returned his attention to his hands, realizing that though he was sharing this grand experience with all of them, really, if he thought about it, he was sharing it with no one but himself. There was no one's hand to reach out and hold; there was no one he could turn to and give a gentle smile to. All that had gone with the memories of the life that he was trying to escape. He bit his lower lip and let out a long breath. Maybe that would change again, but not just yet. He shook his head and looked back out to the city, darkness and light drifting slowly away beneath them. No use becoming even more maudlin; that was not what this was all about. Time to look forward and not back at what had driven him here. In itself, that was the wrong way to think about it too: he had always wanted to embark on something like this, something that would take him out of himself and stretch his boundaries. Well, time was certainly doing that.

Their ship drifted higher, and gradually, the insistent throbbing him, the sound of the rotors steadied, becoming even, present and there, but less insistent to his conscious perception, the ship's forward motion becoming more apparent.

"We are now underway, ladies and gentlemen." Prinsloo's voice over the intercom. "Please feel free to leave your places and move about. So far, forecasts are predicting smooth passage. The weather is fine. No storm activity. We should be clearing the coastline in about ten minutes."

"Ah, that is good," said Max, standing and giving a theatrical stretch of his long body. "Come, Selena. Let us wave bye-bye to this little town." So saying, he reached again for her hand, guiding her to another of the floor to ceiling windows and positioning her beside him and then taking up his characteristic stance, his hands clasped behind his back as he watched the retreating city lights.

Aggie also stood, readjusted her glasses, looked down at her hand and noticed her drink was empty.

"Pavel?" she said, tilting her glass towards him in query.

"What? Oh yes," he said, dragging his attention from the outside view.

"What about you?" she said to Avram, turning his way.

"Um, no thank you. I'm fine."

She shrugged and headed for the bar.

A moment later, Joseph Munine wandered over to sit next to Avram on the couch and placed a companionable hand on Avram's thigh. Joe and Marcus where such a contrast to each other, Marcus with his tall, distinguished good looks, Joe with his more compact body, his dark skin and even darker hair, his rounded face.

"What is it, my dear?" he said. "Marcus and I are worried about you."

Avram glanced over to the chair where Marcus still sat, watching and then shook his head and returned Joe's concerned look with a steady gaze.

"No, I'm fine," he said. "What makes you think there's anything wrong?"

"We've been watching you," said Joe. "Ever since you came on board, you look like you're sitting in a daze. Can't say you look very happy."

Avram gave a slight grimace. "No, no, I'm fine. Just thoughts I suppose. You know."

"If you're sure."

"It's okay. Just being a little self-indulgent."

Joe fixed him with a probing look for a second or two, looking from one eye to the other, then nodded and gave the top of his thighs a little pat.

"Okay, then. But you know where we are if you want to talk." He stood up, and still watching Avram, waited for a moment. "It's not as if we're going anywhere." He gave a little laugh and tossed his head back, then looked over towards the windows. "Well, not anywhere that we are not going together." He turned back to Avram with a gentle smile. "Anyway ..." he said.

"Joe, it's okay. Really …"

"All right then," he said, and then turned and wandered back to where Marcus sat. He retook his seat and they spoke low words together. Joe shook his head and gave a little shrug. Marcus turned briefly to look over at where Avram sat and then turned away.

Just at that moment Samantha gave a scream and clutched the top of her arm.

"He hit me!" she cried. She lashed out with one hand, missing with her slap as Alfred ducked away. The next minute he was racing around the room's perimeter with his sister in pursuit.

"Children," said Max sternly.

"But he hit me," whined the girl, doing nothing to halt her chase.

Selena merely looked over her shoulder and then turned back to face the view. "You deal with them, Max," she said.

Children. Save him from children.

Avram stood. That was quite enough. "I'm going to my cabin for a while," he announced to the room at large. "I'm feeling a little tired. It's been a long day, people."

THREE

"... when the Silver and Bronze ages brought greed and slaughter among them, she exclaimed: "Alas, for this evil race!" and mounted into Heaven."

−The Sons of God and the Daughters of Men

Breath

Perhaps, he thought, he was just merely tired. It had been a long day wandering around the city in the heat, the peculiar scents, the babble of local languages. At least it had been a dry heat. The city, in that Middle Eastern sort of way, was a mélange of faces, oddments and trappings and remnants of history, collected and accumulated throughout the ages and years. All so very different from anything back home. He lay back on his bunk, leaned his head against the wall, feeling the rotor's thrum throbbing slightly through the back of his skull, his ankles crossed, not even having bothered to take off his shoes. Amelia would have castigated him for that if she were still around, but if she had been, then Avram wouldn't have been here for her to admonish him anyway. Ironic in a way.

The cabin was warm. Tethered immobile during the heat of the day, the ship had absorbed enough sun through its thick leathery outer skin to increase the temperature throughout, and Avram was grateful for the small luxuries that came with the accommodations. As he lay there, he pushed his hands into his pockets, staring up at the ceiling and the slowly rotating fan blades above. He'd made the right choice being here, he thought. It took a sizeable chunk from his savings, but it was worth it. At least he could go through his catharsis in comfort, with friends, escape the surroundings of his new and functional apartment with the cheap, hastily-purchased furniture, and full of other reminders that he and Amelia were no longer together. The memories were the things that were not there, things that he would turn around and suddenly miss, bits and pieces that they had accumulated during their married existence, but now lived on with Amelia in his old home and everything that went with it as a part of the divorce settlement.   I t was like that old saying: you don't know what you've lost 'til it's gone. And back home, every time he turned around, there would be something else that wasn't there, just like his erstwhile partner. He would get over that as well, he supposed, in time. He took a deep slow breath and let it out slowly through his nose, closing his eyes.

As he lay there, the random thoughts drifting through his head, considering whether he should doze or not, he flexed his hands within his pockets and stopped. The fingers of his right hand touched something cold and hard shoved down in the depths. He frowned, grasped the object and pulled it out to look, holding it arm's length, bringing his hand in front of his face to see properly. Now what the hell was this? It was a small amulet, suspended on a cord. He frowned up at it. Where exactly had he acquired it and more to the point, why? He had no recollection of buying the thing. For the life of him, he couldn't remember visiting any souvenir stall or such similar and realistically, it was not the sort of thing that he would normally be drawn to anyway. He hated tourist tat.

He looped the simply woven, dark string around two of his fingers, allowing the small pendant to dangle, and rock back and forth. With the fingers of his other hand, he tapped at the setting, making the object pendulum even more. The round stone reflected the light with flashes of violet and green as it moved. He frowned at it and tapped at it again, and with that touch, as the skin at the end of his finger came into contact, noticed a buzz, or a hum, or something that seemed to travel through his hand, up his arm, to flower inside his head. Just as quickly, it was gone. Again, he frowned. The first time he had touched the stone, it had been with his nail, and there was nothing. Now, he tried again with the tip of his finger. Once more, the sensation, the taste of electricity, something else, something other, almost like a numbness that flowed through his arm. He withdrew his hand, swung his feet off the bunk and sat up, cupping the object in his palms. Above him, the fan blade stirred the air, slowly turning. It was hard to tell if the ship's vibration was making him imagine things. He lifted the pendant and placed it beside him, looking down at it. Now that it was no longer within his grasp, the strange thickness he was feeling inside his head seemed to lessen. Still, he could not remember how the thing had come into his possession. It didn't look new, that much was sure; the simple dark woven cord looked abraded in places, as if someone had worn it for long periods of time. Perhaps one of his companions had given it to him to look after, He did not recall having seen it around the neck of any of his fellow passengers, and really, it didn't look like the sort of thing any of them might wear, well, maybe Aggie, but then, not really.

She had a touch of the Bohemian about her, surely, but this looked more local, something completely at home in the Middle East and therefore more likely to come from the city they had just left. What about the Green's girl, Samantha? No, it didn't look like her sort of thing really either. She was more inclined to the new and shiny.

Avram reached up and scratched his head, narrowing his eyes. There was something definitely awry with his thought processes at the moment. He ran his fingers through his hair and then stood. He felt like pacing, but there was hardly room in the cabin to walk back and forth. He compromised and took the couple of steps to the solitary armchair placed at one corner, beside it a small table, and sat. The last thing he wanted was to have picked up some sort of bug in their last port of call. That would not do at all. He closed his eyes again. He couldn't afford to get sick. That just wouldn't be fair.

"Haaaaah ..." A whisper. A breath. A barely noticeable voice and a stir of the cabin's air that was more than the fan, like a gust of wind.

Avram's opened his eyes. There had been a sound; he was sure of it. He looked around the cabin, but there was no one else here, could not be anyone else there. Had he imagined it? He linked his fingers behind his neck, grimacing and gave his head a little shake. So, now he was conjuring things that could not possibly be there as well. He let out a breath of his own, deep with frustration, almost a growl.

"Stop it," he said, and closed his eyes.

"Haaaaah ..."

It felt close, nearly up against his cheek and his eyes shot open. There was nothing there. Nothing.

He stood. Something was definitely not right. Now, whether it was his own imagination, or something in the cabin, it didn't matter. He was alone here.

Imagination. It had to be imagination. He was tired. And yet ...

He lowered his frame heavily back into the chair, running through the events of the day. Had he eaten something, or had something to drink? He knew you had to be careful on some of these visits. The snapshot images of their stopover came haltingly. He remembered them leaving the ship, their second day here, wandering round the Arabic quarter of the city. At first they had ventured out as a group, but gradually, they had broken off, pursuing their own interests and going their own ways. Max and Selena had wanted to shop, dragging the kids along with them. It was something that Avram had no interest in at all. For a while, he had wandered around with Marcus and Joe, drinking in the sights, the remnants of history intertwined with the modern day, stone streets winding between pale-stone cluttered buildings and narrow alleyways. Aggie and Pavel had already left the group early, heading off to visit a succession of museums and art galleries as they always did in each port of call.

Later in the day, as the fierce sun had moved lower, taking the edge off the heat, Avram decided he wanted merely to wander on his own. Marcus and Joe were more content to seek out the local bar scene, the stirrings of evening life to watch the locals and do whatever they did. Joe loved it. He was an artist, a painter, and his favorite subjects were human faces. In a place like that, he had more than enough inspiration and he always carried a small sketch book with him to that end. Marcus, the more taciturn of the pair, was something to do with publishing, but Avram had never been quite sure what, whether it was editorial, marketing, or something else. All he really knew was that it was something to do with books. Avram had presumed always that the quiet reserve would ill fit Marcus for a role in the marketing side of things, so it would be something to do with the production. They made a fine couple, really, and they had, to Avram, always seemed perfectly happy together. He was quite happy to let them disappear off to troll the bars and cafes of the Old Town and head out on his own to explore the ancient buildings and majesty of history through the various ages that was characteristic of the region. Everyone throughout history had been there, visited, set up residence or faded into the past. That sort of legacy always left something behind, he was sure of it. You could feel it within the old stonework, the worn-smooth staircases, echoes of the lives and deaths that had passed there. All of them imbued the place with an aura, some sort of remnant of what had gone on before. Places such as this were more than simply places; they were ethereal repositories of the lives and events that had passed. It was like walking into an old cathedral; you could literally feel the weight of the years pressing down upon you, urging you to silence. You could almost reach out and touch the ghosts of people past in such a place and he loved it.

He could remember doing all the requisite tourist visits listed in the various guides: the African Synagogue, the Great Mosque, the Church of the Ancient, all of the named places, though he would hardly attempt to try getting his tongue around the local names or pronunciations. But then there were the other stops, the unexpected, old buildings or monuments that didn't appear in any particular guidebook. Most of all though, there was the Old Town, in and of itself, steeped in that special atmosphere that he had come to expect from these particular cities. More than simply the heady spice scents and the babble of unfamiliar language—and within the Old Town boundaries there were several—it was what you breathed and walked through, that seeped through your pores and into you like some sort of mystical osmosis. This is what Avram truly loved.

He remembered coming upon the elevated square resting by the old stone harbour that had been used for centuries, the wide hill of steps that led up to the open expanse. Then there had been some sort of building, an empty place, if he recalled, but there was something about it, something special, and he couldn't quite put his finger on it. There had been a small cafe underneath the Moorish arches of an old building near the square, and he had sat there for a while, sipping on a tiny coffee accompanied by an indulgent local pastry, dusted with sugar and overly sweet. He remembered just idling there for a while, watching the passers-by, simply absorbing. And after that ...? After that, he had stumbled upon another ancient construction that definitely hadn't appeared in his guidebook, an old stone building, that for some reason, he felt had extended deep below the stone-paved square. He remembered an expanse, depth, hollowness, and his surprise at the fact that there was no write-up of the place anywhere. It was the sort of place that should appear in guidebooks by rights, but, for the life of him, the details were a blur. He had wanted one last look; he remembered that, so he must have been into the building more than once. What was it about it that had drawn him back? If he could actually recall any of the details, he might have a chance at piecing it all together.

Frowning over at the little necklace that lay innocuously on the bunk, he shook his head. He simply did not suffer gaps in his memory. He prided himself on his ability to recall details, places, contextual minutiae, if not necessarily names, but nonetheless, he was starting to think that something was severely awry.

Pushing himself to his feet, he stepped over to look down at the necklace, amulet, or whatever it was, rubbing at the back of his neck. Right, the answer was simple: get rid of the bloody thing.

He reached down to grab it, planning to walk from his cabin and find some means of disposing of it. Right now, it was the only thing that was out of place and he was starting to believe there was some sort of inexplicable link between the object and whatever it was that he was feeling. He knew it made no sense, but it simply had to be. He wasn't the sort to collect trinkets anyway, and it was of no use to him. He supposed he could give it to Selena's daughter Sam, but, as he'd already presumed, it didn't look like the sort of thing she would like anyway. The child was just like her mother in that regard, always attracted to the glossy and modern.

Resolved, he reached down to grasp the amulet. As soon as he touched it, held it in his hand, that sensation of numbness swept up his arm and blanketed his perceptions. He drew in a sudden sharp breath.

"What ...?"

"Haaaaaaah."

There was that sound again, barely heard, the touch of a breeze on a hot summer's day, an eddy of warmth against his face, a gentle exhalation. He closed his fist tightly around the thing in his hand. The string dangled down, rough, frayed in places. The slightest sense of motion came from behind him and he turned. There was nothing there. How could there be anything there? Though his thoughts came slowly, he considered. Perhaps he should tell the others, but then, they'd just think there was something wrong with him.

"Haaaaaah."

He spun around again, looking for the source of the sound. Nothing.

He opened his fist and tossed the amulet back onto the bunk. As soon as it fell out of his grasp, his thoughts began to clear and he glanced around the cabin, taking in a deep shuddering breath. There was something wrong with him; there had to be ....

"Be still," came a voice, a whisper, but there was no sound. The words had come from inside his head, not from the space around him.

"I ...," he spoke out loud, hesitating.

"Be still."

It was whispered, soundless, drifting through his head, but somehow, he knew it was the voice of a child. The words seemed to pacify him, soothe the growing sense of panic he was starting to feel and he let out a long, slow breath, calming himself.

"Good," came the whisper inside his head. "Good."

"But I need to ...," he said, speaking out loud to the empty cabin, looking around at the walls, the ceiling, the half-open door to the tiny attached bathroom, its interior based in darkness.

"Need ..." said the breath made of words. And then: "All is need. Always need. There is nothing else. Always the need."

He shuddered, feeling something else run through his body, a frisson, a chill, the memory of pressure snug against his neck and yet no feeling at all. The fleetest image of a small child, a girl, came and went, there and then not there. Something he should be remembering, but then....

"I cannot ... do ... this. It isn't ...," he said.

"Shhhhh," said the whisper.

Avram shook his head trying to clear it, closing his eyes and then opening them again. He looked down at the bunk, at the small object lying there. With one hand, he reached down and grasped it, ignoring the strange sensation that came with the touch, and with his hand extended, he crossed to where the inbuilt closet formed part of one wall, opened the door with his other hand. Leaning down slightly, he opened one of the drawers, deposited the object in its depths and then closed it again. That done, he sealed the closet door and breathed out, a gentle sigh.

He stood there for a few seconds, not really sure what he was doing.

"Huh," he said to himself.

He crossed back over to the bunk, eased himself down, and reclined, positioning himself comfortably, crossing his hands above his stomach. He lay there, staring up at the ceiling for a few more seconds, and then gently, gently, without bothering to even switch off the light, he closed his eyes, feeling the gentle thrum of the engines urging him to drift away, the brief episode trailing away like so much smoke.

The bone that has fallen to thy lot, whether it be good or evil, gnaw it.

—The Alphabet of Ben Sira

Avram woke to darkness, the sensation of something running across his chest. Perhaps he had dreamed it. He stayed where he was, still, barely breathing, seeing if whatever it was would happen again. The insistent thrum of engine noise cut through the darkness, almost palpable through the black. He knew that it would be many, many more hours until they reached their next destination. Everything was still. It must be quite late. There was a smell, a scent that filled his nostrils like old dust. A stirring in the air moved silently across his cheek, barely noticeable, but there all the same. He blinked his eyes a couple of times, seeing if there was any way he could get them to adjust before reaching for the light. He didn't want to move just yet, didn't want to make a single noise as he strained to listen. But wait, he hadn't turned out the light, had he?

Something tickled feather soft across his chest, tiny trails moving through his chest hair. Despite himself, he sucked in his breath. He was naked. He knew it now. The pressure at his chest became more defined, took shape, became fingers, splayed, drawing a pattern across his skin, then moving back again, retracing their path. He let out his breath, slowly, with a shudder. The hand, for it was a hand, was elegant, slim, and cold, and yet there was a sensation of warmth —cool fingers painting an involuntary reaction from his skin filling him with heat ... No, this could not be right! He lifted his arm to grab the wrist, but found that he couldn't.

"What?" he said. "Stop!"

"Shhhhhh," came a voice of indeterminate age or gender. It was whispered, gentle.

The hand pressed flat against his chest and then slid slowly down across his abdomen, meandering across his flesh with a gentle touch, side to side and then further down, across his navel, then lower.

The hand trailed through his pubic hair, bumped against his burgeoning erection. Fingers grasped his penis.

In spite of himself, he reacted, driven by that autonomic, primal response.

"You can't," he hissed.

"Shhhhh." and her hand began gently stroking it.

"Nooooo."

And then there was the feeling of lips, cool, moist, and a sensation of hardness behind—something sharp.

He moaned involuntarily. He could feel hair against his belly, draped and moving gently back and forth, another hand sliding up to grasp the skin around his left nipple. This couldn't be happening. Already he was hard, so hard it was almost painful, and yet the ministrations went on. He tried to move, to lift his arms, to push whoever it was away, but they seemed glued in place. He was powerless. He drew another shuddering breath, then swallowed against a mouth gone dry. He could feel his body reacting, tightening. The hand that had been playing with his nipple slid down, moving like a snake, tickling as it went, to cup his testicles, tickling the sensitive scrotal skin. Still, he could not move.

"No," he said, biting his lower lip. "No."

And he was somewhere else.

Avram stood in a wide circular chamber in semi-darkness. Large slabs of smooth gray stone, the surface made irregular over time, stretched from end to end of the chamber, featureless, apart from the occasional pocked indentation in the stone. There was nothing built into the stonework apart from irregularly spaced, high up on the wall, dark metal rings hanging from thick iron pegs, brown-black with age, affixed to the wall. Across the other side of the circular chamber sat a small dark archway, the dim light of the space in which they stood unable to penetrate the blackness. And in that moment, he realized he was not alone. In front of him, a woman stood, or rather the shape of a woman drawn in darkness. Her eyes were dark in the midst of the darkness, and in the dim light, he felt them staring into his face with a gaze filled with intensity. He looked at her, frowning, forestalling the urge to ask her who she was and what she was doing here, what they both were doing here. She gave the barest of smiles, the faintest quirk of her lips and reached up with both hands to undo his belt.

"What the hell are you doing?" he said and she laughed, turning her attention to the clasp on his trousers. They fell around his ankles, the belt buckle clattering noisily against the stonework.

He could not move, could not reach forward to push her hands away.

"Oh, God," he whimpered. At those words, she laughed again. This couldn't be happening ... She reached up with both hands and pulled down his undershorts, then took a step back. She smiled at his face and then looked down and smiled again with a gentle nod. He could feel himself becoming erect, but hardly dared to look down at where she had her gaze focused.

"Why are you doing this?" he asked in a whisper.

She looked up into his face again.

"Need," she said. "Nothing more than need." And with that, she lifted one hand and pointed towards the darkened archway, urging him to look, a expression of triumph on her face.

Though he could move none of his limbs, he felt himself turning. Within the darkness, a deep yellow light started to grow, becoming brighter and brighter, spilling out through the archway and beyond, forming a golden path across the ancient stones, becoming stronger and stronger with every instant, turning from deep yellow to pale white, dazzling his sight, making it impossible to see anything, anything but bright brilliance.

"Need," came her voice from all around him.

With an effort of will, Avram forced his eyes shut, giving some relief from the burning intensity pouring from the archway. With another clenched effort, he turned his face away from the source and the light gently faded. He breathed out, breathed in, held his breath and slowly opened his eyes again.

Breath

He was staring up at the slowly turning fan blades, gently stirring the air above him. Through his bunk, came the ever-present vibration of the engines, barely below his consciousness. He turned his head slowly in one direction and then the other. He was in his cabin, lying on his bunk, fully clothed. The lights were on, just as he had left them. He took another shuddering breath, his mouth dry, a sheen of sweat upon his forehead. Through his foggy thoughts, he came to the realization that he had an erection, pushing hard against his trousers. He sat up on the edge of the bunk, leaning over, his elbows on his knees, and his breath coming in short, shallow gasps. His heart pounded and he could hear it in his ears. He swallowed again.

Was it having been steeped in so much history that was befuddling him, an overload of experience, depth, and sensation? He didn't think so. His mouth felt like a desert and he stood and moved into the bathroom to pour a glass of water at the sink. He could taste the tank in the liquid, but right now, that didn't matter. And the dream, he thought as he swallowed greedily and then took another sip to wash around his mouth. He was not like that. He could never be like that. He gave an involuntary shudder. The woman's eyes had been full of knowledge, of something else ... a ... a hunger. That's what it was. Avram felt unclean, tainted, as if the dream had filled his mind with some evil pestilence.

He closed his eyes, breathed slowly in and out for a couple of seconds and then opened them again. A pale face looked out at him from the mirror, eyes deeply shadowed, haggard in the dim light. He looked like crap. He placed the glass down, stepped back into the cabin and looked at his watch in the brighter light. It was already past 9:00. Not that he felt particularly hungry, but it was probably too late to get something to eat. The barely-seen Ronald (Avram had never heard his last name and doubted that anyone had) who prepared their meals would have disappeared back into his quarters by now, off to nurse a solitary bottle. The deeply-tanned, bestubbled crewman with the lank matt of stringy hair and permanently squinting eyes was hardly ever seen by any of the travelling companions, and then only as if by accident. Nobody ever said anything about it, but it was obvious how Ronald spent most of his time. Avram would just have to raid the larder himself, but first he had to push himself into some sort of seeming semblance of humanity.

Giving himself one last look in the mirror, making sure he was presentable and now halfway decent, he took a deep breath and headed out of the cabin, closing the door behind him along with the now-forgotten object that he had tucked away in the back of a drawer. The dark blue carpet with its silver-gray propeller motifs stretched down towards the spiral staircase that would take him to the area where everyone else was probably gathered at this time of the evening. By the time they reached their next destination, they would have to adjust their watches again, but that was one of the things about their leisurely pace from site to site—plenty of opportunity to adjust to the various time zones. Conventional air travel was all well and good, but there were advantages to be had from taking one's time. A grand adventure needed to be conducted at a civilised speed and with the re-launch of the vast airships, the opportunity had presented itself. He'd been swept up in the romance of it, the sense of adventure and it had taken little persuasion for him to sign up.

At the top of the staircase, he wondered whether any of the party had already retired for the evening, but it would be unusual knowing their normal patterns when they had just left port. He climbed down the stairs to the next level, steadying himself with one hand upon the polished wood balustrade, the smell of polish strong in the air. It was funny, but he'd never seen their crewman—what was his name? Federov. That was it. Alexei Federov—engaged in the act of polishing, but yet the smell was always there.

He reached the bottom of the spiral and turned, facing the end of the corridor, passageway, or whatever he was supposed to call it.

Breath

The carpet on this level was deep red, continuing the propeller design from above. There were definitely voices drifting down from the Observation Lounge and he nodded to himself. May as well get on with it. He took a deep steadying breath and then stepped inside. As he walked through the door, they were all there. Max noticed him first.

"Good God, Avram," he said. "Are you okay? You look like hell." At that, all around the room, the others looked up, all attention focussed on his solitary figure in the doorway.

Avram glanced over to one of the tall mirrors set behind the bar seeing his pallid expression looking back at him from hollow eyes.

"Yeah, I'm fine," he said quietly, stepping fully into the room. "Just a little tired, I suppose. It's been a long day."

"Did you sleep?" asked Aggie, pushing up her glasses and peering at him through the thick lenses, pushing some strands of dark red hair out of her way.

"Yes, yes, for a little while," he answered. "Though I had the strangest dreams. I guess it wasn't much of a rest after all." He moved over towards the bar, avoiding the collective gaze. As he did, he glanced over at the children, still up, playing with some cards on the floor over by the corner near one of the observation windows. Samantha looked up at him, caught his gaze and held it. The young girl's look made him falter in his tracks, memories of the dream images suddenly washing back through his head. He cleared his throat and looked away quickly.

"Avram?" It was Marcus this time.

"Yes, yes, I'm fine. Really. What does someone have to do to get a drink around here?"

Pavel was already behind the bar, fixing something for himself and Aggie. "What would you like?" he asked.

"Um ..." Avram wasn't really sure that he wanted anything to drink after all, but it would draw away some of the attention, he thought. "Oh, what the hell. Get me a scotch will you, Pavel?" They had a reasonable selection of decent single malts behind the well-stocked bar. With Pavel and Aggie on board, it was just as well that it was properly provisioned, although they made few dents in the scotch supply. They tended to drink various exotic cocktails that Pavel mixed up for both of them, the mysteries of which Avram had no real desire to sample.

"Any preference?"

"No. Whatever comes to hand," he said.

As Pavel reached for a dark green bottle to fulfil his request, Avram glanced back over his shoulder at Samantha, but she was back in her game with Alf, and concentrating on her cards. Avram turned back to the bar, his rush of guilt trickling away, though why he should feel guilty about his dream, he did not know. How could he be ashamed of his own subconscious? But he was, and there was still that lingering feeling of discomfort, of something not quite right about it.

"So," he said. "Has everyone eaten?" He took the glass from Pavel and turned to lean back on the bar, looking at them. Aggie was still peering at him suspiciously.

"Yes, of course," said Max. "Everything was cleared about an hour ago. You missed the Captain."

Avram took a healthy sip from the decent measure that Pavel had poured him, feeling the warmth course from his throat to the back of his skull and into his belly. "Well, that's a pity," he said.

"So what did you get up to after we left you?" asked Joe.

"I don't know," said Avram after taking another swallow. He was starting to feel a little more like himself. "I wandered around, as usual. Saw some more of the Old Town. Visited a couple of the buildings. I did stop for a coffee at that little place at the edge of the square. You know the one—all Spanish arches and vaulted ceilings. It was excellent."

"Ah, yes," said Marcus, nodding. "Pity we missed that one, Joe."

Avram thought it had been excellent, his memories were telling him that it had been so, but for some reason, the details were foggy. He remembered having sat there, remembered having coffee and pastry, but though he could recall it, he couldn't see it. Normally, there'd be images in his head, painting the memories with color and life. Instead, it was merely the knowledge that he had, in fact, visited.

"And after that?" said Selena. She was fixing him with one of her looks again.

"Oh, I don't know. Wandered around the square for a bit, sat beneath some of the palm trees I suppose."

"What do you mean 'suppose?'" she asked him. "Either you did or you didn't, Avram."

"It's not important really, Selena," he said. "You know, it was the normal touristy stuff."

"Well, I don't believe you," she said firmly. "How can it be the 'normal' stuff when you almost made us all late, and then when you came back in looking like that? What happened out there?" She had her arms crossed over her chest again, only uncrossing them to flip her blond hair and give her head a little superior toss before she refolded them, obviously believing she had made a point. "Did you visit somewhere special then? Maybe something that made you very tired."

"I told you, Selena; I just did what I normally do."

She was clearly not satisfied. "Listen, Avram. If something happened to you out there ... You come in looking like you are drunk or something, white as a ghost, and then you disappear to your cabin and come out later looking worse. Are you sick? If you have caught something, we need to know, don't you think?"

Avram sighed and turned back to the bar, gesturing with his now-empty glass to Pavel, who took it and turned away for a refill.

"No, I'm not sick. I think it was just a very hot day and we did quite a bit. Perhaps I overdid it." He refused to turn and meet her gaze, but he could see her watching him in the mirror behind the bar. Pavel passed him the fresh glass and Avram took a healthy swallow.

He turned around again only after it was clear that Selena wasn't going to press him anymore.

"All right," she said with a harrumph.

"And what about you?" Avram asked.

"Oh you know," said Max, characteristically leaning back on one of the couches with his ankles crossed before him. "We did some things, saw some shops, bought a few items. Found something for the children. Same stuff what we do every time."

"Ahh," said Avram. "What did you get?" trying to steer the conversation away from his own condition.

"You see what they are playing with now," Max responded.

"They are very nicely looking cards, we thought."

Avram's gambit seemed to have worked. Carefully, he placed his half empty glass down on the bar and crossed to where the children sat huddled together on the floor.

"Hi," said Avram, looking down at them. "Can I see?" He crouched beside them.

Alf held up a card for him to look at. It showed some sort of knight on horseback, his armor brown and finely wrought. Behind him, in the background, stood a castle with flames issuing from its windows. It was indeed a very fine piece of intricate illustration.

"Very nice," he said. "And Sam, can I see one of yours?"

"You want to look?" she asked him.

"Sure."

She held out a card in front of him, holding it flat so he could see the illustration. On the card, there was a small child, slim and pale, standing under an archway. She was dressed in some sort of brown robe. Around her waist was a belt, studded with purple-green gems. One of her hands reached forward, as if entreating him. A sudden chill washed through him. He knew that child, knew it from somewhere. With a slight tremble in his hand, he reached for the card. As he grasped

Breath

it, his fingers touched the end of Samantha's where they held the edge with its finely worked patterns, and her eyes went wide.

Avram felt it too. Something, something in the touch. A flow, a coursing that ran down his arm. Her eyes stayed wide, looking at him, her mouth slightly open. Avram quickly drew his hand back. Samantha's eyes narrowed, fixed on his own.

Very, very slowly, her lips started to form a subtle smile. She held his gaze for a moment or two and then turned her attention back to the card.

**Hast thou seen white and black (combined)?
It (the result) is neither black nor white.**

–The Alphabet of Ben Sira

As quickly as he had withdrawn his fingers, Avram stood. Samantha's gaze tracked his movement, looking back up at him, re-establishing eye contact and with something in her look that could only be called knowing. He tore his gaze away, looking at Alf, but the boy seemed oblivious. Slowly, he looked back to the girl. The almost smile was still there, as if she were smirking at him, bound in her own private joke. Both of the Green's children had always been a little precocious, but nothing akin to what he was seeing now. Behind him, on the couches and beside the bar, the others, including the girl's parents, sat around in idle chit-chat, their attention, at least for the moment, having drifted away from Avram himself. He looked over at them and then back at Sam. There was nothing he could say, really, nothing. She observed his glance and if anything, her smile became more pronounced. Slowly, and with deliberateness, the child placed the card she had been holding down on the carpet in front of her, angled so that the picture was facing him.

"Sam, what are you doing?" said Alf, complaining. "Come back."

Avram feared that there was actually little hope of that.

"Sorry," she said, turning her attention back to her brother, losing the look of calculation.

"You dropped one," he said.

"No, I was only showing it to Uncle Avram." She gave him a little glance, and the quirk of her lips came and went.

He was suddenly not sure that he was very comfortable with the term "Uncle," particularly after the dream images that still played in his mind. He swallowed and turned away. Perhaps that was all it was, a hangover from those awful dreams. Chewing at his lip, he made his way back to the bar.

"They are very beautiful," he said to Max. "Such detailed work. Have you seen them, Joe?"

Joseph looked up at him. "Yeah, they're pretty good. They're fairly accurate representations of the local mythology. Thematically, they get passed down, standard depictions of moral tales. They generally have deeper symbolism woven into the images. If you study them, you'll find that the key image is part of a bigger message and there are all sorts of little icons in them that have meanings of their own."

"Huh," said Avram. "Imagine that." He reached for what remained of his scotch. "Where did you find them, Max?"

"Oh, I don't know," he said. "It was like this little tiny shop in a back street. It was full of stuff. I don't know. The guy was a little ..."

"Strange," said Selena, finishing the sentence. "But it was really good bargaining."

"Yeah," said Max. "It was like he really wanted us to have them, you know? We got a real good deal. Maybe, because of where he was, he does not do so much good business, you know."

Selena nodded her confirmation with the characteristic self-satisfied expression she wore whenever she believed she had managed to one-up a salesman or stall-holder.

Avram wandered over to the window and looked out into the darkness, nursing his drink in one hand. There was only water below them now, a vast skein of blankness, but off in the distance, he could see a few scattered lights, yellow pinpoints in a darkened veil, probably fishing boats. He glanced over at the children, still huddled over the cards, absorbed in whatever game they had invented with them. As if she had felt him watching, Samantha glanced back over her shoulder, catching his eyes and an inexplicable chill ran through him. Just as quickly, she looked away.

Jesus, thought Avram, what the hell was wrong with him? He turned back from the window, crossed back to the bar and placed his now-empty glass back on the polished wood surface.

"Okay, everyone," he said. "I guess I should go and see if I can find something to eat." It was an excuse really. He still wasn't hungry. In fact, food was probably the furthest thing from his mind.

"Sure," said Marcus. "We're going to be turning in soon."
Pavel lifted Avram's empty glass from the bar and tilted it suggestively towards him, his eyebrows raised. "Another one before you go, perhaps? To whet the appetite?"

"No that's fine, Pavel. Thanks anyway." He scanned the assembled travellers. "Well, have a good night people," he said.

"Sure," Aggie responded. "And you get some rest too, Avram. You are still not looking the best."

"No I'm fine," he said, putting a brave face on it once again.

He wasn't fine, but with everything that was happening to him, he didn't want to be forced into detailed explanations. He had to work this out himself.

As he reached the door, the child, Samantha, called out to him across the room.

"Good night, Uncle Avram," she said.

He stopped in mid-step, slowly turned and looked over at the kids. Samantha was looking steadily at him. Alf barely glanced up.

"Good night, children," he said, a deep sense of unease stirring in his chest and turned away, finally stepping out into the passageway.

Damn the child. (If she was not already damned, he thought.)

He stopped where he was, leaned one hand on the wall and let out a deep breath. Just in case the inquisitive Aggie might come and check up on him, he headed down the passageway towards the galley, thinking hard. He could not have been imagining it with the girl. He had seen what he had seen and her looks had been deliberate, knowing. She had been almost taunting him. But that was something different from precociousness. And the look—it had been as if she was seeing inside him, seeing right inside his thoughts, his soul. He swallowed at the memory.

The galley was past the dining area, two doors along the passageway from the Observation Lounge, and as soon as he reached it, he stepped inside and leaned back heavily against one of the preparation counters. There was a small larder type affair and several high cupboards contained crockery, glassware, snacks and various cooking ingredients, but for now, he wasn't particularly interested in rummaging through the contents to find something, even if Aggie should appear to check up on him. Thankfully, of Ronald, the cook, there was no sign either. For the moment, at least, he could be alone with his thoughts. Running his fingers back through his hair, he closed his eyes and tried to force himself to relax.

A bit of cool air wafted against his cheek, chill, and he frowned. Again, it came, stirring the vaguest whisper in his ear.

"Avram ..." It was more than the simple stirring of the air no, no simple breeze or eddy. The whisper was there.

"Avram ...," it came again. The word formed inside of his head at the same time. He suddenly didn't want to open his eyes to verify. A crystal chill flowered in the depths of his abdomen and reached icy fingers deep throughout his chest to tease at his heart. The whisper was directionless; he had no way of telling from whence it had come.

Barely daring to do so, Avram slowly opened his eyes. Without moving position, he looked around, first to his right, and then to his left, emitting a short gasp. She was there, standing by the window. The little girl was there. She was achingly familiar, and yet, at the same time, he had no idea who she was, from where he knew that so-pale face. He licked his lips, his breath coming is short gasps.

"Wh-who are you?" he said, quietly.

"You know who I am, Avram," she said, just as quietly. "You know me, even though you might not know it." There was a deliberate smile on her lips and the chill feeling in his abdomen grew stronger as he realized how alike it was to the faint quirk that had appeared on Samantha's face. He just wanted to run, to leave this place. He bit his lip, closed his eyes and shook his head. This couldn't be happening.

"Say my name, Avram," she said.

He opened his eyes and looked over. She was still there.

"Say my name."

The syllables welled up within his mind, and he found himself stammering out the name. "L-Lilith," he said.

She took a step towards him, and then another. "Very good, Avram."

"But you can't be here," he whispered. "You can't be here."

"I am here, Avram. I am here now and always. I have always been here, but now I am with you." She took another step towards him. Avram tried to back away, but there was nowhere to go. His back was hard up against the counter and the cupboards behind. The girl took another step and was suddenly standing right in front of him. She reached up with one small hand, touching his cheek, gently tracing its shape with the flat of her palm. Her skin was cool. He tried to shy away, but at that moment, all volition seemed to have drained out of him.

"There," she said.

He took a shuddering breath as she lowered her hand again. Those deep, dark eyes were looking into his own, holding his attention. The faint smile still played across her mouth.

"How?" he said. "How did you ..."

"As I said, Avram," she said, not even waiting for the sentence to complete. "I am here, with you."

What was she? Was she a ghost? Avram didn't believe in ghosts.

"Avram?" The voice came from the passageway. It was Aggie, come to check up on him. He looked towards the doorway, suddenly unsure whether he wanted Aggie to see the child or whether she would even see her if she appeared in the galley.

He turned his gaze back, but in front of him was nothing. The girl had gone.

His hand trembling, he lifted it to his cheek where moments before, the small fingers had rested. He glanced quickly around, but there was nowhere to go, nowhere she could have possibly gone. There was a doorway leading into the preparation area, and beyond that, he knew, the space where Ronald spent most of his time, some sort of simple living quarters. His heart still thudding loud in his ears, he pushed himself from the counter and took a step towards that door, but he could already see that there was no one beyond. The dim room was empty. He would have seen if she had gone in there.

This cannot be happening, he thought to himself.

Aggie's head appeared through the doorway. "Avram?" she said. "My God. What is it? You are so white. Are you okay?"

He stepped back from the door and reached behind himself to grasp the counter. "Yes. I guess I must have got a bit too much sun today," he said, the words sounding lame in his own ears. "I was just a little dizzy for a moment there."

"Avram, you need to take care. Maybe you should go and lie down again. Perhaps when we get to our next stop you should see a doctor. I am starting to get really worried about you."

Aggie, though she was the one without kids was always the group's mother—far more than Selena, and the funny thing was, Avram knew within himself that she really did care.

He took a deep breath and nodded slowly in acknowledgement. "Yes, you're probably right," he said.

She stepped through the doorway and moved closer, placing a hand upon his shoulder, studying him, her eyes seeming large behind her glasses.

"You have a drink of water, and go back to bed."

Again, he nodded. "Right."

Despite the sincerity of her concern, Avram really didn't want to be here right now, not after what had just happened, or what he thought had just happened; he still didn't know. He turned, reached up for a glass and filled it, not meeting her gaze. She rested her hand upon his back, urging him on with her gentle presence.

"That's it," she said. "Good boy."

He went through the motions, draining the glass and placing it down on the counter.

"Thanks, Aggie," he said. "I think I'm going to do exactly what you say and go to bed now. I guess I'm still a little bit unsteady."

"Do you want me to come with you?"

"No, no. Please. I'll be all right." It was the last thing he wanted at the moment. "You go back and join the others. I'll be fine."

He turned towards the doorway. She was still looking at him, her expression doubtful.

"Really," he said and moved towards the passageway as she stepped back to let him past. She patted him gently on the back.

"All right then," she said as he stepped out of the galley, into the passageway and turned to the staircase that led to the upper deck and his cabin. "I'm going to check up on you in the morning, you know. If you don't appear all bright and sparkling, there's going to be hell to pay, Avram Davis."

He lifted one hand in acknowledgement without looking back and left her standing there as he headed down the passage.

One by one, he climbed the stairs to the next level, hoping that she wouldn't change her mind and follow him. He needed to deal with this, and he had to do that alone. At the top of the staircase, he paused, resting with one had supporting him on the banister, taking comfort from the feel of the cool polished wood. Of course, there was always the possibility that he was losing his mind. He had to consider that. Had it been a simple hallucination? Somehow, though, he just didn't believe that was the case. Stolid, methodical Avram Davis, wasn't the sort of individual to just lose his sanity and if that was so, then the girl, Lilith, had really been there. At the memory of her hand on his cheek, he went cold again. Flashes of the dream he had welled up in his thoughts. He shook his head. No. No. Again he shook his head as if trying to dislodge those particular vivid thoughts from his mind.

Despite the water, his mouth was dry. The chill still worked inside him. There was no rational explanation for the girl's presence, her appearance, and her just as sudden disappearance. There had to be an explanation, and yet there wasn't one. He walked along the passage to his cabin door, stepped inside and closed himself away. Sitting on the edge of his bunk, he suddenly thought that he should lock the door, but in the next instant, realized, that for some reason, the thought simply terrified him. He was trembling.

He sat there for a while, simply listening, waiting for ... he didn't quite know what. To see if Aggie would come to check up on him? For the mysterious child to appear again? His heart rate had settled somewhat, but there was that continuing feeling of vertigo in his chest and in his guts, as if the solid deck beneath his feet had simply ceased to exist. He gripped the edges of his bunk with both hands, forced himself to breathe through his nose, pressed his jaw tight and lowered his head. He stared down at the indefinably patterned carpeting, fearful of closing his eyes lest something appear when he wasn't looking. The child—he knew her from somewhere, he was certain of that, but he had no idea where and that just didn't make sense. And when she had prompted him, he also knew her name. It was as if there was a sluice of frigid water washing over his recollections and obscuring them behind. He could catch a vague, wavering glimpse, knowing there was something there, and yet being unable to see it sharply enough to know what it was. All he remembered was hollowness, darkness, stone, and ... that was it. It had to have been somewhere in the city they'd just visited. It fit. But, for her to be on board made no sense.

A huge gust buffeted their ship from the outside and the engines below, lifted in pitch to compensate, and then subsided a couple of seconds later. Avram lifted his head and listened. Again, came the wind and the ship swayed slightly, the ever-present thrumming caught and then faded again. He had never really got used to that passing feeling of instability that worked to set your feeling of solidity adrift, but in reality, it paled next to the experience he was undergoing now. How it was possible to be cast adrift from yourself was something he did not, could not understand. He ran his palm over his mouth and chin, thinking about the child, about the city, about the places that he had been, but there was simply nothing that stood out, no memory of where he had encountered her, just those vague impressions of some vast empty space and old, old stone, and impenetrable darkness.

Perhaps, as Aggie had suggested, he needed to rest, to get more sleep. He stood and began to remove his shirt. Just as he did, another blast of wind outside shifted the deck beneath his feet and he staggered, throwing out a hand for support. He waited, expecting another, but it didn't come, and he went back to undressing. Crossing over to the drawers, he removed his night clothes, frowned slightly as something clattered in the back of the drawer, but another gust shifted the deck and he was forced to reach out for something to hold himself steady, distracting his attention. Again, the shifting subsided and he finished dressing, doing up the buttons one by one and staring at the wall in front of him. There was a faint creak and pop in the cabin behind him and he spun around, his heart hammering. There was nothing there, nothing at all. Had it come from the cabin itself, or the gloom beyond the bathroom door? He peered in that direction too, but again there was nothing. Simply the ship shifting and readjusting itself in response to the buffeting outside, he guessed. He nodded to himself as if to reaffirm that thought, waited a few more moments and then crossed over to the bed and drew back the covers.

Sleep. He needed to sleep. And hopefully, during the night, his unconscious mind would do the work it needed to do and he would awaken, and all this would have gone away.

If he was lucky, this time he wouldn't dream those dreams,

Somehow, he wasn't so sure.

The bride goes into the canopy, and knows not what is coming upon her.

−The Alphabet of Ben Sira

Breath

Avram was awakened by a scream. He started upright in the bunk, clutching the bedcovers, bunched in one fist, his eyes wide. Had he dreamed it? But no there it came again. It was a woman's scream and it came from almost directly below his cabin, slightly muffled by the intervening walls, but there all the same..

He tossed back the covers and stood, debating for a moment what to do, and then threw open his door, raced down the passageway to the top of the stairs, took them quickly one be one. The noise had definitely come from the deck below. Reaching the bottom of the staircase, he turned to see a group of people clustered around the doorway to the galley. Max, Joe, Marcus, the kids, most of them dressed, but not all. Some still wore their nightclothes As he appeared, Samantha turned to look at him, catching his gaze and holding it, a half smile on her lips, but he couldn't concentrate on her now; he had to find out what was going on.

"What is it?" he called, heading quickly up the passageway to join them.

At the sound of his voice, Marcus turned, gave his head a little shake.

"Something with Aggie. I don't know yet," he said, turning back towards the galley.

Avram craned over Joe's shoulder, struggling to see what was going on. Inside the galley, just by the door that led to the other section, Selena stood, her hand on Aggie's shoulder, speaking softly. Aggie was leaning back against the doorframe, shaking her head, fanning her fingers in front of her throat and taking in big gulps of air.

"He was just lying there," she said in halting gasps.

Selena rubbed her shoulder and leaned in closer, saying something beyond Avram's hearing.

"What's going on?" he said.

Joe turned. "It's something with Ronald. Don't know yet. We just got here."

Avram happened to glance down. Samantha was looking up at him, watching, the smile still half evident on her lips, her gaze impassive. He met her eyes and something dropped into chill nothingness in the bottom of his guts. He dragged his gaze away with difficulty.

"Maybe somebody should take the children away from here," he said. "Max?"

"What?" said Max, glancing around. He was leaning half into the galley, one hand high up on the doorframe.

"The kids ..."

"Oh yes," said Max and frowned. He pulled himself back from the galley and pushed past Avram and Joe. "Children, you should come away now." He placed a hand on each of their shoulders and turned them to face up the passageway, then gave them both a little push.

"But I want to see," said Alf, complaining. Samantha said nothing. She looked back over one shoulder at Avram, a full smile on her face now, quirked her lips and then looked away.

"No, it is not the place for you to be," said Max. He herded them up the passage.

With an effort of will, Avram turned his attention back to the two women standing inside, and taking the opportunity of Max's departure, slipped past Marcus and Joe to step fully into the room.

Aggie, still fanning herself with one hand, still leaned back against the doorway, her eyes closed, breathing irregularly. Selena continued stroking her upper arm. At that moment, Pavel emerged from the other section, looking down at the floor and shaking his head.

"It is not so good," he said.

"What, Pavel?" asked Avram. "What isn't"

Pavel looked up at his voice. "Oh hello, Avram. So, it is Ronald the cook. There is no question. He is dead."

"What?"

"I found him there," said Aggie haltingly. "I found him. I was looking for him because breakfast was late. I was wondering where he was and I came to look. Ohhh ..." She shuddered and took another gasping breath.

Pavel reached up absent-mindedly and patted her shoulder.

"What happened?" asked Marcus from the doorway. "You're sure?"

Pavel nodded his head slowly, seriously. "Oh yes. There is no doubt."

"Th-that face ..." Aggie stammered.

"Do you know what ...?" said Avram.

Pavel shook his head.

"Perhaps someone should tell Prinsloo," Marcus offered from the doorway.

Pavel looked over at him.

"Look, I'll go," offered Joe and immediately disappeared behind Marcus, heading off to do just that.

Perhaps their part-time cook had finally drunk himself to death, thought Avram, but then Aggie's words put paid to that notion. Something else had clearly happened. He sidled past Pavel and into the small, dim connecting passageway that led to the area beyond the galley. The passage end opened up into a slightly larger, though not by much, connecting room with a door on each side and one straight in front. The door on the left, lay half open, the others firmly closed, so Avram stepped towards that one. Behind him he could hear Aggie's halting sobs, the others' low voices, all strangely distorted and muffled through the connecting narrow space. Swallowing back his apprehension, Avram stepped inside the small, dark, confined quarters where Ronald seemed to spend most of his time. Once or twice, Avram had seen him unsteadily wandering the corridors, but for the most part, except around mealtimes, they rarely saw him. The smell of hard alcohol was in the air, but so was something else, something tainted. Avram held his breath for a moment, realized just as quickly that that was not going to work, and started breathing through his mouth instead.

The unfortunate Ronald was lying back on his bunk, eyes open and unnaturally wide, a simultaneous look of shock and surprise written across his features and frozen there. One arm was flung out to one side, off the bunk, and the other was up against the wall, palm flat against it. There was nothing natural about the pose, nothing at all. There was no question about whether the man was alive or dead. Avram didn't need to reach for a pulse; it was evident. The thing that stood out for Avram was the strange marking upon his neck, like a raised weal. At first, he thought it was a birthmark, but upon closer inspection, it was nothing like a birthmark. It was the sort of impression you got if you sat with your elbow on the top of your thigh for an extended period, a deep red impression, where all around was lighter skin. Towards its center, the mark turned purplish. What could make that sort of mark, he had no idea. Perhaps he had fallen unconscious and in so doing, leant against something that had left the mark, but looking at the expression on the man's face, he decided that was out of the question.

The smell was starting to get to him, and he backed out of the small cabin, and then stood in the connecting room for a few moments. Noises, conversation were still drifting through from the galley. There was something wrong here, something seriously wrong, and Avram knew it, not only from the look of the dead man, but also just a general sense of unbalance working through him. He was considering what he would do next, when Prinsloo appeared in the low passage and shouldered his way past to poke his head inside Ronald's cabin, followed closely by Joe, who pulled up short to stand next to Avram, looking distinctly ill at ease.

"Shit," said Prinsloo, backing out of the cabin, holding a hand beneath his nose, shielding his large white moustache. "Fucker," he said. "He could at least have waited until we docked."

"Captain Prinsloo," said Joe, carefully. "I don't think he really had a choice in the matter."

"Fucker always had a choice," retorted Prinsloo. "Look at his life." He shook his head, lowering his hand from his face and shook his head. "What am I going to do now?"

The question was rhetorical and Prinsloo clearly wasn't expecting an answer, but Joe decided to answer him anyway.

"Well, perhaps you should do something about the body." He wrinkled his nose. "It's becoming a little obvious and I think it should be a priority."

Prinsloo sighed. "Yes, yes, you're right. And I need to notify the port. Make arrangements." Shaking his head again, he crossed to one of the other doors and pulled it open. Behind lay a large freezer, shelves stacked with various food supplies for their voyage. "This will keep him from stinking up the place."

"You're going to put him in with our food?" said Joe in a horrified voice.

"What else do you expect me to do? Shove him out of the ship? You, Davis isn't it? Will you give me a hand?"
Avram cleared his throat. "Um, I suppose ..."

"Come on, man," said the Captain.

Joe just stood there with an expression of disbelief on his face. "For God's sake," he said finally, "Don't tell Selena. We'll never hear the end of it."

"So," said Avram. "Go back there and make sure she doesn't come in."

Joe nodded and disappeared up the narrow passage.

"Come," said Prinsloo. "Help me shift him."

This time, when he entered the small cabin, Avram held his breath. The Captain reached for the upper part of the body, gesturing for Avram to grab the feet.

"Strange," said Prinsloo. "Not quite how you'd expect someone to be found."

He grunted as he moved the arms into position. Rigor had definitely started to set in, working its way down from the head and gradually travelling down the body. Avram knew that it usually took around twelve hours to assert itself properly, and as he grabbed the ankles it confirmed his suspicions. There was still some flexibility in the legs. It had to have been some time in the early hours of the morning, after Avram was safely in bed that Ronald had met his end.

"And, lift."

He took another huge breath of air, clamping his mouth shut as he did just that. As the Captain backed out of the narrow doorway, Avram followed, holding on with his hands beneath the dead man's ankles. There was still enough flexibility in the body for it to droop in the middle between them as they shuffled across the connecting space and into the cooling compartment. Right at the back of the room, Prinsloo dumped his end unceremoniously against the rear metal-shod wall and stepped out of the way. More gently, Avram lowered the man's legs and took his own step back, grimacing and finally letting out his breath.

Prinsloo looked down at the corpse's face.

"Well, it doesn't look like he was happy to go," he said.

"Can we do something about that?"

"What ... oh." Prinsloo reached for a cloth on one of the shelves shook it out and dropped it over Ronald's staring eyes.

Avram backed out of the cooler and stood staring into the room with the now-draped body, rubbing his forehead as Prinsloo stepped out and closed the door behind him

"What now?" asked Avram.

"Now? Now I go back to flying the ship. I will notify the people at our next port of call. Until then, there isn't very much we can do. I suggest you go back and join your friends. This is my problem now."

"But how long before we get there?"

Prinsloo glanced down at his watch. "Another four and a half, maybe five hours. By the time we've docked, maybe six. Fucker," he said again, glancing at the cooler.

And with that, the Captain stepped past him, through the connecting passage and was gone, leaving Avram standing there. Somehow, Avram suspected though that this wasn't Prinsloo's problem alone, no matter what he might think. He stood staring at the cooler door for a few seconds before turning away, still seeing those marks upon Ronald's neck in his mind's eye. Six hours was not too long. At least they'd have a partial resolution to the problem.

Joe was standing waiting for him at the end of the passage. Of the others there was no sign.

"So?" asked Joe.

"In the cooler," said Avram. "It doesn't matter. According to Prinsloo, we'll be there in another five, six hours." He shrugged. "I think I'm going to be a lot more comfortable when we get there though. What's happened to the others?"

Joe waved one hand in the direction of the front. "They've taken Aggie up to the Observation Lounge."

"And the children?"

"I don't know what Max has done with them. I've been here the whole time."

"Okay," said Avram. "Maybe we'd better go and see. Let the others share in the good news."

As he headed out of the galley, Joe following behind reached out a hand to stop him.

"What do you think happened to him?"

Avram turned. "I don't know. I really don't."

Despite the words, there was an uncomfortable suspicion working in the back of his head, one that he wasn't going to voice to any of his companions just yet. One that he wasn't sure he was ever going to put words to. He turned back and headed up the passageway to the front of the ship, Joe following close behind. Vaguely, he noticed that whatever winds had been buffeting them the previous evening had now subsided.

When they reached the Observation Lounge, everyone else was gathered there, but the children were nowhere in sight. Aggie lay back on one of the couches, still looking pale, with Pavel sitting beside her, holding one hand comfortingly. Marcus stood by the bar, staring out through one of the large windows. Selena stood over near the other end of the bar, her arms crossed, merely observing, while Max stood in front of the Bartkos, looking down at the pair of them with an expression of detached interest on his face. He looked across at Avram and Joe as they entered.

"Well?" said Max.

"All taken care of," said Avram.

"I see." He turned back to watching the Bartkos.

"Well, I would like to know what we are going to do about breakfast now," said Selena from her position at the bar.

Marcus turned to look at her, frowning and giving a shake of his head.

"Really, Selena?" said Joe.

"Yes of course," said Max. "You know how they say 'breakfast is the most important meal of the day.' And anyway, we have to think about the children. No?"

Selena nodded.

"Where are they anyway?" asked Avram. Right now, it was the children that he was especially interested in, particularly Samantha.

"Oh, I put them in their cabin. They are playing something now. But they will need their breakfast, definitely." He gave himself an affirming nod as if to confirm his own statement.

"Really, Max?" said Joe, still apparently unable to believe either Max or Selena's responses.

"Oh sure," said Max, seemingly oblivious to Joe's disbelieving tone.

"Well," said Avram. "It's going to be a few more hours until we reach where we're going according to Prinsloo. Why don't you go and prepare something for them, Max, and I'll go and fetch them down in the meantime."

"And I need to go and get dressed," said Marcus.

Pavel looked around at each of them. "We are really going to go on as if nothing has happened?"

"We cannot change it, Pavel," said Selena. He turned to face her, not letting go of Aggies hand. "Whether we sit around doing nothing or get on with what we have to do," she continued, "it makes no difference. We'll be at our next destination soon. You heard Avram. It doesn't matter what has happened. We still have to be ready when we get there for whatever occurs. We are still going to have to leave the ship. We may as well be ready. I don't know about you, but I would prefer to be decent, have breakfast, be prepared. There's bound to be police and questions and other things. I would prefer to look as if I hadn't just left my bed. But, of course, it is up to you."

"Well, I know what I'm doing," said Marcus as he stepped out of the room, and with that he was gone. A couple of moments later, Joe followed him.

"Okay, Avram," said Max. "I will do as you say and go to make some breakfast. Maybe you can do that. Go and get them. Bring them to the dining room."

"Yes, and I'll help you, Max," said Selena.
As they both moved towards the door, Avram hesitated, his gaze on the Bartkos. Pavel still sat there, looking a little lost. After a moment, when there appeared that there was going to be no further reaction, Avram too turned for the door.

"Right," he said. "I'll go and do just that."

As a passing thought, following them both up the passageway, he considered suggesting to Max that he pointed Selena at Aggie instead, never knowing if she might, in the course of seeking breakfast items, stumble into the cool room. He dismissed the idea though. Max would take care of it. He was just about the only one upon whom Selena did not try to impose her will, at least not obviously. He slid past them as they paused at the galley door.

A few steps more and he reached the staircase, mounted the steps and turned into the passage that led to the rest of the cabins. The children, Samantha and Alf shared a double cabin just beyond their parents', both of them being young enough for it not to be a problem yet that they were not of the same the same gender. He paused outside their door, listening. Despite everything that was going on, Avram was still aware of his own state, his feeling of disconnectedness, the apparent lapse in his recollections and the strange, strange looks that the young girl had been giving him. It was one of the reasons he had volunteered; he simply wanted to find out. Taking a deep breath to steady himself, nervous expectation skittering around inside his guts, he opened the door.

"Kids," he said as he took a step into the cabin.

Each child was sitting, Samantha on one bunk and Alfred on the other. Simply sitting, staring across the intervening space into each other's eyes. Between them, on the floor, lay the deck of cards, scattered, their intricate images sometimes face up, sometimes down, partially obscuring bits and pieces of the pictures. Avram barely glanced at the cards, for at the sound of his voice, both of the children slowly, simultaneously turned to face him, and together, slowly, subtly at first and then unmistakably, began to smile. Together, they lowered their faces, each still maintaining eye-contact with his face, and then, in unison, they spoke.

"Hello, Uncle Avram," they said and then turned back to look at each other, the smile never leaving their lips.

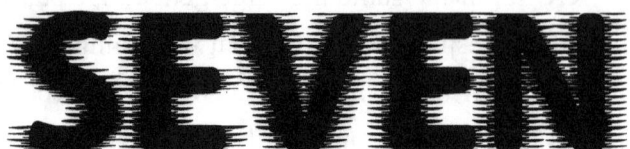

SEVEN

Inquire not into that which is too difficult for thee;
and that which is concealed from thee search not out.
Attend to that which is permitted to thee:
thou hast no business with hidden things.

–The Alphabet of Ben Sira

Together, the children got off their bunks and, joining each other in the cabin's center, stood side by side in front of Avram. Whatever was affecting Samantha had clearly passed to Alfred as well.

"Your father wants you to come down and have some breakfast," he said, his words sounding lame and inconsequential in his ears.

The children looked at each other, and then back to meet his eyes.

"Of course," said Alf, the statement peculiarly adult.

Avram turned to leave the cabin. As soon as he was out in the passage, each child reached out to take a hand. Their grasp was cool, dry, and it reminded him of something, another child's touch, not too long ago. He frowned, trying to dig out the memory. He couldn't go on like this, simply stumbling over the yawning gaps in his recollections. His memory was what he was; it consisted of everything he had ever been. He swallowed back his frustration, more conscious now of the behaviour of his two small companions. That smile, the tone of their voices, the steady gaze, all of it added up to something distinctly not right.

Dammit, he thought; he needed to get a grip on himself.

"So you saw," said Samantha, almost conversationally.

"Saw what?"

"The blessing," she said simply.

Avram stopped dead in his tracks. "The what ...?"

"He has been blessed," she said.

"She has supped of his breath and he is blessed," said Alf. The boy tugged at his hand, urging him on towards the spiral staircase leading down at the end of the passage.

"No," said Avram, resisting, standing firmly where he was. "Who is she?" he asked, though within him, he knew the answer already, and it was a knowledge that filled him with a deeper chill.

Alf looked back, up into his face, with a steady gaze but said nothing. It was Sam's turn to tug at his hand.

"Come on," she said. "We have to go and have breakfast."

It was as if neither of them had said anything, as if he had imagined the words. He swallowed and shook his head. For just a moment, he imagined a stirring of the air along the passageway's length. At least he must have imagined it. All around them, the gentle thrum of the engines continued unabated, pushing them onwards to their next destination.

"No," he said again. "What did you say?"

Samantha shook her head, pursing her lips, almost as if she was indicating displeasure with a young child's stubbornness. She tugged at his hand again and was joined by Alf doing the same on the other side.

"Come on," they said together.

Still he stood firm. His memory might be playing tricks on him, but he had heard what they said. There was no imagination there.

Again, the breeze stirred.

"Avram," came a whisper, a breath, soundless all around him and inside his thoughts. "Avram. Go now."

"What?" he said.

"Go now."

With those last two words, all volition drained from him. He no longer had any desire to resist. Dropping his head meekly to look down at the carpet, the gray propellers criss-crossing the floor, he allowed himself to be led towards the staircase. The children said nothing. The voice was gone, as was the faint stirring in the air. He thought briefly about his travelling companions as they led him down the stairs. Marcus and Joe, Aggie and Pavel, Max and Selena, Samantha and Alfred, Captain Prinsloo, the other crewman, Ronald and himself— that made twelve. Or was it twelve? Wasn't there one more? Even if there was, Ronald was gone now, or at least gone in a way, so it was twelve. Or was it thirteen?

He was still puzzling through the count, a faint frown etched across his brow as they reached the entry to the dining room. Max and Selena were already sitting there at opposite sides of the large polished table. Between them lay a jug full of juice, coffee makings, some milk and a container of cereal. Two place settings sat beside them. As they walked in, Max looked up.

"Ah, hello children," he said. "Come, come, have breakfast.

Max and Selena had wasted no time getting things together.

"No eggs, I'm afraid," said Selena. "Max went to look, but he said there weren't any. We will just have to make do. I suppose they will be getting some more at our next stop."

"Come children," said Max again. "Sit."

"Yes, Papa," answered Sam, releasing Avram's fingers and taking a place beside her father. At the same time, Alf moved to the other side of the table and pulled out the chair next to his mother.

"Avram, please," said Max. "Can we get you something? Of course, we did not think."

Avram waved Max's query away. He could smell the coffee. That would be enough. He did not feel at all hungry.

"I'll grab myself a mug," he said. "Coffee, just coffee."

"Ah yes, there is plenty," said Max.

Avram did just that, crossing the dining room, popped into the galley and retrieved a mug before returning to the dining room, moving to where the coffee pot sat and filling his mug before returning to the seat at the end of the table and sitting, cradling his mug between his hands on the table before him. For some reason, he just wasn't comfortable with the thought of taking the place beside Alf, directly opposite Samantha. As it was, he could feel her eyes on him, observing. He glanced up. She was toying with her bowl of cereal half-heartedly, watching him sidelong. He looked across at Alf to see the same.

Returning his attention to the coffee, he lifted his mug and took a tentative sip. It was still hot and the feeling of the searing liquid and bitter taste in his mouth did something to cut through the embedded fog veiling his thoughts.

"What about the others?" he asked.

"Still in the Observation Lounge," said Selena. "The last we saw anyway. Marcus and Joe had already gone off when we left. We haven't seen them since."

Of course, he knew that.

"Unless they have come back down," offered Max.

But no, Avram would have seen them on his way to fetch the children.

"So I guess the Bartkos are still up there."

"It would seem so."

"What about Prinsloo? Has he been back up?"

Selena shook her head, chewing on her cereal. "It is a pity we can't have any fresh bread here," she said after disposing of her mouthful.

"Wait, wait," said Max. "I know where it is. How stupid of me." He pushed his chair back and disappeared through the door to the galley.

Avram could barely believe how matter-of-fact the pair of them was being. He knew they were like that, living in their own little bubble, governed by their own particular rules, but the apparent bloodless practicality that they were displaying now was a little hard for him to comprehend. Max appeared with a basket full of bread rolls and some butter.

"They are maybe not the freshest," he said as he sat again. "But I guess they are better than nothing."

The man who now lay in the cool room from where Max had obviously retrieved the butter, looking at its hardness as Selena tried to scrape some off the block to spread on her bread, was probably not the freshest either, but it was apparent Max was not going to make any mention of that particular fact. He was probably wise not to do so, but it was no doubt a wisdom born of experience.

"Thank you, my darling," said Selena, reaching for a nearby

pot of jam.

Max simply grunted an acknowledgement.

Meanwhile, as Avram lifted his mug to his lips for another sip, the children continued playing with their food, watching each of the adults in turn. There was something clinical, almost scientific in their observation. Suddenly coming to the conclusion that he couldn't endure the sidelong scrutiny any more, Avram got to his feet, pushed his chair back in, and taking his coffee, turned for the door.

"I'm going to check on Aggie and Pavel," he said. "And then maybe I should get dressed too."

"Yes, probably a good idea," said Max, not even looking up from his industrial concentration on his breakfast. He waved at Avram with a spoon.

Avram left them all sitting there, the coffee feeling like acid in his throat, and by the time he reached the Observation Lounge, of the Bartkos there was no sign. It appeared that Aggie had eventually got over her shock and they had also disappeared to their cabin to make themselves ready. Avram crossed to the bar and placed his coffee mug down heavily, then leaned, both hands supporting him on the solid surface. He turned his head and looked out at the view beyond the windows. It was light now. Intermittent cloud obscured the surface of the land passing beneath them, just as the gaps in his thoughts floated above his memories, hiding them from view. The landscape below was alternately a russet brown and olive green. It rose and dipped, here and there climbing to jagged outcroppings, a darker brown. Down there were roads and villages, cities, people going about their normal lives, but here, for Avram, there was nothing normal any more, or at least there didn't seem to be. It had started with the divorce, that which had ripped away the normalcy of his day to day existence. This journey, this grand adventure had somehow been meant to restore a sense of self-assuredness, a containment of his ability to cope with his own life and turn it back into something usual rather than floundering about trying to deal with the fact that he was no longer a part of something dual, two people, two lives. The events of the last few hours had wrested that away from him and placed him somewhere that was far, far from normal.

And the worst thing was, he had no real idea what was happening to him.

He turned away from the view below and what he knew were ultimately a chain of self-destructive thoughts. His coffee, lukewarm by now, offered some sort of solace, and he lifted the mug and took another decent swallow.

Something about the body, about Ronald's still form was nagging at him. There had been no blood, so it seemed that there was nothing violent about his demise, but that impression could easily have been a false one. Then there were those welts on his neck. No, perhaps not plural; it was one large mark, slightly oval, purplish and bruised, like a deep smudge on his skin. If he took that in conjunction with what the child Samantha had said, and followed by Alf, then it became more than a little suspicious. What did they mean by blessing anyway? He knew that the term bless had its origins in the old word for blood. Blood was used in consecration, hence blessing. But there had been no blood, if you didn't count the bruising. Bruises were blood, weren't they? Some diseases manifested that way, with deep bruising, he seemed to remember. Perhaps it was some sort of exotic disease that had taken the ship's cook, picked up in some strange and foreign port.

He slowly placed his mug back down on the bar. What if it was the same thing that was affecting him?

But that didn't make sense either. The children, the voices, the mysteriously appearing and disappearing girl child, the wind, none of it added up to an illness, unless it was an illness of the mind.

He shook his head, annoyed with himself. They'd be in port in a couple of hours and when they arrived, he'd have the opportunity to get himself checked out. Usually, their stops were a couple of days, enough time to have a decent look around, do the tourist things, take in the sights, and what with the body, who knew if their stay would be drawn out by some sort of officialdom? There were bound to be questions. And, if it was some sort of disease ... they might all be put into quarantine. No, that couldn't happen. Not only wasn't it a prospect he relished, but for some reason, he knew he couldn't allow it. He needed to be out and about, not confined. For some reason, he needed to be able to move freely. He knew that, and yet at the same time, he didn't know why he knew it. The thought of having his movements restricted washed him with a subtle dread. No, that mustn't be allowed to happen at all.

Leaving his mug on the bar, Avram turned away. He was coming to some sort of decision but he was not sure whether it was something he was truly comfortable with. This voyage, this ship, everything about all of it was not turning out in ways that he had envisaged. The three couples, they were his friends, true, and they had supported him without question, but he was still the outsider, the solitary individual in their midst—Poor Avram. Well, he wasn't prepared to be Poor Avram anymore. There was something he could do about that. He would pack, leave the ship, make his way on his own and sort himself out by himself. He could get himself checked out, make sure everything was okay, and then, simply make his own way. A bit of self-reliance never hurt anyone. He felt the new resolve, but only paused for a second to question from whence it had come, before heading out of the Observation Lounge and back up to his cabin to make his preparations.

Once back in his cabin, Avram looked around the space, not sure quite what he was doing. His main luggage was down below somewhere, but he had a leather travel bag stashed in the wardrobe, just in case he wanted to overnight somewhere in one of their several ports of call rather than return to the ship. He opened the wardrobe, pulled it out and placed it on the bunk, then stood considering. He didn't really need to take very much. The contents of most of his drawers, some toiletries: that should be enough. He could supplement along the way, and though it might chip away at his reserves, he had put enough aside to cover any such eventuality. He looked down at himself and realized he was still wearing pyjamas. Well, first he could shower, dress, put on some practical clothes. He had no idea what the weather was likely to be at their next destination. For the last few days it had been all heat and dust, only broken by thick humidity. Now, he knew, they were starting to move into cooler climes, so he might need to prepare for that. Likely, though, they had not yet travelled far enough for that to be a problem. First, he needed to shower.

As he stood under the water in the small bathroom, the glass screen dripping rivulets and patterns in front of him, he continued thinking about the options. This had been the grand plan, the catharsis and he was simply throwing it away? It did not really make sense. It was illogical, and yet, at the same time, certainty filled him. He did not even care that his decision meant that he was virtually throwing away much of the large investment he had made in this trip. He closed his eyes and let the water run down over his face, his eyes and his mouth, as if by doing so he could wash all of the questions away. He finished with the shower, dried himself and then selected some casual but clean clothes, a wearable jacket, shoved his toiletries into a bag and dropped those into the open grip lying on the bed. He then crossed to the drawers and proceeded to empty some underwear, socks, a couple of shirts, some casual trousers. He peered into the drawers, opening them one by one, checking if anything remained behind, but they were clear. For a moment or two, he stood contemplating the rest of his clothes hanging in the closet, then, as a last thought, bundled another jacket on top of the rest of the items he had already shoved inside the bag. That was it. That was everything. The shoes he had on would suffice, sturdy, yet comfortable.

He was standing there, thinking if he could have possibly

forgotten anything else, when a subtle shift in the ever-present vibration through the deck heralded a change in their velocity. It would not be too long now before they made landfall. He nodded to himself. He was set; a new country, a new life, a different direction. Remembering that they would be arriving at a new land altogether, he reached into the top drawer of the table that sat beside the bunk and retrieved his travel documents, slipping them into his jacket's inside pocket and gently patted the place on the outside that not only confirmed that they were there, but gave him familiarity with the feel of their presence, just in case, for whatever reason, they might suddenly go missing.

So, there was nothing else for it. He might as well go and seek out the others, find out what they were up to and if there were any particular plans, though after the events of the past few hours, he thought it unlikely that any of the party's members had even thought that far ahead. In fact, he wasn't particularly sure that he had even thought that far ahead. Not properly.

He made his way down to the Observation Lounge, pausing in the doorway. All of them, each of the couples and the children were arrayed in front of the large windows, watching their gentle descent. The weather had cleared, all traces of cloud gone from the sky, so it was a sparkling view, crystal water glinting in the light and nothing to obscure the vista apart from the haze of city smog lingering like a muddy tissue across the distant urban expanse in front of them. He lingered there in the room, waiting, not wanting to disturb them. He wasn't ready to tell them yet about his decision, nor to have them try to talk him out of it, as he knew they would. That could wait. He moved into the room, quietly took up a position on one of the couches, still able to see beyond the others to the details of their destination gradually resolving themselves ahead. The spires and the minarets, the domed roofs, they were all visible even at this distance. The glittering arc of water cutting through one side and the vast channel, ships like small toys cruising in either direction. At the moment, individual buildings, streets were indistinct, but the landmarks were there, plain to the eye, making the city unmistakable.

Lower and lower, the great ship drifted. Now the sights and building were becoming clearer. Selena was pointing out particular points of interest, and Max, beside her, was nodding. Pavel stood with his arm around Aggie's shoulder. Marcus and Joe had their arms linked. All of them were completely absorbed in the spectacle before them. It was as if none of the events of the past few hours had happened at all. A little to one side, the children stood, impassive, simply watching, or so he thought, but in the next moment, Samantha looked back over her shoulder, meeting his gaze. She lifted one hand, placed it gently on Alf's shoulder before turning and walking across to stand directly in front of where Avram sat. She stood there for a few moments, and then very quietly, she spoke.

"Are you ready, Uncle Avram?" she said.

"What? Yes I'm ready. Why, Samantha?"

"Really ready?"

"Yes, but ..."

"Good," she said. "She waits."

"What ...?" said Avram again, but Sam had already turned and walked back to join her brother. She drew up beside him, reached down and took Alf's hand in her own before returning to watching the approaching city in front of them, gracing him with a single quick glance back over her shoulder before returning to the view below.

EIGHT

She decked them with brightness, she fashioned them in exalted forms, So that fright and horror might overcome him that looked upon them,

–The Babylonian Legends of Creation, by E. A. Wallis Budge, [1921],

Tablet 2

Breath

As they drifted down slowly towards Bakırköy and their eventual mooring spot, the city lay spread out before them, not a detail hidden from view. Shortly before, Prinsloo's voice had come over the intercom, urging them to take their usual positions for docking. There had been no need to move from where they were all gathered, apart from repositioning themselves away from the windows to take seats on the couches. Despite his unease, and the continual feeling of being observed, Avram was still absorbed by the spectacle. It was a beautiful city. Ferries plied the waters between the foreshore near Galata Bridge making their way across the straits to Üsküdar and beyond. The numerous mosques prodded at the sky's clear blue with minarets in profusion, from the huge imposing Sultan Süleyman dominating its hillside above the water, right across to the familiar landmarks of Hagia Sophia and the tourist Mecca that was Sultanahmet. Avram knew that if he wasn't so distracted, he would have been completely captivated by the sights laid out before them. As it was, he could not help shooting the occasional glance in Sam's direction, checking, the echo of those two simple words from just a few minutes before still sounding inside his head. He resolved to put it from him. They were here in a new city; a new page awaited him out there beyond their ship's large windows and he had seen enough there to tantalise him already.

At last their docking was complete, the mooring ropes secured, holding the bloated dirigible in place, but still they couldn't move. Prinsloo asked them to stay where they were in the Observation Lounge until the local officials had arrived to perform their checks. Outside, Avram could see vehicles moving back and forth, a few ground crew in their khaki overalls moving back and forth, making sure lines were secure, shifting things from one side to the other. The weather was clear, but a light haze draped itself across everything out the windows. He glanced around at his companions, but they too were watching the outside world, not paying attention to each other at all.

Eventually, the local officials arrived in their dark blue uniforms and white shirts. One by one, they checked everyone's documents, making a show of flipping through the pages and scrutinising them, comparing the photographs to their faces, and then stamping a page using a portable stamp pad attached to their belts with a flourish. All complete, they backed towards the door, then saluted before disappearing into the passage beyond. Their voices drifted down and then slowly faded as they moved down the passage to the stairway that would take them below, into the gondola and out.

"So," said Max, slapping the top of his thighs. "I guess we can go out now."

"That is perhaps not such a good idea," said a voice from the doorway. "First, there are a few questions."

The man who stood there also wore a police uniform stretched tight around his girth. He had a round face, dark tanned skin and a large moustache, flecked with white. His dark eyes scanned them each in turn, pausing for a moment on the children and giving the faintest hint of a smile before moving on. In one hand, he held a small notepad which he proceeded to flip open and shuffle through the pages with a finger. He turned his attention back to Max.

"And you are?"

"Max. Max Green. And this is my wife, Selena."

"Aha. Yes," said the police official. His finger stopped halfway down a page and he nodded to himself.

"And these are your children?"

"That's right," said Selena. "Samantha and Alfred."

"Very good," he paused for a moment. "By way of introduction, I am Inspector Kaplan. Ali Kaplan. In your language, my name means 'tiger.'"

He beamed at the room in general, obviously pleased with his facility with translation, then each in turn, he verified everyone's identity, mentally checking them off on the list in his notebook. Again he nodded to himself.

"And why do you choose to visit our beautiful country?"

Pavel piped up this time. "We come to your country as part of our trip. We are on holiday. There are many things to see here.

"Yes, Mr ..." he checked his list again. "... Bartko. You are right. There are many, many beautiful things to see here. And how long do you intend to stay here?"

"Not more than a day or so. It is one of our scheduled stops. Normally we visit for a couple of days and then we move on to the next port."

The Inspector pursed his lips and looked back down at his notepad. "I am afraid that this might not be possible. You may be required to stay longer, depending on the outcomes of our investigation."

"Investigation?" said Aggie, a startled expression on her face. Kaplan caught the look and his eyes narrowed. "Yes, of course. It is not as if the death of your crewman, Mr. Cooper, was usual. Of course there must be an investigation."

So that was his name; Ronald Cooper.

Aggie swallowed and looked away, nodding her understanding. She for one had to know that there wasn't anything quite "usual" about Ronald's passing.

"It could be some days before we are done," continued Kaplan. "Did any of you know the deceased before this voyage?" He looked around their faces.

"No," said Marcus. "Never saw him before. Didn't see him much during the voyage either. He kept pretty much to himself."
Joe nodded in agreement. One by one, the rest of them shook their heads.

Kaplan returned to his notebook and scribbled a couple of notes after licking the end of the pencil he was carrying. "All right," he said. "I will let you know. I do not think there is anything to hold you here for, but you will have to leave the ship while we do some more ... how do you say? ... poking around. We will arrange for some nearby accommodation. At the moment, we don't feel that there is suspicion, but we have to be sure, so we would prefer it if you did not leave the city in the meantime. You will have some time to gather your things, and then you will be transported to the hotel where you will stay. In the meantime, our city has many delights to entertain you. I am sure you will not become bored."

He graced them all with a big smile, nodded to the room generally and then turned and left, tucking his notebook to his pocket. One by one they looked at each other, an expression of disbelief on their faces.

"Well," said Max. "We had better get ready."

"Yes, I suppose we don't have much choice," said Marcus, looking at Joe, who shrugged.

"I wonder where they will put us," said Aggie.
Selena, her expression one of clear displeasure sighed and answered. "God only knows. Probably some local dump," she said. "Come, Max, children. We need to get ready."

She stood and took Max's hand, drew him up from the couch and then gestured for the children to join them. As Samantha passed in front of him, she gave Avram a little glance and smiled before looking away. It was almost as if she had been expecting it. But how could she?

Avram thought about it as the rest of them got to their feet and started heading out of the room. It was true; it was as if Avram's decision had played into the circumstance, as if there was some foreknowledge. He was already packed. Regardless, he needed to put on some sort of show of preparing, so he too stood and made his way out of the Observation Lounge to head to his cabin and at least go through the motions of getting ready. For now, at least, the question about when to broach the topic of his decision with the others had been effectively put on hold.

He made his way back to his cabin and simply stood there for a few minutes, looking at his bag, considering the chain of events, the timing of his resolution, everything else that had happened. Still, the strangeness of the children's behaviour and the way in which they had been looking at him ate at his level of comfort. Ronald's demise, the strange welt on his neck, the words and whispers that kept appearing inside his head. Nothing was okay. And there was still the issue of those vacant spaces in his memory, fleeting hints of a set of recollections that were no longer fully there. None of it, none of it at all made any sense and none of it gave him any comfort. He needed time alone to sort all this out, but now, it appeared he was not going to get that chance. His grand plan to leave was nothing more than that, a grand plan. Events had conspired to stand in his way. And, in fact, if he thought about it, he was getting a little tired of fate, circumstance or whatever you wanted to call it, stacking up its own plans to work in opposition to his own.

With a sigh, he closed the leather bag, gripped the handles in one hand and hefted it off the bunk. By the time he got down to the gondola section, everyone else was there, except for the Greens, including Prinsloo, his crewman and a solitary policemen who stood by the doorway looking as if he was guarding the top of wheeled stairs that had, in the meantime, been manoeuvred into place. At the bottom, two white vans sat, people carriers ready to ferry them to their assigned accommodations.

Prinsloo took off his cap and ran his fingers through his shock of silver-gray hair. "I'm sorry about this folks," he said. "It's a little bit out of my control. If it's any consolation, Alexei and I are stuck here on board for the duration."

Selena and Max's voices drifted down from above, and first Alf, then Sam's small feet appeared at the top of the staircase. Sam carried a small pink bag with a picture of a rabbit sitting in a field of yellow flowers on it. Alf had his own, this one blue and decorated with a rocket ship. The children descended to join the others, followed in turn by Selena and Max, each carrying their own designer label overnight bags. Selena stepped precisely, negotiating the descent in her heels with care. Max, in his own usual form took no such trouble, his flat leather sandals taking each step with ease.

Beside Avram, Marcus muttered below his breath. "Typical. About time."

"Hush," said Joe and batted gently at his hand.

"That's all of them," Prinsloo said to the waiting officer.

The uniformed policeman stepped back, holding out one hand to the top of the stairs. "Please to go to cars," he said.

At the back of each van stood a driver, waiting at the back doors to take their luggage. Max and Selena, of course, moved to the first vehicle, the children in tow. Avram decided to join the rest in the second. At the moment, he didn't relish the prospect of sharing a ride in close corners with the Greens, particularly not their offspring. The lead vehicle's driver shut the doors, climbed aboard, and immediately took off without waiting. Avram, after stowing his bag moved up to take the front seat while Marcus, Joe, Pavel and Aggie bundled into the back.

"Well, at least we'll see something of the place," said Joe, always keen to put a positive spin on things.

No one responded, simply looking out of the van windows at the flat expanse of concrete field only broken by large hangars and buildings blocking any view. Beyond, Avram knew, there lay the conventional terminal and standard aircraft, but from this position, they could see nothing of that, only empty space dominated by the shadow of their parturient gray sack that floated in the air above them. As their erstwhile home disappeared behind them, Avram wondered how long it would be before they saw it again—in fact if he would ever see it again at all.

As they drove away from the landing field, there was no conversation. The driver clearly didn't speak their language and he concentrated on the way ahead, zipping in and out of lanes as they travelled at a fast clip along the road leading into the city, the waters of the Marmara spread out to the right, deep blue and clustered with huge tankers heading up to or from the Black Sea. Occasionally Avram glanced over at the other side, but there was nothing much to see, apart from huge commercial buildings and traffic heading the other way. It was a highway like any other, and besides, there was an attraction, a subtle pull that went with large bodies of water. In each place, they seemed to have their own special color, always slightly different than anywhere else in the world, or so he had found, so far in their travels, and the sea here was definitely a different hue to the one they had recently left.

Before long, commercial buildings gave way to city walls, ancient stone encircling clustered buildings like a hungry man guarding his food bowl. Here and there, in places, the stones had crumbled, but mostly, they appeared to be intact. Avram watched the rises and falls, the tumbled spaces, considering time, history, the way the passing of the years can change things, yet at the same time, leave them be while all around other things reshaped and grew, then fell away again. Their vehicle passed through what had once been one of the major city gates and he turned to watch the edifice dwindle behind them. Aggie and Pavel were in quiet conversation, pointing out something here and there to each other. Marcus and Joe sat hand in hand, watching the road ahead, whether the traffic or what lay revealed in front of them, as their vehicle wound through the streets and heavy traffic, Avram did not know.

A few minutes more of dodging in and out of lanes and protesting horns, they finally reached their destination, a small unassuming hotel set at the side of a major artery, complete with tramlines and by the looks of things, a stop just outside. The other van was pulled up in front of the hotel, but of the Greens there was no sign. Apparently they had arrived some minutes before and had not waited.

The hotel was definitely simple, but it looked clean and modern. Avram suspected they should consider themselves lucky if it was courtesy of the local law enforcement; he could hardly expect luxury. It would do under the circumstances. He climbed out and moved to the van's rear to retrieve his luggage, what there was of it, followed by the other two couples. Together, they all trooped inside and lined up to register, filling in various forms and allowing the clerk to take copies of their identification.

"The room is taken care of, but any extras will be added to your final bill," the clerk told them.

"So," said Joe as they all stood around in the lobby space in front of the reception desk looking at each other. "What shall we do?"

"I don't know," said Aggie. "Are you sure we should go anywhere?"

Marcus snorted. "It's not as if they can stop us. As he said, we're not going anywhere. I for one want to take in some of the sights. We've still got most of the day left."

Pavel nodded. "No, Marcus is right. Despite everything, it would be a shame to waste it, no?" He reached for Aggie's hand and squeezed it gently.

"Avram?" said Joe.

"Yes, sure," he responded. "But what about Max and Selena?"

"And the kids," said everyone in unison.

"Listen," said Marcus. "I'll get in touch with them. Let's go and drop our stuff. That's all we need to do. There's nothing going to happen with the ship for a few hours at least, and I'm sure they'll let us know. So, let us do that, and in the meantime, Joe can talk to the concierge, work out the best way of getting around from here. We could take taxis, but depending on Max and Selena, there's really too many of us. Anyway, I for one have a couple of places I really want to see. It will take our minds off everything that's happened." He glanced at Aggie as he said this.

"What's say we meet back here in twenty minutes? If there are any changes to that, we'll call your rooms," he continued.

Marcus was always consistently practical, without being pushy. He looked around and everybody nodded their agreement and without further discussion, headed off to find their allocated rooms and dump their luggage. Avram found his own room on the third floor. It was simple, clean and modern and looked comfortable enough. He opened the wardrobe, looked in the drawers, inspected the mini-bar and then simply stuffed his valise into the bottom of the closet and returned to sit on the edge of the bed, staring vacantly at the wall in front. There was a picture of the Golden Horn, some fishing boats and a mosque sitting in the background against a light blue sky with scattered cloud. Yet another exotic location, another snapshot image. After a while, he looked down at his watch. It was time.

Down in reception, the entire party was gathered, so it seemed that Marcus' efforts had not been in vain. Avram was the last to arrive. According to Joe, the best way to get into the center, and the major touristic requirements, was by tram. He had already arranged some local currency and thoughtfully also popped out to a nearby kiosk and purchased a multi-journey ticket pass that would work for them all. He assured them that if there was any need for any of them to purchase their own passes or change currency, then there would be plenty of opportunities down near Sultanahmet. Avram hadn't even thought of the need for local currency, he'd been so preoccupied. Not even asking where they were going, he was happy enough to be swept along by the group for now as they left the hotel and walked, as a group, down to the tram stop and negotiated the barriers one by one as Joe swiped his card to allow them entrance. They did not have very long to wait, and the next tram arrived within a couple of minutes. Already half full, half of the group managed to find seats, the rest forced to stand as it got underway. Avram held on to a hand strap, looking at the other passengers who seemed to be a mixture of locals and tourists while Joe explained that this was one of the most popular lines, leading right past the Covered Bazaar, Hagia Sofia, The Blue Mosque and all of the favorite destinations.

They left the tram, and after they had alighted, they visited, they wandered and together, they marvelled, taking their minds off the last few hours and washing them away with exotic scents, exhortations to buy, offerings of friendly guides, street sellers, stalls and an array of sights and sensations different to everywhere they had been so far, and very different from what they had left back home. Yet despite it all, to Avram it was a blur, as if made of papier-mâché, each image soaked and laid one atop the other. There was one exception, one thing that stood out; in one area, down by Sultanahmet, he noticed Samantha and Alfred in furious whispered conversation, heads close together, glancing first in his direction and then off to one side. It was more animated than he had seen them in days. He glanced over at Max and Selena, but they seemed not to have noticed the change at all, being too absorbed in the grandeur of the ancient basilica in front of them.

He glanced back at the children again, and then he felt it, a subtle tension working through his limbs and a tightness in his skull. Samantha looked up at him, caught his gaze, fixed it, held it. Without breaking eye contact, she reached for her brother, turned him to face Avram as well. Two pairs of eyes, holding him, deep and piercing as if looking into the very depths of his being. He tried to move, found he couldn't.

With an effort of will, he tore his gaze away and gasped reaching to the side for something to steady himself, but there was nothing and he staggered. A passer-by shot him a curious look. He regained his balance and then simply stood there, taking deep breaths, steadying himself. What the hell was that? Barely daring to do so, he looked back over his shoulder towards the children, but there attention had turned to something else, and in the next moment, their parents had called them over. He watched them as they walked calmly across the square to Max and Selena. They did not even walk like children. They were confident, purposeful, still, looking straight ahead. They simply walked like small and not yet fully-formed adults. For some reason, it gave him a chill.

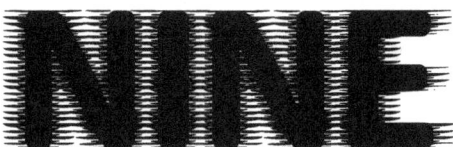

NINE

If it afflicts him in his sleep and he gazes at the one who afflicts him, it flows over him and he forgets himself…

—Assyrian Diagnostic

Breath

He barely remembered the tram ride back to the hotel, getting back to his room and somehow collapsing on the bed. The rest of the afternoon had been little more than a blur, a succession of daguerreotype images on laid on top of the other and bleeding at the edges. Somehow, he had managed to purchase his own tram pass, navigate his way back without getting lost after begging off further landmarks or museums. He had made it through Topkapi, and the small cafe down near the water at Eminönü, but after that the bands around his skull had started to tighten and his spine had felt like there were metal clamps gripping it at each end, stretching it taut. By the time they reached Kabataş there was nothing more he could do but stumble off on his own and rely on what he could remember of their path to retrace his way back to the hotel. Thankfully, it was a single line, no changes, with a few distinctive landmarks on the way. On the way back, he avoided the eyes of his fellow passengers, keeping his head bowed, only looking up to verify his progress and check whether he was anywhere near his final stop. By the time he finally reached their accommodations, the sun was starting to dip below the line of the minarets, tingeing the sky with purple and orange. Gratefully, he closed his door and locked himself away to lie there, staring at the ceiling. After a while, he dozed and before long, he had fallen into a deep black sleep full of shining eyes and dark wings beating blasts of air against his face, stirring the scent of damp and rotting leaves with the taste of dust.

He awoke to darkness and the feel of a presence close beside his bed. His mouth was dry; his tongue thick.

"It is time, Uncle Avram," the young voice said. It was Samantha.

How had she had gained entry to his room? More to the point, what was she doing here? His half-conscious mind stumbled through the thoughts, not coming up with any satisfactory answer.

His eyes were starting to adjust to the gloom and he could just make out her pale form like a ghost in the darkness.

"What do you want, Samantha?" he asked with difficulty.

"You have to come now," she said simply, without a trace of emotion.

Avram was still lying on top of the covers, fully dressed, and for that much, at least, he was thankful. Images of that early dream flashed through his head, making him swallow, an action that hurt with the dryness of his mouth and throat. He pushed himself upright and swung his legs off the bed so that he was sitting facing her. He still wasn't quite sure that he wasn't still dreaming.

"What are you doing in here, Samantha? Where are your parents?"

"They do not matter," she answered, confidence drifting into her voice. "They are asleep. You have to come, now." The last word came out as a breathy whisper.

"No, I'm sorry. This is not right. You should go back to your parents, Sam. I am not going to come with you and you should not be here."

Samantha took a deep breath and lifted a hand to his shoulder, saying nothing in response.

And with that touch, something ran through him, flooded through his shoulders, into his chest, into the back of his head and following behind came the words of another, different voice.

"Go with her, Avram. Go with her now."

Urging, insistent, the voice whispered through his thoughts. Though he clutched at it, his resistance started slipping through his grasp and dissipated in fragile strands. He found himself standing, turning at the side of the bed, stepping forward into the room. Sam reached for his hand and drew him forward, past the bed, around the corner to the door. Fumbling, he opened it and stepped out into the corridor. There, a few steps down the hall stood Alfred, looking at him impassively. Avram stood where he was, returning Alfred's gaze, numb, not knowing what to do. Further up the corridor came the muted sound of someone talking in a room. Gently, Samantha closed the door behind him, handing him his key, which he took unthinkingly and slipped into his pocket.

"Come," she said, reaching for his hand again and led him down the hall towards the stairs.

As they drew abreast of Alfred, the boy reached for his other hand. This could not be happening, but it was. Avram's thoughts came slowly, but still he tried to rationalise what was occurring. He was dreaming. He wasn't really there. And yet he was. Step by sluggish step, the children led him to the stairs, down, one by one, to the ground floor and then the lobby. As they passed the reception area, the man behind the desk looked up, saw the children and smiled. Then they were outside and they led him along to the tram stop. Barely knowing what he was doing, he passed them in and then entered himself. It was late, dark, but there was still traffic on the road and the trams still ran. Before long, one was with them and together, they boarded.

During the entire journey, not a word was said. The hum and whir of the tram rose and lowered, the doors hissed open, stop after stop, but Avram merely watched blankly as the streets and buildings rolled past. He did not count the stops, did not take note of where they were, he simply watched, and then finally, the tram drew to another stop and the children were urging him to disembark, pulling gently at his hands and guiding him to the door. Together, they stepped out and waited for the tram to depart. He knew this place. Knew where they were. It was Sultanahmet, the place they had been much earlier in the day, if it was still the same day, another thing he didn't know.

The streets were dark, one or two people wandering around. Orange tinted lights illuminated the nearby mosques, and reflected slickly from the black expanse of roadways, casting glimmers from the metal tram tracks. A faint humidity haze fogged the light beams and draped the trees in milky coronas. He could smell the heat, the moisture in the air, mixing with the scents of dirt and civilization. The children led him down the street to an intersection, then up another street to the left.

"Where are you taking me?" he asked.

"Shhhh," said Samantha in response.

He halted, resisting their pull, gaining some of his self-will momentarily.

"No," he said. "Where are you taking me?"

"Come, Uncle Avram," she said, pulling at his hand again, and once more, all volition left him and he meekly followed, doing merely as he was instructed.

Halfway up the street, they came upon a small building, low, squat, stone. Signs were affixed to the wall beside the door, brown with gold lettering, but in the darkness, even though he had no capacity to do so, he could not read them. Around them the streets were empty. The children led him to the door, waited while Alf stepped forward and pushed it open. Samantha led him forward. He did not question, did not think to question that the place was unlocked.

Inside, the entrance area was dark. Faint illumination seeped in through the doorways from the streetlights outside, but all that Avram could make out was some sort of desk, a windowed cubicle and a stand with pamphlets arrayed on it, all shadowed edges in the darkness. Heat rose from somewhere within and the sound of water, not running water, but a steady drip, echoing. At the other end of the small entranceway lay a staircase leading down, a colored glow, orange/red illuminating what lay beyond.

"Come, Avram. She waits," said Samantha.
He looked down at her, met her gaze and noticed absently that her eyes seemed filled with a faint inner light. He looked slowly over to Alfred and saw the same. Together, the children turned away towards the staircase and led him forward.

They descended wide wooden steps, one by one, to a platform halfway down, and then the stairs turned, descending further. Down here, the sound of drips echoed. A deep blanket of humidity reached hot clammy fingers to envelop him. Further down they went, and as they moved further, a vast open space lay revealed, stone pillars stretching in several rows off into the darkness, half illuminated by reddish lights along the edges, a vaulted stone ceiling above enclosing the space. The smell of wet stone and water was all around him. The pillars shone with seeping moisture, and all around, the constant drip and plink of drops from above falling into a dark, slightly rippling expanse of water, stirring sluggishly between the pillar bases. The place was old, very old, and he could feel the centuries pressing down upon him along with the humid air. The children led him forward.

Halfway along the stone platform that ran along this end of the chamber, a wooden walkway stretched out between the pillars, barely above the water's surface. It was towards this that the children led him. They urged him forward, steering him onto the walk and further, towards the other end, lost in distant shadow. All around, the tall stone pillars stretched, but closer now, he could see they were irregular, not all the same shape, mismatched cylindrical stone chunks stacked one upon each other, discolored with dark staining. As he took a step forward and then another, other sounds drifted through the darkness, noises and stirrings, unidentifiable and distorted by the cavernous space, floating through the constant moist drip, drip, drip of the water.

Brother and sister were behind him now as he took one step forward and then another. Around him, on either side, the water stirred sluggishly, and it seemed that above and beyond it the shadows moved too. Avram was starting to feel something else now, despite the loss of his capacity to resist, despite the fog that worked across his thoughts, and he recognised the feeling, vague as it might be; it was a growing sense of fear. Definitely now, there were other movements in the darkness, and he knew, then, that they were not alone down here. He swallowed drily and took another step, and then another.

Halfway along, connecting walkways ran off to the right and

the left, but they moved past the junction and continued forward. The wooden slats seemed to go on forever, but a few moments later, their ending started to resolve, a wall at the end defined in darkness beyond. Now, Avram could see that the walkway split into a square enclosing two larger pillars at the end and what looked like a sort of platform to one side. On the platform there were clustered shapes, still indistinct, but they were figures, simply standing there, still in the darkness and waiting. At the base of the first large pillar, was a shape, becoming clearer now, a large chunk of stone, carved, stained green by water and age, a vast head, ancient and inverted, looking blankly at him with cold stone eyes. The carving drew him, holding his attention, drawing him forward to see.

"Avram, welcome," came a voice, a child's voice, and his attention was wrested away from the stone head and to the platform and the clustered figures. They were children, all of them and slightly in front of them, in the center, stood a familiar form, arms held out in front, palms up. It was the girl. It was the child called Lilith.

"Come to me, Avram," she said.

Despite himself, Avram took one halting step after the other moving closer. Behind and around her stood the others, the same, familiar impassive expressions on their faces. They wore normal street clothes, all of them, both boys and girls. There must have been a dozen of them. Every eye was upon him, and every eye held the barest hint of a faint inner light. He could feel their gaze upon him.

"At last, we are here," said the child called Lilith.

A sudden rushing motion from the darkness to one side seized his attention and he turned, not quickly, to see a small shape flying towards him.

"No!" said Lilith, throwing up one hand.

The boy, for it was a boy, stopped, letting out a long exhalation filled with disappointment. His teeth were bared, and a faint light played within his eyes. He stood in place, his arms outstretched, slightly hunched over, a mere three steps away from Avram. Slowly, he took a step back, his face filled with ... Avram was not sure what.

"No," said Lilith more calmly. "He is one of us now. He is with us. Now ... and always."

Avram turned back to face her. From beside him, the boy let out another low, sighing breath.

Lilith looked at Avram and smiled. "I am glad you have come to me," she said. "You will be with us in the journey ahead and we will be with you."

She gestured around her at the other children. "These, and others now," she said. "So many others."

Avram looked around at the children, still all watching him. He looked to the side, but the boy who had rushed upon him was now standing, gazing at him, just like all the others.

"I ... I ...." The words died on his lips. He did not know what it was he wanted to say, what he wanted to ask her. His thoughts still came slowly, and here, close to her, he could feel the damping of his self, his will. But he wanted to ask ...

"I ..." Again, he started and again the words halted.

"Hush ..," she said. "We are here because of you. And now, because of you, there will be more here and elsewhere." She stepped forward and reached up to place the tips of cold fingers upon his lips. "Hush."

She stepped back and then looked him slowly up and down, inspecting him. There was no judgement in her gaze. She looked back to his eyes, and licked her lips slowly.

"There is much to do," she said. "So much to do."

"But what?" he finally managed.

"When the time is right, you will know," she said and smiled again. "Too many questions now. You have no need for questions. You will be among us, and you will know."

Very slowly, he looked around the faces of the other children standing unmoving behind her. He turned to look at the boy off to one side, and then turned in the other direction to look at Samantha and Alfred. Alfred's face was expressionless, but Samantha was smiling.

"You have been blessed, Avram," Lilith spoke again and her words drew his attention back round to look at her. "Take your blessing and travel far so that others might be blessed," she said.

The words were strange, archaic, adult and strangely disconnected from the girl who stood before him. He stared into her eyes, struggling within himself, and then, with an effort of will, haltingly, the words came.

"I do not understand," he said. "How are you ... who are you?" The next welled up inside him and burst forth from his mouth in a shout that echoed around the vaulted stones above them and bounced back from the walls. "Who the hell are you!"

She laughed, then. Simply laughed. And then, after a brief pause, still smiling, she said, "You know who I am, Avram."

"No!"

She tilted her head to one side, as if suddenly interested in his outburst, and then straightened again and spoke. "Go now. Very soon, you will leave this place. These two will go with you. I will be with you. I will always be with you, Avram. When you leave this place and go the next, and the one after that, we will be with you."

He stared at her, and in the next instance felt small hands taking his own on either side, drawing him to the side and back up the long wooden walkway and away. Behind him, the stirrings in the darkness went on and all around, the echoes of dripping water continued.

TEN

Knowing no care, they grind the land like corn. Knowing no mercy, they rage against mankind. They spill their blood like rain, devouring their flesh and sucking their veins.

–Babylonian Tablet

Avram barely remembered the trip back to the hotel, and of the meeting in the ancient underground cistern, he only retained fleeting impressions and images. Children, lots of children. He did remember that much. After he'd returned, he sat in darkness in his hotel room, staring into the black in front of him until eventually, he had lain back and drifted into unconsciousness. His sleep was without dreams, black as the darkness he lay in.

"Avram! Avram!" A pounding on his door dragged him from the deep pool and shoved him into consciousness.

"Avram, are you in there!?" It was Aggie's voice.

"Yes, yes, I'm here," he called out, struggling upright and realizing that he was fully clothed, including even his shoes. Befuddled, his eyes half closed with sleep, he staggered to the door and opened it.

Aggie stood before him, her eyes wide, panting. "Oh my God, thank you, thank you," she said reaching for his hand. "You have to come."

"Wait, wait," he said, looking around for his door key, then finally touching his crumpled top pocket, realized he still had it on him. The tugging at his hand was insistent, and he let himself be dragged into the corridor. He'd been going through quite a lot of that lately.

"Aggie, what is it? Calm down."

"It's Pavel!" she said desperately.

"What about Pavel?"

"I don't know what to do. I don't know what to do. Please come."

A chill feeling opened up deep within his abdomen as he allowed himself to be led further down the corridor and then to the Bartko's room. The door was closed and Aggie fumbled the key, then dropped it on the floor in front of the door, before letting go of Avram's hand and crouching on the floor, patting at the carpet as she unsuccessfully tried to retrieve it.

"Oh God, oh God, oh God," she said.

"Here, let me," said Avram, stooping to scoop up the key and push open the door.

"Oh God, oh God," she said. "This can't be happening."

Avram stepped into the room, Aggie close behind him, her hand fluttering at her throat. The thin slight form of Pavel Bartko lay stretched on the bed, the covers thrown back. He was staring up at the ceiling, eyes open, unmoving, and on his lips lay a smile. Avram quickly absorbed the picture, realizing that Pavel's pyjama bottoms were open, his genitals on display. On his neck, a deep red and purple weal marked his skin, rounded, looking like a birthmark, except that Avram knew that Pavel had no birthmark. This was something else.

Aggie gripped his shoulder from behind, craning over to look. "Avram," she said. "What are we going to do? What am I going to do?"

It was clear that Pavel wouldn't be moving or offering any answer.

"Wait," he said, detaching her hand and stepping over to the bed. Aggie did as she was told, remaining by the doorway, her breath coming in short, shuddering bursts, her fingers of her right hand still tapping at her throat.

Despite his reluctance, Avram crouched beside the still form and, loathe to touch Pavel's neck with its tell-tale marking, he reached for the wrist. Pavel's skin was cold, some latent warmth from the bed radiating in contrast, from where Aggie had clearly been lying. He felt for a pulse, knowing that he would not find any. Slowly he stood, rubbing the back of his neck. He didn't know what to say. He felt Aggie taking a step towards him, but he gestured behind with one hand.

"No, stay there," he said, thinking. Almost as an afterthought, he reached down and pulled the cover up over Pavel's exposed parts. He looked up into Pavel's face, focussing despite himself on the smile.

"Oh God, Aggie," he said, running his fingers back through his hair and then turning around to face her.

"What is it?" she said. "Tell me. What is it?"

"You have to come away now, Aggie," he said gently, reaching out with both hands.

"No!" she said, withdrawing from him.

"Aggie, listen. We can't do anything here. Come with me now."

"But we have to do something. There must be ... oh God, oh God." Her hand lifted to her mouth, stopping the words, as she stood there, gulping air.

He reached behind her for the door, taking her shoulder in one hand and turning her, leading her gently out of the room.

"We need to talk to the hotel. Come with me now."

"Oh God," she said quietly again, her eyes closing as he drew her into the corridor.

He had seen this before; she had seen this before, back in the ship when she had discovered Ronald, but now ... now this was Pavel, her partner, her husband.

"Come on, Aggie, we'll deal with it," said Avram. "We have to deal with it."

"But how, Avram?" The words came out haltingly. "How?" She kept her gaze on the floor before them as they moved further down the corridor, shaking her head, every few steps punctuated with an almost whispered "oh God."

Eventually, they reached the lobby and Avram placed Aggie on a nearby chair, where she sat trembling, her arms wrapped about herself, staring at the floor in front of her and rocking slightly back and forth, whispering those words over and over. Avram realized he had no idea what he was supposed to be doing. He stepped across to reception. As the man behind the desk looked up, his face flickered with concern, first taking in Avram's appearance and then looking across at Aggie seated there behind.

"Sir?" he said, frowning.

"We need help," said Avram. "There's been an accident." How

else could he describe it? "Room 326, the Bartkos."

The clerk shook his head, not quite understanding. "What sort of accident, sir?" he said.

"You'd better come," said Avram.

"I will send someone to the room."

"No!" he said through gritted teeth. "You have to come. And get someone to stay with her," he said gesturing over in Aggie's direction and hissing the last from between his closed teeth.

The clerk ducked his head, quickly turned and disappeared to a back room, emerging a few moments later with a short, uniformed woman. One after the other, they moved out from behind the desk, the woman crossing over to where Aggie sat and crouching down beside her. The clerk held out one hand in the direction of the upper floor access.

"Please show me, sir," he said. "Have you got the key?"

In that moment, he realized that he had no idea what he had done with the key. He looked across at Aggie, but her hands were empty. Of course, he had been the one with the key; he had used it to open the door. He shoved his hands in his pockets, but there was nothing there. He checked in his shirt pocket, but there was only the one there, the one to his own room.

"Shit," he said.

The woman from the hotel was murmuring quiet words to Aggie, one hand on her arm, the other holding her hands in front.

"A moment," said the clerk who ducked back behind the desk, grabbed a set of conventional keys which also had a passkey dangling from the ring. "Come," he said when he had moved out from behind the desk, again indicating the way with one outstretched hand.

Avram followed the clerk towards the elevators, up to the floor and along the corridor, leaving Aggie sitting in the hotel woman's care. There was nothing much else he could have done in the circumstances. At the Bartko's door, he waited behind the clerk as he positioned the pass key and pushed opened up the room. The clerk stood there, holding the door open with one arm.

"Sir?" he said.

"Come and look," said Avram

The clerk gave a little frown but stepped inside. "Siktir," he said as he looked at the bed, and then remembering himself said, "I'm sorry, sir. This is a problem. What happened?"

He stepped forward and looked down, inspecting Pavel's staring face, then turned away.

"Have you checked? Is he ...?"

Avram nodded. "Yes," he said simply.

The clerk gave a big sigh and shook his head. "We will have to inform the proper authorities. If you will come with me please, sir." Then he seemed to remember, and he paused. "You are the people from the ship," he said and then nodded as if confirming to himself. "I will need to inform someone else in that case. Please, sir, please come with me. This is most unlucky," he said, almost as an afterthought.

Back in the lobby, the clerk positioned Avram on one of the large, comfortable chairs positioned around the space, but one with a clear view of the reception desk, and vice-versa. Avram suspected that it was the latter that was the real reason for his choice. The clerk then disappeared behind the desk and rapidly got on the telephone. What ensued was a lengthy conversation, with the clerk shooting glances in Avram's direction all the while. Eventually, he put down the phone. Avram made to rise, to go over and find out what was happening, but the clerk gestured for him to stay where he was. He could just see where Aggie sat from his position. By now, the woman from the hotel had found another chair and drawn it up alongside her and was sitting there stroking her hands. If they were saying anything, Avram couldn't tell. Aggie still looked as if she had her gaze fixed on the floor in front of her, her slightly hunched position betraying her distress. Poor Aggie. Avram could barely comprehend what it must be like.

Breath

It was about half an hour before there was any response, and all the while, the clerk kept shooting him glances. Avram kept his eye on the large clock above the reception desk ticking through the minutes, something to occupy his attention while thoughts of what was happening to them, to him, kept running through his head. What had they done? Why was this happening to them? He barely wanted to consider what part the children were playing in all of this. He thought about the possibility of discussing it, but who would he tell? They'd look at him as if he was crazy, and in reality, he might just be that. As the seconds ticked away, his thoughts grew darker and more despairing. He had to do something, but he didn't know what. He hadn't even told any of the others. What about them? First Ronald, and now Pavel. Was it a sickness? In his heart of hearts he knew it wasn't anything like that.

Any further contemplation was broken by a large black sedan pulling up in front of the hotel doors, a flashing light on top. All of its doors were flung open, and four men got out, two in uniform, two in suits. They trooped into the hotel lobby, headed straight for the reception desk and spoke to the clerk who motioned over in Avram's direction with a few words. In the next moment, one of the men detached himself from the group and strode over in Avram's direction, leaving the other three standing by the desk.

Avram watched the approaching man. He wore an obviously hastily thrown-on brown suit, with cream shirt. As he got closer, Avram recognised the face with its large flecked moustache. He stood.

"Mr. Davis, isn't it?" he said to Avram.

"Yes, that's right."

The man nodded. "I am Kaplan," he said, "if you remember. Like the tiger."

Avram had forgotten the name, despite recognising the man himself.

Kaplan looked him up and down, and then met his eyes with his own dark, assessing gaze.

"One is unfortunate. Two, and so close together, that is more than unlucky, wouldn't you say?" he said. "Now, it becomes a little serious. We had already discounted the possibility of disease. We have confirmed that it was some kind of violence in the other case. Perhaps we should go and see what has happened here. Yes?"

At least that much confirmed Avram's own suspicions.

He gestured behind himself and motioned for one of his men to join him. The other man dressed in a suit crossed over to where they stood, leaving the two uniformed men to take up position on either side of the hotel's front doors.

"This here, is Akin," said Kaplan. "He does not speak very well your language, but he is a good man." Again he motioned to the reception, waving the hotel clerk over as well. "Let us go and see."

All the while, as the four of them traipsed off and out of the lobby area, Avram felt Kaplan studying him, scrutinising and assessing and for the trip up to the Bartko's room, he kept asking little questions, conversationally, as if there was no particular significance to the things that he was asking. After each answer there came a little nod, a consideration as though Kaplan was filing it all away, compiling a dossier in his head.

They reached the room and the clerk opened the door for them. Kaplan said something and the clerk withdrew, heading back down the corridor, Avram presumed, back to his place at the reception desk. One by one, they stepped inside the room. Nothing had changed. Pavel still lay where he had left him. Kaplan stepped forward, looked, tilted his head first one way then the other, and then crouched down beside the bed and went through the same motions.

"Yes, I see," he said. He then started speaking to the other man, Akin, words that Avram could not understand. Akin intermittently nodded. And then Kaplan stood, drew back the covers and sucked in air through his teeth and shook his head. He said something else to

Akin, raised his eyebrows and then pulled the covers back up in place.

"And, Mr Davis," he said. "This is how he was found?"

Avram nodded slowly.

"It is unusual for one unusual death, but to have two unusual deaths in the same party is more than unusual, wouldn't you say?" When Avram simply nodded again, Kaplan continued. "So far we have not determined the cause of the death on your ship, but this would look very much the same ..." He cleared his throat. "... despite the, um, obvious differences."

Avram didn't know how to respond, so he just kept mute.

"All right," said Kaplan with a sigh. "We will have to look at this with more attention. Do you know anything that might assist us? What about the wife? She was the one who found him, no?"

"Yes," said Avram, finally finding something he could usefully respond to. "But you could not suspect Aggie of anything. It's not in her nature. Besides, how do you explain that thing on his neck?"

"I do not, Mr Davis," Kaplan responded. "However, it was the wife who found the other one too, was it not?"

Avram paused. He hadn't considered that. Kaplan was right. Regardless, that didn't make sense, and, more importantly, Avram knew things that Kaplan didn't, that no one else did, apart from Samantha and Alfred as far as he was aware, things that he wasn't going to blurt out to the police inspector in a hurry. Well, at least he thought he knew them. He reached up with one hand, rubbing the back of his neck and grimaced.

"Is it something you have thought of, Mr Davis?" asked Kaplan.

"No, no. It's just ... well, I can't explain it. It's just strange. How can this be happening?"

"My question exactly, Mr Davis. My question exactly." Kaplan nodded to himself as if he was very satisfied with the statement he had just made.

"Well, there is one thing we know for sure," he continued. "It appears there is no sign of a ... how do you say? ... infection. So that leaves only one other possibility. There have been some other signs though. Perhaps signs of suffocation. If a man drinks a lot, becomes deeply drunk, it might be possible that could happen, but this man here, he is in bed, with his wife. There seems to be no explanation. And, as you have said, how do we explain this mark on his neck? No, no. It is very strange." He gave a deep sigh and looked at the ceiling.

"So, what happens now?" asked Avram.

"We will, of course, have to do some more investigation. I will have to ask you to stay at least a few days more in our city. We will let the others of your party know, of course, but until we have a better idea, there is no choice. I thank you, Mr Davis. That is all for now. If I need to ask some more things, we will locate you. The same thing for other members of your group. I will need to locate them now and ask some things too."

"So, how long do you expect we are likely to be stuck here?"

There was a flicker of a frown on Kaplan's face. "It is difficult to know, Mr Davis. Very difficult to know."

With that, he turned back to the body and starting conversing with his companion in his own language. Avram had clearly been dismissed. He backed out of the room, stood in the corridor for a second or two, wondering what he was going to do, and then, decided. He had to talk to the others, but whom first? And in that moment, he realized. Now, with this, he couldn't afford to keep quiet any longer. Whatever was going on with Samantha, Alfred, the girl who was not a girl, Lilith, he had to tell someone. He let out a deep breath. Max and Selena first then. Really, it had been obvious and now that he had finally decided, he didn't understand why he hadn't done so before. Berating himself for stupidity, he turned and headed up the corridor to the floor where the Green's room lay. He wondered if they knew, if anyone had informed them yet.

Outside their door, he hesitated. He could hear them inside, the stirrings of morning. It was still early. No, there was nothing else for it. He lifted a fist and rapped gently on the door.

"Yes?" Max's voice.

"Max, it's Avram."

In only a moment, the door open and Max stood there, a hotel robe wrapped around him, looking at Avram with a quizzical frown upon his brow.

"Avram, what is it?"

He swallowed, paused and then spoke in a low voice, trying to peer over Max's shoulder to see if the children or Selena could hear.

"It's Pavel."

"What. What is with Pavel?"

"He's gone, Max. The same as Ronald. That policeman is here. Kaplan."

"Ah, shit," said Max. He looked past Avram, glancing up and down the hallway and then stepped back. "You had better come inside."

The Green's room was much bigger than Avram's, naturally, and as he stepped inside, he looked around. Selena sat up in bed, looking half asleep, confused. Over the other side of the room were two single beds and the children sat on the edge of each, looking at each other. As Avram entered, slowly, their faces turned together to look at him. They said nothing.

"Come, come," said Max, closing the door behind him. "What has happened?"

"What is it?" asked Selena from the bed.

"It's Pavel," said Avram again. "The same as Ronald on the ship. There's something going on. The local police are here and Kaplan's definitely suspicious." He stood there, in the center of the room looking from one to the other, not quite sure where he should position himself, if he should stand there where he was, go and sit in the chair. Instead, he simply clasped his hands in front of himself, waiting for them to react, sneaking a glance in the children's direction.

Selena's hand had moved to rest at her throat. Max was scratching at the back of his head.

"There's something I need to talk to you about," said Avram.

"What?" said Selena. "Something else? Isn't that enough?"

"Yes, yes," he said. He darted a look in Samantha's direction. "Yes, surely it's enough, but I think it's connected."

"Do they know what it is, what caused it?" asked Max, still in the previous chain of thought.

"That's what I want to discuss," said Avram.

At that moment, Alfred stood, crossed and took Avram's hand, looking up at his face. "What is it Uncle Avram? Are you upset?" The words were innocent, a child's words, but the look on Alf's face was something else, filled with knowing.

"I ... I ..." Avram felt the compulsion to speak going out of him, the resolve dissipating through his limbs as if it were simply draining away. Samantha stood now and crossed, taking his other hand, also looking up at his face, and then the words grew, first as a whisper then more clearly, in a voice that didn't belong in that hotel room at all, a quiet and confident little girl's voice. He knew what he had to say next. The whisper had told him.

"We have to get out of here," he said. "We need to leave."

"What do you mean?" asked Selena from the bed.

"We just have to leave," he said. "We cannot stay here. You know what it is like: foreign country, local police. I just think we need to get out of here."

The children dropped their grip on his hands and moved back to their beds, moving out of Avram's sight, but just before they did, Avram caught a smug little nod from Samantha, a look of approval.

"Yes," said Max, who had started to pace. "You are right. But how can we do so? The police. They would not like this. And what about the Bartko woman?"

"Aggie," breathed Avram. Of course; he hadn't thought about

her. "I think she would want to stay, to be with Pavel."

Max nodded. "And the Boys?"

"They need to come, of course."

"But how do we tell Aggie?" said Selena.

"I think we can only write her a letter," said Avram after a moment. "She will be a mess anyway. She won't be thinking straight. I'll do it. Leave it for her. I feel kind of guilty, but I don't think we have a real choice."

"Yes, good," said Max with a nod. "I think if we talk to Prinsloo, he will do this too. All we have to do is slip away," he gestured with his hand, "get on the ship, go."

Avram looked across at the children.

"We could be home in a few days. It would be a pity, but it is what we must do," Max continued. "Once we are home, we can sort everything out."

Samantha was looking at her father, listening, her head tilted slightly to one side, a speculative look on her face.

"So," said Max. "You will go and talk with the Boys?"

Avram nodded. "Yes. Meanwhile, I think you should get your things together. Don't make it too obvious. Remember, Kaplan and his men are still here."

"We will have to wait for them to leave," said Selena.

"Yes," said Avram. "And no doubt they will want to talk to you, and probably to Marcus and Joe as well. Expect a visit, but I imagine that will be soon. And speaking of Marcus and Joe, I'll go and talk to them now, tell them what we're planning. Hopefully, Kaplan isn't already with them."

"Selena, children, we should get dressed," said Max.

And with that, Avram left them, closing their door quietly behind him.

As he walked slowly down the corridor, he wondered briefly what he was doing, where this sudden resolve had come from, but the thought only lasted a moment.

ELEVEN

... and he burned the chariots of the sun with fire

−2 Kings Chapter 23

Thankfully, Marcus and Joe were alone and already awake when he reached their room and somehow, he managed to avoid both Kaplan and any of his men on the way down. Joe, naturally, was more obviously affected by the news, whilst Marcus merely went very, very quiet. After the initial impact had faded, Avram spent a few minutes explaining their plans. Neither of their reactions was quite what he expected. Marcus simply said nothing and stood there, subjecting Avram to a thin-lipped gaze, before looking away, pushing aside the curtain with one hand and staring out the window. Joe, on the other hand, grabbed Avram's upper arm and pounded him with a barrage of questions—what about this, what about that, not a single one of them about Aggie, and shaking Avram's arm with each one until Marcus turned from the window and snapped at him:

"Joe, shut up. It's what we've got to do. We don't have a choice."

The torrent of words stopped and Joe released Avram's arm. He bit his lip and stepped back.

"So how will we know when …?" said Marcus from his place by the window.

Avram hadn't thought that far.

"I guess I will try to keep an eye out. I'll let you know."

"And in the meantime?"

"Just stay here. I expect you'll be getting a visit soon."

Marcus nodded slowly. "Yes, of course."

"Meanwhile, I'm going back to my room to write something for Aggie. I'll check on progress while I'm out there and also see if I can quietly what's happened to her at the same time. Wait to hear from either me or Max."

Marcus simply nodded. Joe, by now, had moved to the end of the bed and was sitting there, his head in his hands, saying nothing. It appeared that the initial torrent had subsided.

Avram left them there and made his way cautiously down to the lobby. Finding Kaplan's men still there, he headed back to his room to write the promised letter. Maybe soon, he would work out what the hell was going on within himself, but he didn't have time to pursue it right then.

What was he going to say to her? What could he say?

He made several false starts, scratching away at the hotel stationary and crumpling his attempts, tossing them into the waste bin under the desk. Finally, he settled on a version that he thought was acceptable under the circumstance:

My Dearest Aggie

I cannot imagine the pain and loss you are going through right now. We all feel so bad, but it cannot equal what you are feeling.

As a group, we have taken a decision. We must leave this place. We hope you will understand. Together, we decided that you would want to stay with Pavel, to deal with what has happened. It is the right thing to do. When all this is over, you will know where to find us. We just hope that you will forgive us for what we must now do.

With all my love and sympathy,

Avram

He sat back and stared down at the note, wondering still if it was enough. He ran his fingers back through his hair and then plucked at his bottom lip. It had to be enough. Anything longer would be stretching whatever he was trying to say, making the unpalatable even more unpalatable. As an afterthought, he decided to take the last 'my' and change it to 'our.'

Painstakingly, he rewrote it on a fresh sheet and crumpled the original. This too he tossed into the waste receptacle below the desk. With care, he folded the new version and placed it inside one of the hotel-provided envelopes before carefully lettering Aggie's name on the front. He sat there for a few moments, and then stood, scanning the room, looking to see if there was anything he needed to gather. Strangely, it was as if he hadn't been here at all. There were hardly any traces of his occupancy. The bed lay undisturbed, the covers still in place with the slight impression of his body in the center and the depression caused by his head still on the pillow. It would take only moments to pull his few things together before departing.

At the last minute, he had another thought. If they were going to absent themselves, then he'd be stupid to leave the pile of crumpled false starts in the wastepaper bin. He dug them all out and crumpled them in a tight ball which he shoved into his trousers. He'd dump them in a waste receptacle out on the street.

He slid the envelope into his inside pocket—he thought it unwise to leave that lying around either—and left the room, heading once more for the lobby to check the on-going presence of the local constabulary.

As he left, thoughts of damage and loss walked with him. He really could imagine what Aggie must be going through. The unexpected departure of a loved one was something he could relate to, though not something he had experienced directly, not in the same way. His separation from Amelia, the pain of the divorce, the blame, it all had similar characteristics, even though it was not quite the same or as extreme, but he remembered the hard knot of resentment that had lived inside him, tearing away at his insides and his capability to function normally within the world. Of course it was not the same, but it had to be similar, pale by comparison, but similar all the same.

Down in the lobby, he ducked his head around the corner to see, but the two policemen were still in place. He withdrew quickly, patted at his jacket pocket to ensure that the letter was still safely there, and then turned around. He could go back and see Marcus and Joe, or he could see how the Greens were getting on, but somehow, the latter prospect filled him with a strange reluctance. He had been going to tell them something, he was sure, something else, but he couldn't seem to remember what it had been. In the meantime, he would simply have to return to his room for a while and wait it out, spend some time puzzling through the absences in his thoughts. He was sure he had been doing things over the last couple of days, things that were not directly related to the death aboard their ship, nor, now, to Pavel's demise, but all he had were blurred impressions, pictures of the city, buildings, old things and places … and something about a child. A child but not a child. He shook his head. What did that mean?

Back in his room, Avram sat in the armchair just staring into space, thinking about nothing in particular and just waiting it out. Occasionally, he glanced down at his watch, or stood, crossed to the window and easing the curtains aside with a couple of fingers, looked out, but the view from his room afforded him nothing. Each time, he returned to the chair and sat. After a full two hours had passed, he decided it was worth another check and got up again. First he would recheck the lobby, and then go and find out how the others were doing, first Marcus and Joe and then the Greens.

When he reached the reception area, there was only one of the policemen left, leaning over the reception desk, casually chatting to the young woman with the flame-red hair that stood behind it. The policeman barely glanced at him as Avram casually walked past and out the front door. Once outside, Avram checked up and down the street, but there was nothing. Kaplan's car had gone, which further supported the casual attitude of the young policeman inside. In the meantime, he suspected that they had arranged to have Pavel's body removed and of any further activity there was little indication, but under the circumstances, he was not going back up to the Bartko's room to check. He wondered if Aggie was even there. Perhaps they'd taken her away, either to a hospital or to police headquarters. Neither prospect was very attractive. He entered the front door again and strolled back past the desk. This time the young policeman didn't even look. The girl behind the desk glanced at him, but she was tied up in her conversation. The phone rang and she lifted a hand to the policeman telling him to wait a moment, and proceeded to answer. Satisfied,

Avram left the lobby and wandered over to the elevator, keeping his movements calm, unhurried, just a local tourist wandering around. Clustered on a group of couches near the elevator area sat a collection of people, perhaps a family. They too barely glanced in Avram's direction as he passed. He wondered if they were coming or going. There was no sign of luggage. Either way, he thought they might be useful as a distraction, a group their size. He would have to time it right though.

Marcus and Joe were ready. Avram slipped into the room checking around himself before speaking.

"It looks like Kaplan's gone for now, but I think we might have to be quick. It will be better if we leave individually rather than as a group. That's going to attract attention, particularly if we are carrying luggage."

Joseph stood and crossed to the window, looking out. "Yes," he said. "That makes sense." He seemed to have pulled himself together in the meantime.

"I think it would be wise to meet up the street a bit," offered Marcus from the chair. "It's going to be a bit obvious if we all meet in front."

"Okay," said Avram, rubbing his chin. "Maybe if we go in the direction of the tram stop. Enough people, things in the way. The next corner up in that direction."

Joe turned away from the window. "We are going to need more than one cab."

"You're right," said Avram. "But I'm a little worried about the Greens. With the children, they're going to be a little hard to miss."

"Perhaps you should follow them out," said Marcus, standing. "That way you can check that they get out all right. We can go first, get the lay of the land. If it looks like there's going to be a problem, we can come back in and let you know before it turns into something."

"Cabs shouldn't be a problem," said Joe. "I've seen plenty of them cruising up by the tram stop." He looked over at Marcus who answered with a short nod.

"All right, it's settled," said Avram. "Give me about fifteen minutes to line things up with Max and Selena and then you head out." He looked down at his watch. "I'll get them to follow five minutes after that and I'll be close behind. If there's any trouble, I'll try to get out, meet you up there and let you know. Meanwhile, I'll pop the letter under Aggie's door. I don't know if she's still there. If I was in her position I wouldn't be, but you never know. Either way, she'll get it, one way or another. Either she'll pick it up, or Kaplan will show it to her. He's going to hit the roof is my prediction."

He looked down at his watch again. "Okay, fifteen minutes. Let's do this."

Slipping out of the room again, he checked up and down the hallway and, finding it empty, strode quickly in the direction of Max and Selena's room. Upon reaching it, he knocked gently, briefing Max rapidly at the doorway and checking his watch again. Behind Max, he could see both children sitting quietly, looking at him past their father's tall frame. Avram shook himself, a slight shiver running through him and turned away from their gaze. He took a deep breath, nodded at Max and then turned, quickly making his way back down the corridor in the direction of his own room. First, he would grab his bag, and the last thing he would do would be to slip the letter under Aggie's door. One quick last glance around his room when he reached it and he took his valise and moved back out to the corridor, shutting the door gently behind him. A few moments later, and he was outside the Bartko's door. He stood and listened for a couple of seconds, but if anyone was inside, there was no sign of movement. He checked his watch, waiting, and then, judging that enough time had passed, withdrew the letter from his inside pocket and gently slipped it under the door. Quickly, he turned and walked rapidly away.

As he reached the stairway, he slowed his pace, calmed his

breathing and descended. He checked around the corner, and the policeman was still there, still talking to the girl behind the desk, still seemingly unconcerned by anything. Of Joe and Marcus, there was no sign, so he presumed they had got out safely. The family that he had seen before had disappeared, and he grimaced a little at that. One more opportunity gone. The Greens had still not appeared, so he took up a position on one of the couches affording him a view of both the elevators and the front door, including most of the lobby area. A couple of moments later, a waiter appeared and asked him if he wanted anything, but Avram waved him away. The waiter bowed, clutching his tray in front of himself, and then turned and disappeared somewhere. Avram gave a sigh. Right now, his heart was starting to race again, and he could feel his palms growing damp with sweat. There was just so much that could go badly wrong.

Five minutes later—Avram confirming with constant glances at his timepiece—the Greens arrived, children in tow, characteristically some minutes behind schedule, not that Avram had ever known Selena to keep anyone's schedule but her own. They exchanged the briefest of looks before they moved past him, not even acknowledging his presence. They turned the corner, their designer luggage trailing behind and headed for the hotel front doors. For just a moment, Avram thought everything would be All right, that the Greens would get past without problems, but then the girl behind the reception desk tossed her chin in their direction, indicating their presence to the young policeman who was still nearby. He turned, took in the picture and immediately crossed to confront them, standing in their path to the door. He held up a hand, as if directing traffic. Avram caught his breath.

In the next instant, Avram barely understood what took place, it happened so quickly. Leaving their bags where they lay, the children moved, quickly, without a word. Samantha stepped past her mother and took the policeman's hand, looking up into his face. At the same time, Alfred crossed to the reception desk, stood in front of it, staring over the edge into the face of the girl, his hands crossed behind his back. She looked down into his eyes as if drawn to them. Not a word was spoken, but then the receptionist turned, stepped through a door into the back office. Samantha withdrew her hand, watching as the policeman turned, walked around Max and Selena and headed through the lobby to the back of the hotel. Just as quickly as it had happened, it was over. Sam and Alfred returned, retrieved their luggage and the Greens were out the door and gone.

Avram sat where he was for a couple of seconds, just blinking at the empty lobby. What the hell had just happened? Whatever it was, he didn't have time to wait around, so he too grabbed his bag and walked rapidly to the entrance following the Greens up the street to the corner where they had agreed to meet. He had no idea what the children had induced nor how long it would last, and he quickened his step, closing the gap between himself and Max and Selena and the kids walking passively along beside them. He could already see Marcus and Joe up ahead, Joe with an expression of relief at the sight of them.

As they clustered there, making up their minds to act, another thought came to him.

"Aren't we stupid going back to the ship?" he asked. "Don't you think the police will still be there?"

"It is just a chance we will have to take," said Max.

Samantha looked up at him then.

"Everything will be fine, Uncle Avram," she said.

He frowned down at her, not at all sure, but he let himself be dragged along by the others all the same.

As Joe had promised, it didn't take long to flag down a couple of taxis, give the directions to the airfield and climb aboard, the Greens in one cab, Avram, Joe and Marcus in the other. Following one after the other, the taxis made the big U-turn that would take them back out through the city walls and away. As their vehicle wound in and out of the traffic, Avram desperately craned for a view of the hotel's front, checking for any activity, his heart pounding, his mouth dry. It couldn't be long; it shouldn't be long.

"That was a little bit too easy," said Marcus from the back seat.

Avram said nothing.

Joe had turned around to look out the back window, watching the traffic behind for any signs of police. Avram turned back, keeping his eye on the cab in front, watching as it passed through the city walls, taking the left hand road beyond to enter the highway that would take them to where their ship, and ultimately escape, at least a partial escape, awaited them. Avram didn't know what had happened back there in the hotel lobby, but there was no time to think about it. Right now, the only real thing on his mind was getting away. He glanced at the driver, but the man was concentrating on the road ahead. Hanging from the rear-view mirror dangled a blue and white circular object patterned in circles, a local evil eye symbol, rocking back and forth with the car's movement. Avram stared at it and swallowed. He turned to the driver once more and pointed.

"What is that called?" he said.

The driver glanced at it. "Nazar," he said simply. "Evil eye," he followed in heavily accented English and then turned his attention back to the road.

There was something about it, something that triggered a faint tendril of memory in Avram's head, but he couldn't grasp it. It was something he should remember, he knew, but it slipped away again and he was back to concentrating on the cab in front.

After several minutes of discomfort, an empty feeling in the base of his stomach, a chill in his chest, they reached the outskirts of the airfield. The lead cab turned in through the gates and pulled ahead, just starting to traverse the flat expanse of concrete leading to the spot where there ship lay tethered. There it was, in front of them, the vast sack gray, distended against the pale blue sky. Avram felt the relief start to wash over him. He stared forward at their ship, fixated, but then, there was something else, something not quite right. An orange discoloration marked the even gray at one end. As he watched, it grew in size, expanding, replacing the dark skin with flecks of yellow and deeper brightness. Avram struggled to work out what could make it look like that and then … a vast gout of flame erupted from the ship's side, expanding, consuming, enveloping the whole. It blossomed outwards, and then drew in, gouting black smoke amongst the flames.

Slowly, ponderously, the great ship canted and then crashed burning to the ground. As the dark gray skin was burned and consumed by the growing conflagration, the ship collapsed in on itself leaving blackened spars pointed upwards at the sky, like the ribcage of a burning witch. Avram simply stared in disbelief.

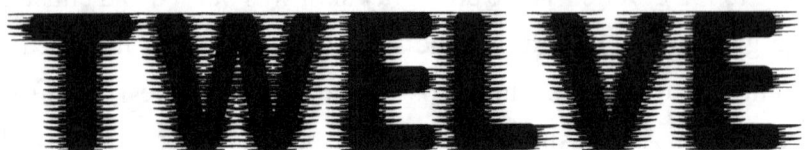

TWELVE

For it is the side of Lilith you have reached, the dark side, from which it is dreadful to escape.

–19th C Eastern European Folk Tale

The lead cab was still circling on the apron in front of them. Avram could see Max and Selena, craning, tracking the remains of the burning ship as they went round and round. Their own cab had slammed to an abrupt halt, the driver spouting a string of what Avram presumed were curses, his eyes wide. Avram threw open the passenger side door and stepped out, his hand over his forehead, shielding his eyes. Even at this distance, the heat from what was left of the balloon was palpable and thick dark smoke now rose from the wreckage, filling the air with a noxious chemical taint.

Now there are four, came the thought.
Four what?

Then he realized the answer to that too: four bodies; Ronald, Pavel, and now he presumed, Captain Prinsloo and his crewmate. Four deaths in such a short space of time. How many more would there be?

Up closer to the conflagration, little men were scurrying about. Off in the distance, a vehicle with a flashing orange light was approaching. Avram was suddenly conscious of their exposed position. They were supposed to be getting out of here, and yet here they were, standing on an exposed flat space, just begging to be noticed. Thankfully, the lead car had stopped circling by now and the front door opened and then Max's gangling form stepped out. Max stretched as if straightening out the kinks from the cramped space inside the cab, but he was still watching the ship, or what remained of it.

"Max," Avram called and he turned. "We have to get out of here."

"Yes, you are right," he said, looking around the field. "We should go back the way we came, but where?"
One of the back doors opened and Samantha got out.

"Sam, get back in here," Selena called from inside.
Slowly, deliberately, Samantha walked towards Avram, not even sparing a glance for the scene of chaos behind her.

"Samantha, do as your mother says," said Max in a voice more stern than Selena's frowning, though he made no move to physically stop the child. Samantha waved her hand behind her as if dismissing Max's words. He frowned, shook his head, glanced back behind him.

"Samantha?"

Again she waved him away, continuing her approach. In a moment, she was in front of Avram and she reached for his hand. The touch brought a sense of charge, electricity through Avram's fingers and up his arm, and in the next instant, his head was awash with a quiet, whispering voice, a little girl's voice and it was all too familiar.

Avram, said the voice. Time for you to leave now. The station. Of course. They could get out of here by train.

We would have you travel by land. Our touch will be greater.

He didn't really understand the import of the last words, but already he was making plans. There would be too much activity, too much attention here; it was better if they got the hell out of the vicinity as quickly as possible.

Samantha turned and without a word, headed back to her own car where her father still stood outside, glancing nervously behind him while he watched the girl.

"Max, tell the driver to head to the station. We can all take a train."

Max nodded and moved to step back into the taxi. Samantha had already got in and closed the door behind her. Avram boarded his own cab and closed the door.

"What's going on?" said Marcus from the back seat. "And what the hell just happened?"

"I don't know," said Avram without turning around. "We're going to the station."

"But …" said Joe.

"We have to get out of here," said Avram, cutting him off. "Look at that. We don't have a choice."

Their taxi driver was still muttering whispered curses, his

attention focused out the front window. Avram reached out and touched his shoulder, getting a wide-eyed glance in response.

"Station," said Avram, slowly, clearly. "Main station."

The driver narrowed his eyes, processing and then nodded, repeating Avram's words. "Main station."

"Yes."

The driver gestured towards the burning ship and the columns of smoke with his chin, but Avram gestured with both hands, a shooing motion.

"Station," he said again, and the driver nodded and shifted the cab into gear.

As they drew out from the port, each of the cab's occupants looked back, watching out the rear window, seeing the growing cluster of vehicles, flashing lights and frantic movement of people running around the site. There was the sound of sirens now, both distant and closer, growing louder.

"Where are we going to go?" asked Joe, his voice full of concern.

"I don't know yet," Avram responded. "Let's work that out when we get there. That's the first concern."

That seemed to still Joe, at least for the time being.

"We can't do this," said Marcus quietly.

"What do you mean?" asked Joe, starting up again.

"We just can't do this," he said again.

Avram swung around in his seat, looking back at Marcus's serious face. "What choice do you think we have now? What choice do we have, Marcus?"

His words were met with a stare, hard and fixed. "It's not right."

"What? You want us to wind up in a local jail, at best? Think of the consequences. Especially you two. Think about it. You remember the films don't you?"

"And what about Aggie?" Marcus said, his eyes narrowing.

"We spoke about that. We all spoke about that."

"Yes, of course we did. But now …" He looked behind himself, but they had at last drawn out of the gates and were well along the road back into the city. The only indication of what they had left behind was a plume of black smoke rising into the sky behind a wall of buildings.

Slowly, he turned back to meet Avram's gaze.

"None of this makes any sense."

Joe reached a hand and placed it on his partner's thigh. Marcus glanced at him, his expression a little sad then turned back to meet Avram's eyes.

A fire engine screamed past, travelling in the opposite direction klaxon sounding and fading as it disappeared behind them. Avram tracked it briefly.

"No," he said. "You're right. None of it makes any sense, but we need to go, we need to get out of here. There's nothing else we can do."

Marcus's lips narrowed into a fine line and he turned to stare out of the side window, his jaw working. Joe watched him with an expression of concern and worry on his face. There was clearly going to be no further discussion, so after a couple more seconds, Avram turned to watch the road and cars ahead, keeping an eye out for any that might have the hint of police around them. They were retracing their route and that gave him concern. What if they were spotted travelling back past the hotel? He thought about that for a moment, thought about trying to tell their driver to take another road, but then realized that any such attempt would be futile with the language barrier they faced. He was right to feel worried. As they swung past the hotel, there was definite activity. The familiar black sedan was outside and so too were two police cars. Unconsciously, he sank down further in the seat, tracking the cars out the side window. So, it seemed that Kaplan had been alerted, and he had brought his men in force. Avram swallowed and turned back to face Marcus and Joe over his shoulder.

"So it would appear that they know already," he said.

"Of course they bloody know," Marcus snapped. "This is just madness, Avram. What the hell are we doing?"

Joe stroked Marcus's leg to try and soothe him, but Marcus merely shook his head, disgustedly.

"Listen," said Avram, glancing nervously at the cab driver to see if he was actually following any of the conversation. "You've seen the movies. We all have. This is another world, Marcus. And, as sophisticated or urbane as this police inspector seems, it doesn't work the same way. We're better off out of here and you know it."

There was some sort of logic to what he was saying, but it didn't sit comfortably. There was a presumption there that he didn't particularly like. Regardless, he just knew that they had to leave and that for them, the station was the right way to do it. A few moments before, he had known the reason why, but now, he just couldn't quite put his fingers on it.

"Listen, once we get to the station, we can explore our options, and from there …"

"We disappear into the wilds of Eastern Europe or Asia," said Joe. "Just as likely to be never seen again."

Marcus gave an exasperated sigh. "Well, it's not that bad yet," he said.

In the meantime, they had lost sight of the other car. Avram scanned the traffic around them, but there were too many taxis. He kept an eye out as they passed through the city walls and moved into the old city proper, but of the Greens, there was no sign. For the time being, Marcus and Joe seemed to have subsided into some sort of grudging silence, merely staring out at the passing buildings and cars.

Before long, they reached the front of the old Serkici main station, its brick and stone façade echoing the 19th Century grand building style typified by the start of European Orientalism. Avram knew all this. He always researched a city well before they were due to visit. The usual herd of people wandered back and forth in front of the edifice and drifted in and out of the large main entrance doors. Their cab pulled up, Marcus leaned forward and paid the driver, and then, together, they all got out, retrieved their minimal luggage from the rear and then stood looking around. Of the Greens, still, there was no sign.

"Where are they?" said Joe.

"Typical," muttered Marcus, almost to himself.

Avram scanned the surroundings. Despite the many people, Max, at least would be easy to spot in the local crowd.

"Perhaps they've gone in already," he said. "Let's go inside."

"I'll stay out here and wait, just in case," offered Joe, looking up and down the street and around at the passing faces.

"Right," said Marcus and headed towards the main building, not waiting for Avram. Avram turned and quickened his step to catch up.

"I'm sorry," said Avram weakly as he drew abreast.

"You don't have to be sorry," said Marcus. "I just don't understand why we're going through this shit. This was supposed to be …" His words trailed off and he merely pursed his lips and shook his head. "I don't get it."

Inside the building, it was like entering some sort of bizarre architectural pastry, all pinks and creams and brown wood. The upper level of the main hall was surrounded by Ottoman style archways and the high ceiling and broad floor filled the space with echoes. Avram quickly scanned the people, looking for the Greens and spotted them almost immediately, hovering around near the ticket area. Samantha's pink travel luggage blended strangely with the overall color scheme. Both he and Marcus strode over to where they were standing. Avram glanced down at Samantha who looked up and gave him a little smile.

"Hello, Uncle Avram," she said.

Avram tore his gaze away from her and tried to focus his attention on Max.

"So …," he said.

"So …," said Max in return. "You are finally here." He moved on from the implied minor admonishment and looked up at the displays surrounding the ticket area.

"Did you know," he said, "that you can catch the Orient Express from here?"

"Yes, I knew that," said Avram. "But it hasn't run since 2009."

"Ah," said Max. "What a pity. It would have been so nice … But I see here they are still advertizing it."

"No," said Avram. "It was withdrawn from service. The one they're talking about is run by a hotel chain. It runs maybe once a year."

Even in their current circumstance, Max and Selena were still thinking about being tourists, wrapped up in their own little world.

"Pity," said Max, his gaze still roving the displays.

"Where do we want to get to, apart from away," asked Marcus.

"I would still like to see some things," said Selena, also scanning the pamphlets and posters.

"Fine," said Avram. "I know," he said, drawing once again on the research he'd done, "that at least from here, there's still a train that runs at least part of the route the Orient Express used to travel. I think they call it the Bosphorus Express. Runs through Bulgaria and on to Bucharest with a few stops on the way."

"Ah, that is interesting," said Selena. "Yes, we could do that."

"I did some reading before we got here," said Avram lamely with a shrug.

"And then from Bucharest?" asked Marcus, his expression becoming less and less impressed with each interchange.

"Look," said Avram. "Go and get Joe. We'll sort out the tickets, or at least try to. We can work out the rest later when we get out of here. I don't know, but somehow, I seem to remember there was a major representative of our travel company in Paris, but we can talk about that later."

"Ah, Paris," said Selena. "I like Paris."

Avram sighed. "Go, Marcus. Get Joe," he said. "We'll meet back here."

Marcus ducked his head and headed off to do just that.

"Come, Max," he said. "Let's sort out those tickets."

Max joined him, and as they walked to the ticket counters, Avram had a funny thought. It was most unlike himself to take charge of things. He usually preferred to hang back, go with the flow, but here he was organising the group, directing them. Maybe it was just a symptom of the crisis. Stressful situations did funny things to people. Still ...

After much discussion, they managed to acquire the tickets, first class, sleeping cars, because it was an overnight journey, though in the current situation, Avram doubted that he'd be doing much sleeping. The tickets, which Max paid for, were surprisingly cheap. Having organized that much, together, they went back to join the others.

"And once we get to Bucharest?" said Max.

"I guess we'll have to find somewhere to stay. We only arrive at around six-thirty, so we should have time."

"Well, I hope there is somewhere decent," said Max. "I am not so happy with these crappy places."

"Yes, Max, I understand. I'm sure we'll find something up to your standards."

By the time they re-joined the others, Marcus and Joe had come back inside.

"We have a little bit of a problem," Avram announced to them.

"What?" asked Joe, looking worried. "Don't tell me we're stuck."

"No, no, nothing like that. The problem is that the train doesn't leave until ten o'clock tonight. We have to kill a few hours. We need to keep our heads down though. They could be looking for us by now.

Why don't we do this? I'm sure there are some locker areas here. Let's track those down, stow our bags and go separately. I don't think we should stay here in the station. Especially not together. If they come looking for us, we'll stand out like a sore thumb, and this is going to be one of the places they're likely to look. If we split up and regroup here at say nine thirty or thereabouts, we can pick up our bags, get to the train and get settled in before it leaves. Whatever we choose to do, we shouldn't do it together. From what we've seen, there are enough tourists around to lose ourselves in the crowds. They're hardly likely to suspect that we are going to be off taking in the sights."

"Yes, it makes sense," said Marcus.

"Okay, then settled."

It didn't take long to locate the lockers, but it was a few minutes before they found enough that were free to accommodate all their luggage. After sealing his own locker, with a click, taking note of the position and the number, Avram stood and looked around, as much checking that there were no nearby police to worry about as trying to work out what he was going to do for the next few hours. Marcus and Joe had already left, but the Greens were clustered together at the end of the row. The noise of the station, trains, the squeaking wheels of a trolley, voices and the general blurred hum of accumulated noises in a vast high-ceilinged place surrounded him. He could smell food from somewhere, machinery, people. He walked over to join the Greens.

"Have you worked out what you are going to do?" he asked.

"We will find something," said Max. Again, Avram could barely believe how little all of this seemed to affect them.

"Okay, well, I'm heading out," said Avram. "See you back here."

"Don't go too far, Uncle Avram," said Samantha, looking up at him.

"No," said Alfred, also chiming in. "We wouldn't want you to get lost."

Breath

Avram looked at both of them, from one face to the other and back again, narrowing his eyes. The children merely gave him a knowing smile.

"Right," he said and turned away leaving them standing there, his belly feeling strangely hollow inside. He glanced back over his shoulder as he neared the main hall. Max and Selena were in discussion, but both of the children were still watching him, tracking him in tandem as he moved away. The chill in his guts grew stronger, but he still really didn't know why. The feeling nagged at him all the way out of the station and beyond, working in the back of his head. Something definitely wasn't right, not the circumstance, not the events leading up to now—all that was clearly not right—but something more, something stirring like black smoke shadows inside him, and no matter how he tried, he could not shake the feeling that was stalking him.

THIRTEEN

In heaven they are unknown, on earth they are not understood.

−Assyrian Tablet

Breath

For a while, Avram merely wandered. After some time spent traipsing through the old Spice Bazaar, though he couldn't work out exactly how he had ended up there, it all became a little too much for him. He, among the many other tourists, walked up and down the narrow high-ceilinged passageways, assailed by colors and scents, bins and baskets full of multi-colored exotica or stacks of the cubed lokum in multiple colors and flavors, dusted on the outside with white powder. The stallholders watched him as he passed, speculatively, sizing him up, predatory gazes. One or two approached, hitting him with lines of patter, but he waved them off. It was humid inside, adding to the overall miasma. He had had quite enough of speculative gazes, pairs of eyes sizing him up, looking at him knowingly; quite enough. He pushed his way past some locals, past a couple of tourists, and out through one of the many entrances, seeking fresh air, feeling as if the breath was being sucked from his body.

It was hot outside, the early afternoon sun beating down upon him and he stood just outside the entrance for a few seconds, bent over, his hands on his thighs as he tried to regain his wind. It made him feel a little better, but his head was buzzing and he staggered away from the crowded building and across a square, finally finding a small area where a tree was enclosed with a concrete wall, high enough to sit on. He lowered himself with one hand, then hunched over, his head in his hands, breathing deeply. A nearby simit cart was plying its wares and the smell of bread and sesame wafted his way, almost making him gag, but it too passed in a moment.

What was going on with him? There were holes in his memory, gaps, periods of time that he couldn't explain. He was doing things that seemed as if they were almost not of his own volition. Even some of those actions, he thought, were not things that he would normally do. Witness his taking charge in the station and in the hotel. It was as if he was being driven to act by someone, by something else.

Slowly he raised his head and scanned the square, tracking the people walking past, looking for…he didn't know what. Something familiar? Something he could hold on to? Over the other side, near the road, stood a policeman, watching the traffic. Avram almost ducked involuntarily as soon as he noticed him, but the policeman was more interested in the passing cars than some out-of-breath tourist struggling with the heat. Avram looked away and turned his gaze to the sky, clear blue and here, near the water, populated by wheeling gulls. Wings, flight, air—there was something there, but nothing he could grasp, nothing he could understand. All this had started back in that last city, back in the depths of history that had built that city; of that much he was certain. All he could remember was some sort of building and something to do with a child, a girl, he remembered that much, but details there were none. He rubbed his forehead as if the pressure would force the memories out of his head, but it did little good.

With a deep sigh, he turned his thoughts back to the more recent events and narrowed his eyes. One by one, he focused his attention on his companions, looking for something in their actions that might lend him a clue. Max was as Max ever was, seemingly oblivious to the world and generally only concerned about his own needs and those of his family. He dismissed Max, and then in turn, Selena, Joseph and Marcus. Nothing in their behaviour was anything that he would not have expected. That only left the children, Samantha and Alfred. As his thoughts turned to them, the looks, the gaze, the knowing smiles, the words and more than that, their touch, his insides went cold, but in the next instant, he found the thoughts slipping away again. Desperately he struggled to hold on to them.

Children. And then, the little girl. A child's voice in his head, filtering through the veils of unknowing. He took a sharp breath.

That was it. It had to be.

Slowly, he gazed around the square again, looking for children. He spotted one or two, a couple over the far side playing, another being dragged along by its mother, but if he expected to find anything unusual, there was nothing. Somewhere, vaguely, he seemed to remember a lot of children, boys and girls, all together, somewhere dark and moist, perhaps the sensation of underground, but he couldn't give it shape. He grimaced and gritted his teeth. He had a few more hours yet. Perhaps if he retraced his steps .... The police would hardly be looking for him in the regular tourist spots, because, ultimately, that's all they had done here, played at being tourists, visiting the sites. He wasn't too far from the main cluster of landmarks, and it would take him maybe half an hour to walk to the first of those. If he did that, there might be something that would jog his memory and start to repair the continuity of his thoughts. It was worth a shot. Right now, anything was worth a shot. He was a man out of place, in a foreign city, and at this very moment, out of his depth. With a sense of resolve, he stood and looked around, confirming the direction he needed to take. He had to put this to bed, and he had to do it now. The rest, the deaths, the ship, everything else, all of that could wait. At the moment, he simply had to fix the gaping holes in his head.

It was a healthy walk to Sultanahmet, and all the way, he was trying to piece together the events that had led him to this state. Finally, up the final hill, past the tourist-geared restaurants, carpet and souvenir shops past a couple of tram stops, along an ancient wall, behind which lay the entrance to Topkapi and other museums, and then into the square and park that fronted both Hagia Sofia and the Sultanahmet Mosque. He stood there, out in front of the former looking at the tourists, a Japanese group with their guide holding an umbrella aloft, a queue of people waiting to get into the entrance, the palm trees, the seats, the simit and chestnut carts, but there was nothing there that triggered anything. Slowly, he turned around and around, seeking something, anything, that might unravel a thread of familiarity. Nothing. And then he saw it: one of the signs pointed to something called the Basilica Cistern. He couldn't remember having visited it on their previous sightseeing expedition, but there was something about it.

He turned in that direction and wandered up the street, curious now.

The street led to a small squat building to one side, nothing grand, but as soon as he saw it, he was struck with a pang of familiarity. He crossed the street and stood at the entrance for a few moments, considering. If he was going to find out what was going on, then he had to do more than stand there. Fumbling in his pocket for his wallet, he stepped inside. The entrance area seemed familiar too, but there was something different about it. He looked at the ticket booth, and then handed over the ten Lira required for entry, took the ticket and stepped in direction of the sign pointing to a stairway leading down. This was right; he knew it was right. As he descended, into humid semi-darkness, the sound of dripping water echoing off stone floated up around him.

He had been here before, he knew it, but still the details were struggling to come. The sound of voices echoed around the chamber, a few groups of tourists clustered at various spots along the wooden walkways. The smell of damp stone and moss filled the humid air. He stopped at the bottom of the steps on a broad stone platform and stared along the long central walkway leading to the end, the rows of irregular columns leading off into the dim reaches beneath a vaulted ceiling. Yes, he knew this place. Swallowing, he took the first step onto the walkway.

It did not take him long to reach the other end, the small square platforms, the sign pointing with the single word "Medusa" pointing the way. He waited patiently for a large group to move out of the way and then stepped forward to take his place in front of the column, staring down at the inverted moss-stained stone face, the snakes almost seeming to writhe around the blank features. Yes, he knew this. He looked around the dim space. He had been here at night. It had been darker, and he had not been alone. He looked over at a spot on the wooden platform. There, there had been a child, a child that had … he couldn't quite remember. He looked at another spot. And there had stood … Lilith. That was her name. Lilith, the girl, the young girl, and he had seen her before. It started to take shape in his head, and then came the memory of the voice, that whispering voice inside his head— her voice.

Lilith. A child and yet so much more than a child. She was the reason that he no longer … he no longer what?

He stared at the spot for several minutes without moving, the deep moist air flowing in and out of his lungs. Then, finally he turned and made his way gradually back along the walkway, barely even registering the tourists who moved past him as he did. Slowly, he made his way back up the steps, out past the ticket office and back into the air, hot and dry, but feeling like a relief after the underground humidity. He glanced down at his watch absently and then frowned. He had been in the place for well over an hour. How could that be? But at least he had some idea now, at least a cord of memory that he could reel in and tighten, drawing things together. He looked up and down the street. For now, there was no clear answer. They still had to get away, get out of the city, all of them, but it was no longer as simple as that. He needed to regain control of himself, needed to be able to trust what he thought and remembered, and right at the moment, he had no confidence in either.

This time, he wandered up the hill a bit further, past the tourist shops, the tram stop. He had no intention of making it as far as the Grand Bazaar. His experience with the Spice Bazaar had been quite enough and the other one was many times larger. Instead, he turned into one of the many side streets, clustered with restaurants, all with their bills of fare posted outside in multiple languages and picked one of them at random. As it was, the one he chose was decked out in sombre black and white, less garish and glaring than most of the others and more in tune with his current mood. Nor did the waiters descend upon him like a pack of vultures. They waited patiently whilst he chose a spot and settled himself at a table that had a view of the street, but was slightly off to one side and set back a little from the front doors.

He needed to eat, he knew that. The empty hollow in his belly was more than the uncertainty and fear he was feeling. He still needed fuel. The waiter brought him a menu, asked him if he wanted something to drink, and then withdrew discretely while he scanned the photographs and descriptions on the glossy card. He ordered a simple local salad to start with; they were generally fresh and good, mixed with lemon juice as part of the dressing, and then decided on a local fish, grilled. The waiter, having poured his water and taken the order, proffered a wine card in front of him, but Avram waved it away. Wine would not be a good idea, nor beer, nor any other alcoholic beverage. He needed to maintain his current clarity if he was going to work through this.

He spent some time picking through his salad. It was good and fresh, but he still needed to kill some time here. At the moment, he wanted to focus his thoughts on the young girl, Lilith. Sam and Alf were enough of a concern on their own, but all of it was linked to that strange little child who had seemingly appeared out of nowhere. Deep within himself, he knew that to be the case, but there was nothing logical that told him that apart from the half vague memory of a group of similar children clustered in the darkness beneath the city's streets in that ancient underground cistern. He pushed his fork back and forth across the now-empty bowl's surface, leaving glistening oil trails in its wake, willing the memory to focus, but it was as if his own mind was determined to betray him. Finally, he lay his fork down and pushed the bowl away. The waiter was with him in a moment, ducking obsequiously and removing the empty dish, hovering to see if there was anything else Avram wanted. It was no wonder; he was the only patron in the place, but he shook his head and once more the waiter withdrew.

The voice; if he could focus on the voice.

All he had was a whispered impression, something hissing through his consciousness in the voice of a child, not even the words themselves.

Breath

The waiter appeared again bearing a large oval plate with the grilled fish, a few chipped potatoes and a slice of lemon. He placed it down in front of Avram with a flourish. Avram nodded at him and he withdrew once more. Grasping his utensils, Avram proceeded to clean the fish, sliding the flesh away to reveal the bones and the spine, lifting it to one side and then forking a mouthful of the succulent flesh to his lips. It was as good and tasty as he had expected, but he barely noticed it. Normally, he would be digging into it with relish, always appreciative of good fresh, local cuisine, and here you could hardly go wrong.

The child's voice was not going to give him anything. He chewed slowly, considering.

Back to the ship; perhaps there was something there. All he kept seeing when he thought of the ship was the slow-motion collapse of the burning shape as it fell to the ground. He reached for his water and took a long sip as if trying to wash the memory away. Placing his glass down again, he turned his thoughts further back, back to when they had boarded, when he had boarded in their last night before making the journey here. He had been somewhere on his own, doing a bit of last-minute exploring. He knew at much. He had arrived back at the ship and borne the brunt of the others' annoyance, because, because … for some reason he had been late.

Done with his fish, he sat back, waiting for the waiter to notice, which he did in short order, rushing over to clear the plate away. Avram ordered a baklava and a local coffee, feeling that the sugar rush might do something to help his errant synapses to fire a bit more efficiently. He toyed with his water glass, pushing it back and forth across the plasticised tablecloth while he waited.

The baklava arrived, dripping with honeyed syrup and he prodded at it with a fork, and then took a mouthful of the cloying sweetness, followed by a sip from the equally sweet coffee, washing it around in his mouth and appreciating the sugary bitterness. On the ship there had been something, but each time he thought of that, images of

Ronald, of Aggie's fluttering hands, and then of Pavel lying exposed on the bed, staring beatifically up at the ceiling filled his mind.

Finally, it was that particular image, the sight of Pavel lying there in compromising disarray that triggered the memory of his dream, if it was in fact a dream. With Pavel's memory floating in his mind, he began to wonder. Instant by instant, the dream images played back through his head.

He was lying there, in bed. Someone was touching him, gently, the feather contact drawing frissons of electricity from his skin. Without volition, he moaned and it was deep from inside him, something primal and animal. He could feel hair against his belly, draped and moving gently back and forth, another hand sliding over his chest and down. He was hard, so hard it was almost painful, and still the sensations went on. He tried to move, to lift his arms, to push whoever it was away, but they seemed glued in place. He had no willpower to do anything else as if all strength had been sapped from him. He drew a shuddering breath, swallowed against a mouth gone dry. He could feel his body reacting, tightening. The hand that had been playing across his belly slid down, moving like a snake, tickling as it went, to cup his testicles, tickling the sensitive scrotal skin.

He sat back, swallowing hard, glancing around the empty restaurant guiltily, but there was no one to notice. He tried piecing the images together, and then felt the pit of his stomach give way, dropping into a deep abyss. The woman from his dream. It had been a dream hadn't it … nothing more than a dream. But this woman, this woman shape in darkness, how was she linked to the child, Lilith. Unless … He closed his eyes and took a deep breath.

It simply couldn't be so. Could it?

Lilith was no simple child, that much was clear.

FOURTEEN

Terrible are her deeds. Wherever she comes, wherever she appears, she brings evil and destruction ... A flesh-eating, blood-sucking monster is she.

–Die Labartu Texte

Avram sat there at the restaurant table for nearly an hour or more, ordering a succession of coffees, processing the images that kept replaying in his head. Finally, he called the waiter over and paid, leaving a reasonable tip and wandered out into the little side street, his heart pounding with the overdose of sugar and caffeine that now coursed through his veins. The Lilith child—that was the answer, and somehow, some way, Max and Selena's children were connected. He had to put a stop to it, at least for his own sanity as much as anything else. But, and it was a big but, he could hardly tell the Greens. Max and Selena were stoic, unconcerned and so bound up in their own little world that it would be highly unlikely for them to give any credence to his suspicions. Nonetheless, he thought, glancing down at his watch, they had other concerns right now, and it was about time for him to walk back to the main station and meet the others, to finally make good what amounted to their planned escape from this city. As it was now, he would barely make it in time. He had spent much longer than he intended in the restaurant.

As he walked down the hill, he quickened his pace, but all the time, the dream images kept floating up in his head, leaving a deep dread as he processed the implications. He was not like that. He could not have done that. He could not have allowed that to happen. And yet he had. The self-recriminations rolled around and around in his thoughts.

He barely glanced at the two mosques, at the short piece of road that led to the underground cistern where he had had the encounter, or at least thought he had. He turned away focussing on the street ahead, chewing at his bottom lip. A tram rolled past, whining to a stop further down the road, and its bell rang sounding loud in the evening air. The doors hissed shut and it whirred into motion again, clanking as it slid around the corner at the bottom of the hill.

As he passed that bottom corner in turn and started to travel along the lengthy array of shops and eateries, another suspicion came to him. If he did not know any better, he would think of vampires, those blood sucking creatures of legend that controlled and manipulated and fed. But there was no blood, nothing but those staring eyes. There were those marks on the neck of both Ronald and Pavel, but the skin had not even been broken. But, mind control, manipulation, taking over someone's will; that was all part of the legend wasn't it? He shook his head. No, all that was nothing more than superstitious folk tales. And yet ... and yet, where were they now headed? To Romania, to the birthplace of that legend. Was it coincidence, or something more sinister. Again, he shook his head. No, he was starting to see significance in places where there simply could be none. He did not know enough. Their new destination was something that he could not have known, so he hadn't done the requisite research and reading that he would normally do before visiting somewhere. Besides, the vampire legend went way, way back, didn't it? Far further back than what had been popularized in literature. He seemed to remember something about Greek culture and maybe even Chinese ....

Avram walked around the final curve and saw the station squatting there before him in all its faded glory, the candy-striped brickwork in even bands drawing the eye to the ornate front entrance. He paused, looked at his watch again and then decided it was close enough to time, negotiated the traffic and crossed the street. Not wanting to draw undue attention, he quickly adopted a measured, strolling pace as he headed towards the main entrance, glancing around casually as if merely taking in the sights. A few people were walking around, and by now, the last traces of daylight were starting to fade. Along the waterfront, the multi-colored lights of the restaurants beneath Galata Bridge were already alight, and even at this distance, Avram could see the gray barbed smudge indication the rows of locals, leaning over the edge of the bridge with their fishing rods. He drew his attention back to the station entrance, but of the others there was no sign. He hesitated and then finally decided he should go inside and wait if they were not already here. What, after all, was more natural than someone waiting in a station? It was probably the reason why so many main stations were home to the dispossessed, finding warmth and shelter beneath the vast echoing roofs in a place where they were less likely to be moved on unless they made nuisances of themselves.

Still, as he stepped inside, his breath was short, his pulse racing. By now, he wasn't sure whether it was the coffee and the dessert, or even merely his own uncertainty about what he was starting to suspect. Perhaps it was a combination of both. Passing through the main entrance hall, he sought out a map. He hadn't even taken the trouble to trace their journey, another fact that confirmed for him that he was not himself. It was those little things; failure to do what he would normally do. Avram had always been a creature of routine. At least he could do something to approximate some sense of normalcy. After a period of wandering back and forth across the station's hollow expanse, he found what he was looking for and peered up at the large map attached to the wall, seeking their particular route amongst the many. He traced the line with his finger, noting the number of side-branches that split off from the line. After Halkalı, the first stop was Alpullu then Pehlivanköy, where the line branched off again and headed north-west to Edirne. After Edirne it arrived at the town of Kapıkule on the Turkish-Bulgarian border. In Bulgaria, Svilengrad, then Dimitrovgrad. After the city of Gorna Oryahovitsa, the line arrived at the city of Ruse on the Danube river, then Giurgiu, and finally continuing to Bucharest. It was a good journey, one that he might have chosen to make on his own, potentially passing many sights that he would not have normally seen in the day to day course of his life. His finger paused on the final stop on the journey. Bucharest. Romania. Again, he thought about the stuff of legends— Transylvania, Vlad Tepis—and his hand dropped from the map and moved to his throat. There was not a connection, could not be a connection. Now he really was starting to imagine things.

"Ah, there you are," a voice said from beside him, making him start. Avram turned to see Max staring up at the wall map. "Yes, not bad," said Max. "We should have a good time."

He turned to look at Avram. "We are waiting for you near where the luggage place is."

"And the others?"

"Yes, the Boys are there too. Shall you come and get your bag?"

With one last glance at the small dot marking Bucharest, Avram turned and followed Max towards the luggage lockers. As Max had said, Marcus and Joe were there, Selena, the children, all waiting with their small pieces of luggage either gripped or lying on the floor beside them. Avram nodded, took a moment locating his own locker and then withdrew his valise.

"Do you know which platform?" he asked.

"Yes, of course," said Max. "This way."

Taking Max's lead, they followed as a group, no one saying a word. This was it. They were finally getting out of the place. At that moment, thoughts of Aggie filtered up through Avram's consciousness and he could not help but feel a sense of guilt about what they were doing. Though he tried, he could not get rid of it. Ultimately, he, Avram, was to blame.

As they reached the platform, Max stopped, dug around in his pocket and withdrew his tickets and looked down at them, then gestured with his chin and along the platform where the long, dark blue train sat already, waiting. Their compartments were about halfway down, and Max again led the way with the rest of them trailing along behind, luggage in tow. One carriage, three compartments. They climbed aboard, negotiated the corridor and found their places. Looking around, and finally peering into his own allocated space, Avram doubted that Max and Selena would be overly impressed. It was hardly the level of luxury that the Greens expected for themselves. The long seats were decked out in dark blue fabric, a thin curtain covered the window and the fake veneer walls, a pale yellow. It was a train, that was all. Avram shoved his bag inside and took a seat, pulling the curtain aside to look out at the station, the movement all around them, another train pulling in and passengers piling out, many of them carrying large plastic-wrapped bundles or assorted pieces of luggage. He moved away from the window, leaned his head back and closed his eyes, waiting. The smell of the carriage, musty, old sweat stained upholstery filled his senses. After a couple of minutes, he opened his eyes again and glanced down at his watch. There were still a few minutes to go and he sighed. They just needed to get out of here. From the adjacent compartments, there was little noise, nothing to indicate that there was anyone else even aboard the train. He wondered if the others were feeling the same things he was, the nervousness, the uncertainty, the confusion about what they were doing and what had brought them all to this point. At least their journey would be mostly through the night, and if he was lucky, he'd be able to find some sleep, though that was another thing that was distinctly uncertain.

A noise outside and then someone slid open the compartment door. For an instant, Avram panicked, the blue uniform, the hat making him see a policeman, and he gripped the edges of his seat, the next instant realizing that it was just the conductor coming to check his tickets. He relaxed a little, fumbled around inside his jacket and then handed them over, his heart still pounding. The conductor scrutinised the papers, handed them back and nodded and then tipped his hat before withdrawing once more and closing the door. A couple of minutes later, and the carriage lurched and the train began pulling out of the station. Avram leaned back once more, closing his eyes and trying to steady his breathing. The first step was done. As the train wound its way out of the station and through the suburbs of the vast ancient city, Avram's tension started to trickle away. They were on their way and no one had stopped them. Soon, soon, they'd be across the border and in another country, away from everything that had happened, and perhaps then they might have a chance, he might have a chance to work out what the hell was happening to them. With the train's gentle rocking, he finally allowed himself to drift.

For a couple of hours, he dozed fitfully, occasionally opening his eyes a crack and once or twice pulling the thin curtain to one side to peer out at the darkening landscape. He was too drained even to lie down, just letting the exhaustion take him where he sat. There were a couple of stops along the way, but they barely roused him.

About two hours into the journey, Max poked his head through the compartment door and asked him if he wanted to join them in getting something to eat, but Avram merely shook his head, mumbled some excuse and went back to watching until he started drifting again. The meal he had consumed earlier forestalled any hunger pangs and at the same time, the mere thought of food was distasteful. Much later, the train lurched to a stop and moments after, a series of clanks, shaking and other noises brought him fully awake. A gentle knock at the compartment door came a couple of minutes later. He slid the door open, revealing a man decked out in an unfamiliar uniform. He asked Avram for his travel papers. Avram handed over his documents and then waited nervously while the man checked them over. He gave a little frown, looked up from the passport at Avram's face, back down at the document and sucked air through his teeth.

"Wait a minute," he said.

Avram's heart lurched into his throat, and he felt himself go cold. Just at that moment, a small shape appeared beside the border guard, lifted on arm and touched him gently on the hand. It was Samantha. The guard seemed to shake himself, almost as if he had forgotten what he was doing, then looked down again and cursorily checked the passport, nodded, handed it back and then moved on. Samantha stood there for a moment or two, simply looking at him, and then withdrew, back up the corridor.

Again the carriage shuddered, jumped and then lurched forward. They were clearly at the border, he suddenly realized. Across the other side, the rail system was different and they had to change the engine. That had been the cause of all the noise and movement. He moved back to the window and peered out, but all he could see were a few shadowy buildings, some bright lights above and behind them and the nearby rails catching the light off their surface. Of the border patrol, there was no sign, and Avram found himself able to breathe again. Within minutes they would be in Bulgaria, the next country on their route and effectively, they would be away. He settled back in the seat once more to wait. For about fifteen minutes, nothing happened. Avram presumed it was to give the border officials enough time to perform the rest of their checks. Then, a quick jerk forward, a creaking of the carriage, and the train slowly started to accelerate forward, the noise of the diesel engine thrumming through the darkness ahead of them. They were off, and in that moment, Avram felt some more of the tension draining away. The further away they got from Istanbul, the better.

At last, he allowed himself to remove his shoes, his jacket, lay them out on the seats opposite. He found the pillow and blanket in the small storage space above the seats and spread them out. It was late and time that he got some proper sleep. They had several hours before morning and several more before they reached their final destination. There, away from the immediate danger of restraint or worse, he might have a chance to work out what was going on. He knew that there would be more engine changes, more carriages to separate travelling to different destinations along the route, but for now, he was tired enough that none of that would matter. He needed to sleep and as he climbed beneath the blanket and pulled it over himself, he felt the waves already washing down upon him.

"Avram," said a voice, softly, gentle in its tone. "Avram."

There was a hand against his cheek, cool, dry, small fingers tracing patterns.

"Avram."

The hand was too small, smaller than it should be. Slowly, he opened his eyes. She was there, sitting at the edge of the couch bed, her hand held up against his face, watching. Was he dreaming?

"What," he said, his sleep-filled state being replaced by confusion. "What are you doing here?"

"Hush," she said.

"Who are you?" he hissed back through tightly closed teeth. "who the bloody hell are you?"

"You know who I am," she said. "My name is Lilith."

"You cannot be here," he said, trying to rise, but for some reason, could not perform the action.

"Oh, but I am here, Avram," she said. "Here with you."

He shook his head. At least he could manage that much.

"No," he said simply.

"Shhh," she said again. "I have felt you, Avram. You are trying to fight against me. That is not possible, I'm afraid. You are with us now. With all of us."

"But why?"

"You are the one who gave me release. You are blessed and so we are with you, but it is a greater blessing. Different from the blessing that gives us life."

"This doesn't make any sense," he said. "You cannot be here. How can you be here?"

She smiled then, a small girlish smile. "I am here and I am in many places. All of it is possible." She reached up with her other hand and pushed her hair back from her face, taking her eyes off him and looking up instead at the ceiling.

"Many years and many places," she said quietly, almost to herself. "The Shedim, the Ruchin, the Lilin, my children, all of them. We travel with the wind. We are the wind. We flow across the hot desert from whence we came. We are the breath of the world and there are no barriers to where we are. Not any more, thanks to you. You took me from that dark place and you set me free."

She returned her gaze to his face, looking at him now with almost fondness. "And now … now we will travel the world together to spread our blessing and multiply."

"The children …" Avram whispered.

She simply smiled.

For a few moments, words were lost to him. Again she stroked his cheek gently.

"I am with you Avram Davis. I am with you now and for always. You must not fight. You must accept. Enjoy that which I bless you with, for there are years to come. So many years. And you are fortunate. There are so few who are blessed."

There was a sadness in her eyes along with the depth, the knowingness. She withdrew her hand.

Avram closed his eyes, squeezing them tightly shut, and then slowly opened them again. She was gone.

He sat up, looking around the compartment, but there was no sign, no sign that she had even been there. He felt the place where she had been sitting, but there was nothing to indicate her presence. Where the cover lay upon the bed it was smooth and its temperature was the same. Had he been dreaming? It couldn't be so. He had felt her hand on his cheek, he had heard her words. She had been here. It was not something conjured up by his subconscious, reacting to his own efforts to tease out the memories of what had been happening to him. No. That was not sufficient. She had been with him, talking to him.

He took a deep, halting breath and closed his eyes again, the hollow in his abdomen like a chill cave. Around him, the carriage rocked gently back and forth, the sound of the wheels on metal rails rhythmically clattering around him, joined by the sound of wind rushing past the closed windows. He opened his eyes again, focussing on the noise of the wind.

He thought about rushing air, he thought about the wind, and he swallowed and gave an involuntary shudder.

FIFTEEN

These are the angels who have descended from heaven to earth, and have revealed secrets to the sons of men, and have seduced the sons of men to the commission of sin.

−The Book of Enoch

Their train drew into Giurgiu about six in the evening. Avram had slept little until the early morning light and banishing the darkness had offered him some solace. Though there was the passing landscape of new countries outside the train windows along the way, he had little interest and only watched the fields and villages and smudges of landscape in the distance with half an eye. He remained buried in his encounter, or was it the dream, from the previous hours. The girl child Lilith had filled him with hopelessness. Could he discuss any of it with the others? He simply did not know, although with the events, Ronald, Pavel, who knew how many more, there was a possibility that they might give him some credence. The first problem was how Max and Selena might react to him damning their own children, because up until now, there was nothing that told him that they had noticed anything unusual. Perhaps they too were in some sort of thrall, conditioned to accept and to comply. There was about half an hour or so before they reached their final destination in Bucharest, so if he was to do anything, he should really do it now. He left his own compartment and headed towards the Greens'.

"Max," he said after first knocking and then poking his head inside the compartment. The Greens were busy pulling their things together, the children sitting watching, as if fixed in place. Max looked up with a semi-distracted expression on his face and at the same time, both children turned to look at Avram leaning in the doorway. Samantha's eyes narrowed slightly.

"What is it, Avram?" said Max. "We are nearly there."

"Yes, I know," he said. "I just need to talk to you for a couple of minutes."

It was Max's turn to frown. "Can't it wait?"

"I would rather we didn't, Max," responded Avram. He stepped back from the doorway as an invitation to follow. Selena's face was now echoing Max's frown, but taking the hint, Max left what he was doing and followed Avram out into the corridor.

"Don't be too long, Max," said Selena, but Max just waved behind himself and then pulled the compartment door closed.

"So," said Max, standing in the corridor and making no move to follow.

"I would rather we discussed it in my compartment."

Max sighed and then followed him down the passageway to Avram's door and stepped inside as Avram let him past.

"Please, sit," said Avram, closing the door behind them.

"Well, what is it?"

"I don't quite know where to start, Max," he said. "I just … I just need to know if you have noticed anything unusual about Samantha and Alf."

He leaned back on the door watching Max's expression, unsure about how he was going to react to the question.

"Unusual? What do you mean?" Again, there was a flicker of a frown. He sat there his arms resting on his thighs, his fingers clasped in front of him, his head slightly bowed. "No, no, nothing." He shook his head and then looked up, meeting Avram's gaze before lowering his head again to listen.

"Hasn't their behaviour been strange? Have they said anything out of the ordinary? Have you felt anything?"

Max's eyes seemed to glaze over for a minute. He sat there unmoving simply staring at the floor, barely breathing, his mouth half open and just hanging there. A moment later, he shook himself, struggling back to reality.

"What was that?" he said.

"I asked if you had felt anything unusual."

"Felt? What is there to feel? Of course the children have been a little quiet I suppose, but under the circumstance we would expect that, no?" He looked up at Avram and fixed him with a probing look. "What is it you are suggesting?"

Avram chewed at his bottom lip while his thoughts raced.

"Okay, let me ask you something else. What about you and Selena? Have you been experiencing anything unusual, losses of time, doing things that you might not normally do? It's hard to explain."

"So it seems," said Max, his eyes narrowing. "I still do not understand what you are talking about, Avram. If you have something particular to say …"

Avram sat heavily on the opposite side from Max with a sigh. "Okay, just listen to me."

hough he found it a struggle to get the words out, briefly he recounted his experience of the night and what he could remember of the last few days, the snatches of memory, the bits and pieces that he still had hold of. As he spoke, Max's eyes grew wider and then he slowly started to shake his head.

"So you think this is all real?" said Max, his expression had now become one of concern.

"How else do you explain everything that's happened? What about those marks on their necks? The ship, everything. Why did we end up catching a train? Why couldn't we find some faster and easier method of transportation and get the hell out of there, Max? What's your explanation?" Avram could feel the growing hint of desperation in his own words.

Max looked at him for several seconds before answering.

"I do not know where you are getting this stuff. You have always been so rational, Avram. I suppose this is a lot to take in. We have to find ways to cope with everything that has happened. I think, maybe, it might be an idea for you to seek some help when we get to our next destination."

"But what about your children?"

"What about them, Avram?" Max stood and slid open the compartment door. "I don't want you to talk about this with Selena. I think you need to do some thinking. We are your friends, Avram, you know that, but this is just weird stuff. You need to get a hold of yourself.

In the meantime, also, please stay away from the children. Just do that for me until you sort this out in your head. You need to get yourself together."

Max stepped out into the corridor, his features etched with a look of concern, and then he closed the compartment door behind him, leaving Avram staring at the space where moments before his lanky form had been sitting.

Avram shook his head. So that had gone well. Perhaps he should talk to Marcus and Joe, but doubtless they'd have a similar reaction. At least he'd been sensible enough to talk to Max rather than Selena. He could only imagine her response.

"Come on Avram," he said to himself and the empty compartment. "What are you?"

Apparently he knew the answer to that and it did nothing to make him feel proud of what he was.

Already they were on their way north to Bucharest. Outside, the signs of civilization grew denser. What he was going to be led to do now, here, in the heart of the land of legend did not bear thinking about. Gradually, the train wound its way around the city, the tracks finally swinging south east and into the main station, Gara de Nord. He could not stop the pounding of his heart. He seemed unable to control his breathing. He dragged the curtains aside, seeing apartment blocks, concrete spires, rail tracks, the cluster and density of another city, sketched in strokes of an Eastern European legacy flavored with concrete. He stood there watching, his palms planted on the base of the window steadying him, as the train moved over criss-crossing tracks, lurching gently from side to side. With the sound of metal upon metal, the train applied its brakes, slowing and finally stopping with a final lurch. Down the corridor, a man walked knocking on each compartment along the carriage.

"Final stop," he said in three languages at each compartment.

The knock came at his door, and he stood upright, took a deep breath and then sought out his luggage. As if it were a defence, his mind turned to practicalities, seeking normalcy amidst the strangeness. He needed some more clothing, or at least to get what he had cleaned. He had grabbed precious little from the ship when they had left, what seemed like weeks ago and anything else that had been there was now gone.. He needed to check whether he had enough toiletries to last. He knew he was okay for toothpaste, but not so sure about deodorant. What else did he need?

"Final stop," came the voice again. "Bucharest. Please leave the train."

And where were they going to stay? They had no idea about this city; nothing was planned.

He hefted his valise, gave the small compartment one last scan and then stepped out into the corridor and out towards the door at the carriage end. He stepped down from the carriage and out onto the platform, looking around at a major station just like any other, long gray platforms extending out beneath a covered roof. The rest of the group were clustered at the other end of the carriage in the platform's center and he made his way over to join them.

"So, what now?" he said as he neared.

Max gave him a look before speaking, as if checking if Avram was about to say something out of the ordinary.

"Well, let's see if there is a hotel board or something. Normally they have such things in a main station. We can choose a place to stay and then work out what we are going to do next. I propose we spend a couple of days here. At least make use of the opportunity. I doubt we will get another chance like this."

Selena nodded her agreement.

"Chance?" "Opportunity?" What particular reality were the Greens living in?

"No, it makes sense," said Marcus. "Somewhere decent though."

"What about Aggie?" said Joe, always the caring one.

Max turned to him. "It is probably not a good idea for us to try to contact her. At least not yet. For the moment, we should be looking after ourselves."

What else did Max and Selena ever do?

"No, he's right," said Marcus, reaching for Joe's arm. "Okay, let's work out where we're going."

He lifted the bag that had been lying near his feet and swung it over his shoulder.

"This way, I think," he said as he started walking down the length of the platform towards the station entrance.

"We will need to exchange some money," said Selena.

"There will be a currency point somewhere here," said Max in response, his children trailing silently behind, their own bags in tow. "Or we can find a bank."

"Not at this time," said Selena.

"No, no, you are right," Max affirmed.

At the end of the platform, multiple stalls ran the length of the station, signs hung from the ceiling beams advertizing various things and above, the arched ceiling was criss-crossed with a red framework of support. Down the center, a glass skylight illuminated the space, clearly showing the people moving up and down and back and forth across the broad lobby, standing looking at signs, purchasing items from food stalls or simply browsing. Marcus had gone on ahead and he spotted the rest of the group and waved them over. He'd located a tourist information booth and now stood beside it with a bunch of pamphlets in his hand. As they drew near him, he was peering down at an unfolded map in his hand. Around them the station noises echoed from the ceiling and the smells of food and machinery were filled the air.

"There's a couple of possibilities," he said. "Probably a few too many, but this one looks All right. It's right in the center in the Old

Town. And apparently the area is pedestrianized. That should suit our purposes."

Max craned over his shoulder to see. "Yes, look—there is a church and a monastery nearby."

"What is it called?" asked Selena.

Marcus frowned down at the map. "Hotel Rembrandt. It's in a street called Strada Smardan or something. Wait a moment. I'll see if these guys can make a booking for us."

"Wait," said Selena. "Is it any good?"

"Seems okay," said Marcus. "There's a couple of pictures here." He held the pamphlet over so she could see. "It looks very woody inside, but it also looks quite up to standard."

"Yes, it looks all right," she said.

"Okay, wait here me." Marcus turned back to the front of the booth and started conversing with the woman who sat there. Moments later, she reached for the telephone, entered into a conversation, leaned forward, asked a couple of questions and then spoke once more into the phone.

Avram turned his attention away and continued scanning the station, the people walking back and forth, the travellers. As he did so, he felt something prickling in his awareness and narrowed his eyes, trying to shut out the cacophony of sensations and concentrate. It was as if someone was watching him. Though he looked from end to end of the station, he could not see anyone. He looked down at the children, but their attention was focused on Marcus's interactions at the information booth. He looked back out at the length of stalls and tracked along their entirety, right to the far end where they were distant enough that their signs became an indistinct blur.

"Right. Done," said Marcus as he re-joined the group. "We will need to get a taxi down there, so we'll need to change some money. The girl says there's a place just down there where we can do that, but if not, there are some bank machines nearby. Does anyone know what the local currency is or how much it's worth? I might have enough cash on me until we can get into the center. What about you Max, Avram?"

"Sure," said Max dismissively.

Avram merely nodded.

Together, they wandered down to the currency exchange booth and one by one made their transactions soon finding out about what the local currency was called and how much their foreign cash would buy them. The country had not yet joined the single currency, so for now and for the next couple of years, they still dealt in the local Leu.

Having completed their transactions, following Marcus's lead, they headed to the station entrance, out under the vast stone pillars of the front portico that formed a façade to a squarish building with a clock tower constructed of yellow stone. A broad street ran out front and a line of taxis sat at one end. Avram stopped as he realized that nearly every single one of the taxis was uniformly yellow. They weren't in New York or somewhere. Perhaps those cultural signposts spread by some sort of international osmosis. What was the unspoken agreement, the global driver that standardized these things from country to county? His surprise revelation was momentary. The feeling of being observed was still with him, and he scanned the surrounding area, but still nothing. Above them, atop the clock tower, fluttered the country flag, stirring in a slight breeze.

Again there was wind, and again Avram felt the chill creeping up inside him. He dragged his attention away with an effort and followed Marcus and Joe to the second in the waiting line of cabs, wondering that even amongst all of this, everything that was happening, he still had the capacity to be surprised and fascinated by those strange differences that existed from country to country, from people to people. And then another thought struck him; this was about people, all about people, but in ways he didn't yet understand.

This time, Marcus climbed into the front of the cab giving directions and pointing to the map. He also pointed to the cab in front that was already pulling out, bearing Max and Selena towards their destination. As they too drew away from the station front, Avram looked back. He wasn't sure, but just for a moment, he thought he saw a small girl standing in the station entrance by one of the pillars, watching them as they drove away.

The blood of other winged animals may be taken, in the same manner, with the proper solemnities.

−The Key of Solomon

The hotel was, as Marcus had said, very woody in appearance, dark, polished floors, strips of wood set artistically above the bed. A pale yellow bedspread added to the darkened appearance, though the sheets were crisp and white. Avram dumped his bag on the bed and walked back and forth, his footsteps echoing from the shining floor. Looking out the window, he was greeted with nothing but old buildings, a street below and the barest patch of sky above. He turned back to the bed and proceeded to dump out the contents of his valise. A couple of shirts, underwear, socks, his toiletries, all fell out to form a scattered pile on top of the bed. He really ought to get himself cleaned up, change his clothes, but first he needed to put this stuff away. One by one, he found places for each of the items lying on the bed. As he tugged at the last shirt, preparing to hang it in the wardrobe, something that had been hidden, concealed within its folds tumbled out and lay there accusingly. It was a small amulet of some type, a little pendent on a simple, dark woven string. He stood there looking at it, chewing at his bottom lip, trying to remember where he had acquired such an item. He frowned a little as vague recollections teased at his memory.

Back, two cities ago now. Somewhere underground. It was not the cistern, he knew that. Then before. He reached out to take the thing, to get a better look and then hesitated. Again he frowned. He had no idea what had made him pause like that. He reached for the trinket once more. As his fingers made contact, a frisson of something, almost electric, ran through his hand and up his arm and he withdrew his hand suddenly, jerking back. It was as if he had just received a tiny shock. With everything that was happening, perhaps that wasn't so strange. Shaking his head, he reached for it again. Perhaps he had imagined it, a twinge of his nerve or something. He cupped it in his hand, continuing to feel that charged tingling seeping through the skin of his palm. Within his head, a buzz, well, almost a buzz. He tried shaking it away, but it remained barely below the level of awareness. He turned his hand first one way then the other, looking at the object. As he peered down at it, an image floated up in his mind's eye, somewhere deep, cool, large stones and a small child, a little girl and her name had been … Lilith.

Somehow, this tiny object was connected to her.

Avram opened his case and gingerly placed the amulet in one of the internal side pockets and snapped it shut and quickly stepped back. He could work out more of the details later, understand the connections, but for now, he just wanted to have a shower. He had had enough of this child, this young not-young girl who was haunting him. He just wished everything would go back to normal, but somehow, he didn't think there was any chance of that. He grabbed the shirt, smoothed it on the bed, then took the bag and carried it over to the small stool affair created just for that purpose and placed it down. He stared at it for a moment or two, suspiciously. What did that thing have to do with the girl? No, he wasn't going to fathom it out like this. A shower, clean clothes, and he would go down to the lobby, meet the others and work out what they were going to do.

The steaming water did something to restore a semblance of humanity. At least the shower was good. Sometimes, in hotels, they were less than perfect. As he wiped away the condensation from the mirror with his towel, he looked at himself, at how pale and haggard he looked. He had lost weight over the past few days, it would seem. It was no surprise, really. Every time he started to think about the things that had occurred on the ship and then after, an empty hollow opened up in the pit of his stomach, a hard knot of tension in his chest. He dried himself, turning away from the mirror. He had had feelings like that before. In the midst of his divorce, in the deep pool of loss and separation, he had felt like that, black, empty, and it had led to thoughts of self-destruction, thoughts that he should not have been having, ever. He had to get a grip. Dropping the towel on the bathroom floor, he went back to the bedroom and dressed.

This particular hotel had old style keys, a large metal oval engraved with the room number attached. He grabbed it now from the desk and shoved it into his pocket. He would meet the others, say nothing about what had been happening, just let himself be swept along with the flow. Perhaps then, it would all simply go away. He knew, within himself, that it was a vain hope, that he was fooling himself, but it gave him a shred of comfort nonetheless. Leaving the room, he pulled the door closed firmly behind him and walked down the corridor to join the others in the lobby.

Down on the ground floor, he looked around, but there was no sign of the others at all. He looked into the bar, around the corner, but apart from a pair of Japanese tourists, there was no one else. He couldn't be early. With his shower and everything else, the others must have had time to make their preparations. Frowning, he made his way to the front entrance and looked out. On the street, tables with umbrellas stretched to either side of the hotel's façade, and next to it, on the right hand side hung a sign, naming the next-door establishment as the Grand Café Van Gogh. There, at one of the tables, sat his group, the Greens, the Boys, Marcus and Joe, already with drinks in front of them. Typical Max and Selena. They had not even spared a thought for him, bothered to inform him of their intentions. He grimaced, then shook the reaction away. It was probably unplanned, and in his current mood he was making things out to be more than they were. It was much more pleasant out here than in the depths of the hotel lobby. He picked his way between the other tables to join them.

Selena, a tall latté sitting before her, was poring over a selection of pamphlets. Max had another in front of him. Marcus and Joe sat with coffees, Marcus stirring his idly and looking out to the street, watching the evening passers-by. The children, who but weeks before would have been running between tables making a nuisance of themselves, were sitting impassively, watching their parents. As Avram approached, Samantha looked up at him, met his eyes and then looked away. Avram pulled out a seat and sat. He motioned for a waiter, ordered coffee, and then turned his attention to the group.

"What have you got there?" he asked.

"Oh, just some pamphlets, some tourist stuff," said Max.

"Some we got from inside the hotel, but I picked up a couple at the station too. This one shows all the trains from Bucharest. You know, it's a pity, but we could almost do the old Orient Express route from here. It is a shame it no longer operates."

"So what are you suggesting?" asked Marcus. Max made a great show of rubbing his chin thoughtfully. "Well, you know, I think from here we go maybe to Budapest."

"Oh yes," said Selena.

"And from Budapest," Max continued, "Vienna, Zurich and finally Paris. That should give us enough to see and do and wait for this entire furore to die down. We can connect with the travel company and find a way to get home."

"I don't understand why we just don't go straight home," said Marcus.

"Well, you know," said Max, looking up from his timetables.

"I am not going to throw this away. We have the children. There is school. We have to take this chance now. It might be years before we get such a trip again."

Avram glanced over at the children. He had forgotten that they even went to school. He wondered briefly if they would ever attend a school again. Their father's words washed over them as they watched the conversation flow back and forth.

"I wonder how Aggie is doing," said Joe glumly. Marcus reached for his leg and squeezed it gently.

"She'll be fine," said Selena. "Do you know," she said looking up and turning to each of them, "this place was once called 'Little Paris?' Funny, no? We are going to Paris and yet we are in Paris They even have an Arc de Triomphe here except they call it something else." She looked down again. "Arcul de Triumf."

"Huh," said Marcus.

"Anyway," she continued. "There is lots to do here. I would like to see Revolution Square. You know, the place where Ceausescu finally realized it was all over. Maybe the Athenaeum, the Royal Palace, a couple of others. But this one we have to see …" She held up the guidebook and turned the page so that each of them could look at the photograph. "Listen to what it says. 'The People's Palace took 20,000 workers and 700 architects to build. The palace has 12 stories, 1,100 rooms, a 328-ft-long lobby and four underground levels, including nuclear bunker.'"

Avram reached over. "Can I see that again?"

Selena handed over the pamphlet and Avram looked at the photo. The place was just creepy. Marcus leaned over to look over his shoulder.

"Oh God," he said. "That's scary."

"Yes," offered Joe. And if Ceausescu built it, I bet it took more than 20,000 workers. Or better, it might have taken that many, but you've got to wonder how many of them made it through the job. The man was a tyrant, a monster. I bet it's scary in more ways than one."

"Ha," said Selena, reaching for the pamphlet again. "There's more than one monster. Maybe we can visit the Jewish Quarter too. It was quite big. It started around the 16th Century so it says. Very old. Of course, not too many survived. Well … you know."

"Hmmmm," said Joe. "You know, there's quite a lot not to like about this place."

"Oh, come on, Joe," said Max. "It's just history. Everything is just history."

Joe sighed. "Typical, Max. Just because it's history doesn't mean that it didn't happen. Or that it can't happen again. You can just brush it off like that, make light, but these things leave an impression. You can feel it in a place."

Max snorted. "Right, and next you'll be telling me the city is haunted."

"Well, maybe it is," said Joe. "Maybe it is." He held Max's eyes for a moment, and then looked away.

Selena looked at Max and smiled, giving him a little shake of her head. Marcus narrowed his eyes at her, and then he too looked away. If Selena noticed, she gave no further sign. The pair of them, Max and Selena had always somewhat existed in their own little bubble, their own version of reality, and now it seemed that particular tradition was going to continue unaffected by anything else.

"Come on, Selena," said Avram finally. "Doesn't anything affect you guys?"

Selena looked at him as if not understanding. "Sure," she said. "The things that matter." She looked over at her children.
Avram followed her gaze. Samantha met her mother's look and smiled. A moment later, Alfred did the same. Selena turned back to look at Avram.

"See," she said, as if that was explanation enough.

Avram pursed his lips. Yes, more than you might imagine, Selena, he thought, but he wasn't about to say anything. Not now.

"So," said Max after taking the last sip of his drink. "Perhaps we should find somewhere to meet. We can look at some more things over dinner, and then, I don't know, make some plans for the morning. We can go to the station later in the day, maybe book some tickets for the next part of our grand adventure. But for now, let us find something to eat."

By the time they got up from their table and paid, the sky was filling with a bruised purpling, beckoning the onset of evening. It did not take long to find a local establishment, one that boasted local, rustic fare and they wound up in a cellar, vaulted ceilings and dark wooden tables and chairs. The meal proceeded quietly, filled only with Selena and Max's suggestions for the following day. Avram picked at his food, drank sparingly, and it seemed that both Marcus and Joe were unenthused about the dishes set before them. Max and Selena, however, ate with gusto. Avram watched the children throughout the meal, but if they actually ate anything, he could not tell. Nor did they seem to drink much throughout. Avram consumed a lot of water and little else. Eventually they decided that the meal was over, and after settling up, they made their way back up to the street and along the pedestrian street to head back to the hotel and sleep.

On the way back, Avram excused himself. He's spotted a tiny bric-a-brac cum antique shop. He didn't know quite what possessed him, but he wanted to acquire a particular object, a very special object. The others wandered off and left him to his own devices.

The shop was lit in yellowish light, the glass fronted window cluttered with various objects, porcelain, metal, wood. A number of religious artefacts, perhaps old, perhaps new, sat amongst the piled shelves. Whatever it was, he knew that he could acquire what he wanted within. As he stepped inside, a bell chimed in the rear and a small man, his face deeply lined, his brown leather face dark. Within the face sat dark, dark eyes that immediately fixed on his face, narrowed and then took on a normal gaze. His mouth opened with a wide smile, revealing yellowish teeth, large within his face.

"English?" he asked.

"How did you …?"

"Oh I can tell this," he said and his grin grew even wider if that was at all possible.

"I am looking for something," said Avram, glancing around the small shop.

"Many things. Perhaps some memories of Romania. Something to remember." The little man gestured around the shop with an expansive wave.

"No, I am looking for something particular," said Avram. "I need a cross. Maybe something old."

Perhaps he was crazy, but here, Bucharest, all of the legends, he had read the stories, heard the tales. Vampires. A cross would provide some sort of protection, or it was supposed to do so.

The shopkeeper's face became serious. "Yes, of these we have," he said. He fixed Avram with an intense look. "Something for a gift, or …"

"No, no," said Avram distractedly looking up and down the cluttered shelves. "It is for me. Something, I don't know, something old perhaps." He didn't know why, but that seemed right.

"Are you religious man?"

"No, not particularly," he answered dismissing the question absently, still scanning the shopkeeper's wares.

The little man went quiet for a moment, looked away. The next he spoke without looking at Avram directly.

"You need it for some other reason."

"Yes, yes," said Avram, still not seeing what he wanted. The shopkeeper cleared his throat. "Wait," he said and disappeared into the back of the shop. He reappeared a few moments later, clutching something within his hands, resting it on one palm and stroking it gently with the other.

"This," he said.

Avram looked at the object the shopkeeper was clutching. It was a simple wooden cross, no adornments, the surface shining in places where the touch of many hands had held it. It was a cross, that was all, but somehow Avram could tell it was old, well used, something special.

"Is very old," said the man. "Is blessed."

Avram watched as he continued stroking it. The word 'blessed' shot a chill through him. That particular word was far too familiar.

"I'll take it," said Avram.

"Are you sure?" asked the little man, pressing the question with his expression, filling the simple words with import.

"Yes, yes. I'm sure."

The man nodded, moved over to a short glass-topped counter and display case and started to wrap the piece in tissue paper. Avram barely registered the amount, shoved across a sheaf of bills and shoved the wrapped item into his pocket.

"No bag?" asked the shopkeeper.

"No bag. Thank you," said Avram and turned towards the door.

"Take very good care," said the shopkeeper behind him. "Take very good care in the night."

As he pulled open the door and stepped back out to the street, Avram considered the strangeness of those last words. He looked back through the glass door and the shopkeeper was watching him, his hands clasped in front of himself an expression of solemnity on his dark and wizened face. There was a depth of concern, of seriousness in that gaze. Avram swallowed and turned away, heading down the street and towards their hotel. All the way, his hand was shoved into his pocket, his thumb stroking the solidity of the object sitting there through the paper wrapping, feeling the smooth hardness and in places the wood grain. What he had said was true. He was not religious, not at all, and yet this thing, this religious object was giving him some sort of comfort and he didn't know why.

Back in his hotel room, he pulled out the package, unwrapped it, shoving the paper into the waste paper basket below the desk. He placed the cross carefully in the center of the bed and stood looking down out it for a couple of minutes wondering what it was he was doing. Finally, he picked it up again and slid it underneath his pillow. Partially satisfied, he started to undress and get himself ready for bed.

SEVENTEEN

[The Shedim] souls were created by God, but as the Sabbath intervened before they received bodies they had to remain without them.

−Beresh, raba c.7

"Avram Davis."

The words cut through his sleep like a chilled knife, dragging him to consciousness. He had not been deeply asleep, skittering in and out of semi-consciousness, though there were dreams. At first he thought they were more dream words.

"Avram," her voice came again. It was she, Lilith, here in his room.

He struggled with the bedclothes and then remembered, grasping frantically beneath the pillow, feeling the solid wood connect with his fingers. He dragged out the cross, held it gripped firmly by the base with one hand thrust forward, and only then did he open his eyes, barely daring to look.

The room was in semi darkness. It had to be shortly after midnight, but she was here, again, through a locked door, standing at the foot of his bed watching him with that intent adult gaze in that young and innocent face, but he knew it was not innocent, not at all.

Still she stood there watching him and then she laughed. She actually threw back her head and laughed.

"Oh, you poor man," she said. She shook her head, a look of slight pity on her face, if he could interpret the look properly.

"Really, Avram?"

"Get away," he said. "Leave me alone." He thrust out the hand with the cross again.

She shook her head slowly, the look of pity growing more pronounced.

"I know not what you are thinking, Avram," she said. "Of course, you will clutch to those fragile beliefs fostered by a too young religion, but no. You think we are our lesser brethren, our poor cousins?"

She looked thoughtful for a moment. "Yes, here in Romania, where many of them were spawned. We pity them, you know. These poor shadows you call vampires. Doomed to exist upon the blood of animals, the blood of humans, bound to their need. We are not their kind. They are young. We are old. We have existed from the dawn of memory and will continue long after they, poor creatures, have passed. We are Shedim."

Gradually, he lowered the cross his hand trembling, his heart beating in his ears and let it fall from his hand.

She gave a look of gentle satisfaction. "And so, you understand," she said.

"But I don't understand," he said, whispering the words.

"But you must. It is time for you to come."

"Come? Come where?"

And then, as if something had distracted her attention, she paused, her eyes narrowing. She tilted her head a little to one side as though listening, then, with her eyes still narrowed, she turned her face slowly, scanning the room, her lips open, almost sniffing the air, tasting it.

"What do you want?" he forced out, the words full of breath.

For a moment, he thought she was going to approach him, but then, an instant's hesitation, and she was gone. Her form shifted, changed, became shadow that drifted away in fragile tatters, leaving not a trace of her shape or presence.

In the next seconds, there was a gentle tapping at his door. His breath caught in his throat. He reached for the cross again, but then thought better of it, leaving it where it lay, tumbled away from his hand on the bed. Again came the tapping, light, but insistent. He threw the covers back, swung his legs out and padded over to the door, gently opening it a crack to see Samantha standing there looking up at his face.

"You have to come now, Uncle Avram," she said softly.

Avram glanced behind himself, expecting to see Lilith's shape, her presence there again, but there was nothing.

"No," he said simply. "Go back to your room, Samantha. Do

you want me to call your parents?"

"Avram," she said, closing her eyes and then opening them again. She was clothed in a white dress. Funny that he should think of it now, but he could not recall having ever seen it before. He shook his head.

"You must come."

Again he shook his head. Her hand darted like a snake through the slim crack, touched his leg and with the touch, all volition suddenly washed out of him. He stepped back from the door, and she slipped inside.

"Get your clothes," she said simply.

Doing as he was told, Avram turned, seeking the clothes he had removed before going to bed and pulled them on. He had to search for his shoes in the gloom, but he didn't even think about turning on the light as he felt across the floor. All the while, Samantha simply stood there watching him, her back against the door, holding it lightly shut with one hand. Seemingly satisfied with his preparations, Samantha stood back and held the door open.

"Come now, Avram." There was no inflection in her voice; the words were flat and emotionless.

It was as if he was walking through a dense fog, but one that sparkled with ice crystals, a pale white veil across his senses. He tried to ask, to enquire, to demand, but the power of speech seemed to have deserted him as had any ability to fight against the compulsion that drove him to follow the child's instructions.

We are Shedim kept repeating in his head as a soft whisper, over and over again. The words had her voice. Her voice.

Avram knew, now, he should be in a state of panic, but the thought trickled away with any sense of real emotion, hidden beneath the covers of this dream state that was yet not a dream. Mechanically, he followed the child out to the corridor, down to the lobby and out. The hotel reception was empty, and of people on the street, there was no sign. As they walked, he wondered where they might be heading, but that thought too fluttered away from his fragile grasp.

They crossed a square. One or two people walked with purpose away over the other side, not even noticing their passing. Avram registered their presence, vaguely thought that he might call out to them, but that idea drifted away as well. They wound through streets, across a bridge. Before them lay a large park. Struggling, Avram finally managed to force a few words from his unresponsive vocal chords.

"Where are we going?"

"Come now, Avram," was the simple response, nothing more.

Despite the streetlamps, the night was still dark, and as they passed through the trees and gardens, long shadows stretched like black fingers across the pathways and walls. At the other side of the park, across a road, Avram saw their destination. It could be the only place they could be heading towards. There was nothing else around. The huge structure loomed over the surrounding area, looking bone-like in the evening darkness. He'd seen the picture before in the pamphlet that Selena had been passing around. This was the People's Palace, that folly of construction, sweat and tears that spoke of another era and a darker history. Even though he was now seeing it from the side, it was unmistakable. Avram swallowed despite himself, for although his senses appeared fogged, he could still feel. The sight of the building, especially its pale stone reaching against the black, hundreds of blank, eyeless windows looking out was something of dread, intimidation, enough so that it drove inside of him and hunched with a chill, hard feeling.

"Come now, Avram," said Samantha again.

Unhurriedly, they crossed the road that led around the building's side and to the front entrance. The vast construction was set upon a small hill and a bent path drove at an angle then straight towards the front. The security gates lay open for some reason, and there was no one around, no uniformed guards, no police; it appeared totally devoid of life, until, that was, they neared the front of the building. A tall columned portico fronted the monstrosity, at least three stories high and in its shadow, on either side of a set of double doors stood at least half a dozen children in solemn lines, the girls wearing the same white dress that Samantha wore, the boys in black suits with plain white shirts. As they neared, all faces turned to him, expressionless, merely watching as they approached. Though there was nothing, Avram almost believed that their eyes were glowing with a vague inner light. He could have been imagining it. Samantha led him past the twin lines, right to the door and in order, the other children fell in behind. Together, they passed through the double doors and moments later, they were inside proper.

The interior turned out to be as ornate as the exterior was forbidding. A large circular lobby area, all polished tiles stretched beneath a dome, their footsteps echoing hollowly in the empty space. Shiny white columns surrounded the space at regular intervals and to each side, stretched passages sealed off by arched, dark wooden double doors, all closed. From behind one or two of the columns, other children appeared and unhurriedly crossed the floor to fall in beside them, all decked out in the same black and white clothing. They said not a word, no greeting, no signs of recognition between them. Avram's breath was coming in short gasps, struggling to pull in enough air.

"Come now, Avram." The words were flat, seemed almost automatic.

She led him towards one of the sets of double doors leading further into the dark complex. Moulded and painted ceilings stretched above them, ornate, yet not overdone. They walked, together, through corridor and passageway, past multiple doorways, and down, down into the depths of the vast building. At last, they came to another huge set of doors that now stood open and that led further into another complex of rooms, the thick walls evident, pale emergency lighting daubing the solid surfaces with a yellowish red glow. Behind them, the rest of the children walked silently in step.

Samantha led him through a passage into a central chamber, large, but contained, the ceiling comparatively low. He smelt … nothing. There was an almost clinical absence of smell, but he dismissed the observation as he saw another cluster of individuals before him, and there, in their midst, she stood. More children gathered around her, both boys and girls, and as he approached, she smiled.

"Welcome, Avram."

Though his thoughts came sluggishly, he could not help identifying this scene with the last, brief subterranean meeting in the last city, but this time, there was no dripping water, no smell of wet stone. As his fragile awareness picked out details, his apparent lack of control, he drew in an involuntary gasp. There, to either side of the group stood Joe and Marcus. How had they come here? And then he saw Alfred, standing next to Joe, gently holding his hand. The boy looked up at Avram and his lips quirked in a smile.

Lilith opened her arms, spread her hands in a gesture that took in the assembled children.

"You see, Avram, now we grow. And now we will grow more and manifold." She lowered her hands again. She fixed his eyes and then she too smiled. "You can speak," she said quietly and without any ceremony.

"Why here?" he said haltingly. There had to be some reason for these choices.

"We are at home here among the dead as we are at home among the living," she said. "It reminds us of their mortality, of your mortality, and of that which we never had. Perhaps we are sentimental," she said with a little shrug.

"But why me? Why them? What do you want of us?"

She responded with a short laugh. "The reasons are different, Avram Davis. You … you were there at the beginning and you will remain with us. It is you, Avram, who help spread our blessing. My blessing.

You are like a beacon to me."

He frowned, not really understanding.

"But these …," she continued, gesturing at Marcus and Joseph in turn. "These are beyond their use for us. I thought to give you a lesson, Avram, show you our blessing so your understanding would grow. And so, they become useful again."

She smiled at him indulgently. "Poor man. You need tutoring. What better place than here amongst the forgotten dead." She looked around the chamber as if seeking those dead. "They are here."

Still Avram had difficulty moving, but with an effort of will, struggling against the immobility, he took a step forward, towards her. She lowered her gaze, fixed him with a steady look, and he stopped, unable to take another. Volition drained away from him again. He looked at first to Joseph, and then Marcus. Both were staring blankly in front of them, their faces expressionless.

Lilith raised a hand and all at once, the children began to move, clustering closer around Joe and Marcus in turn. Whatever they were doing, it was clear that both Alfred and Samantha were taking the lead. Small hands reached up, manipulating clothing, opening catches and buttons, pulling fabric away, leaving exposed naked flesh at their throats. Avram struggled to look away, but he could not. He had to watch, was compelled to watch as small fingers ran across their faces and necks, across skin and hair and flesh. The expression on Joe's face changed, the blankness replaced by something else, a look of bliss, of something like rapture. His head tilted back, his mouth opened, his eyes closing as he faced the ceiling. He turned his gaze to Marcus, and it was the same. Together, the children lowered them both backwards, together supporting their weight until they were lying flat upon the solid floor and still the ministrations continued. Avram tried to tear his gaze away, but there was nothing he could do. Inside, he felt something, a growing sense of wrongness, of abhorrence, a need to reject what he was seeing, but he could not look away.

"No," he said from between closed teeth, trying to lower his face, to look away, but unable to muster the will.

"But yes," said Lilith, an indulgent grin upon her face as she seemed to study his reactions.

oe was in his focus now, and Samantha moved around, her face positioned near his throat, exposed as he arched backwards, his body rigid, fingers and lips working at him. His body arched further. A moan escaped his lips as he tensed every muscle in his legs roped and tight. His mouth grew wider, his teeth exposed, his face stretched, and then, at that moment, Samantha's face dipped to his neck and she supped, her lips pressed against the flesh of his throat, her eyes watching Avram. Joe let out a cry, something between agony and rapture and as Avram watched, Samantha's eyes, rolled back, showing nothing more than blank whiteness, staring at him. Across the other side, Alfred lay stretched across the floor, his face at Marcus's neck, his face ecstatic, and then, together, Marcus and Joe collapsed back to the floor, their bodies having given all.

"And so," said Lilith, "we sustain, we celebrate your lives, your pulse, the warm beating of your passion, and your breath. It is like a warm wind across the desert and it stirs our souls. It is the life force that courses through all things."

Together, Samantha and Alfred stood, turning to face Avram, twin looks of contentment on their face.

"No," said Avram again.

This couldn't be happening. He simply could not have just witnessed what he had. The sense of revulsion worked within him. Marcus lay where he had fallen back, a look of ecstasy sat upon his face, his eyes open wide, staring up at the blank ceiling in the dim red-yellow light. And upon his neck lay a familiar purple weal, broad, dark, bruised, the size and shape of an open mouth. He saw now what it was. Slowly he turned to look at Joe. The picture was the same. Avram shuddered and took a deep halting breath and finally managed to look away. One by one, the other children climbed slowly to their feet, turned until, as a group, they were all facing Avram, looking at him. Slowly, slowly, he scanned the faces and with every set of eyes he felt the breath drifting out of him to be replaced by a deep and insidious chill.

"Why?" he whispered. "Why?"

The horror of what he had just witnessed washed through his skull, through his body. "They were my friends."

"Friends?" Lilith laughed. "They were as cattle," she said.

Ronald, Pavel, and now Marcus and Joe—how many more were there? Aggie was the lucky one. And what about Max and Selena?

As if reading his thoughts, Lilith spoke once more.

"Now you have seen. Now you know. You and the others will continue your journey, travel together with these two ..." she gestured to Samantha and Alfred who both stepped across to join her on either side, both continuing to keep their gazes fixed on Avram's face. "And as you pass across the lands and people, our blessing will be spread. We will sup and grow stronger. It has been a long, long time, far too many years, but again, we are free." She smiled at him indulgently. With an effort of will, he managed to shake his head.

"No," he breathed.

"But yes, Avram. Go now. You have many places to see. And we will be there with you."

Alfred and Samantha stepped forward, each taking one of his hands, turned him and gently led him away, out of the deep underground room and beyond, into the depths of the night. Inside, the black filled him like clouds, not a single flickering star to illuminate the darkness. Behind him, he could sense her presence, like a chill beacon, long after she was out of sight.

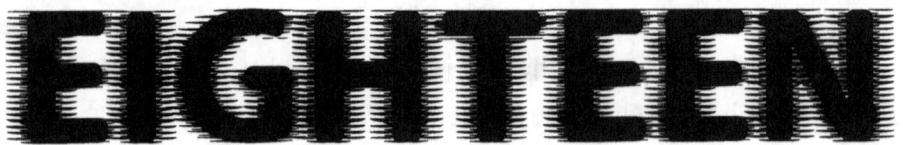

EIGHTEEN

Their face is a burning wind and their voice the hissing of serpents.

–Malleus Maleficarum

Avram wondered, as he stared down at the bed, at the old wooden cross that still lay there, if he was still in the midst of some kind of thrall, whether last night had been merely another dream. He knew better though. This was beyond dreaming. Any other thought was merely some way for him to come to grips with what was happening, some state of denial. He knew, without having to check, that Marcus and Joseph would not be in their room, would never be in their room, or any other room again. He picked up the cross, turned it one way and then the other and then, in a fit of anger, hurled it across the room. It clattered against the wall and then fell against the polished wooden floor, sliding along the surface to rest, accusingly where it lay. She'd been right; what had he been thinking? There had to be some way out of this, some escape, but more than that, he had to find out a way to do something about her, Lilith, her army of what he presumed had become Shedim, or whatever she called them, for they were clearly children no longer.

Then there were the Greens. If he had understood correctly, then Max and Selena were somehow useful to her. They had always been somewhat removed, but it was clear to him that something else was going on there. That few instants of their apparent fugue when he had confronted Max, their refusal to notice anything different in their children's behaviour, all of it pointed to something deeper and more sinister than their normal self-obsessed attitude to the world. Despite that cavalier attitude, that … ignorance …Max and Selena were good people; he knew that. He had been friends with them for years, and through the hard times their support had been solid and constant.

Still the crucifix stared up at him accusingly from where it lay on the floor. What had she said? A young religion. Something like that. Well, if he wasn't going to find the answers in the trappings of Christianity, he was going to have to look elsewhere. There were older traditions here in Bucharest, he knew that …

The images of what had happened to Marcus and Joe played

out through his head and he grimaced, turning away from the bed, into the bathroom and leant over to splash some water on his face. It had not been a dream, could not be a dream. He stared at his own haunted eyes in the mirror above the sink. What should he do ... tell someone, announce to the world that he was delusional? That she should use children. It made it all the worse, though he knew now that they were not mere children. They just wore their form. They were so much more than children. Here, in the hotel room, right now, he felt that he had some control over his own actions, that he had a semblance of self-possession. That was a good word, possession. That was exactly what it was. Gradually, as he was losing his capacity to act, his will, his volition had been possessed by something that he found it impossible to fight against, and that something was Lilith. He considered his efforts, those brief periods where he had attempted a struggle. Was there even a hint that his own will had been increasing, that he was less a slave to that control? Maybe. Or perhaps he had only been imagining it.

As those thoughts continued tumbling through his head, he stood under the shower, letting the water pound down on top of him, washing his body automatically without thinking about it. He dressed, grabbed his room key and then headed downstairs. He could at least see how Max and Selena were doing. By now, he knew they would be at breakfast, as regular as clockwork.

They were there in the breakfast room, as predicted, both Samantha and Alfred sitting there with them. Max and Selena were chatting to each other as they buttered pieces of toast, reached for condiments, sipped at their juice, nothing to say that there was anything out of the ordinary. Together, the children looked up, watching Avram as he neared the table.

"So, Avram," said Max. "You are going to join us for breakfast?"

"Yes, sure," he replied distractedly, pulling out a vacant chair. "I'm just going to have coffee."

"Well, you know," said Selena. "Breakfast is the most important meal of the day. If you are sure you know what you are doing."

"Yeah, sure. Coffee is just fine."

"Hmm," she said, turning her attention back to her toast and eggs.

If Avram hadn't known any better, it would have been like any ordinary day on their journey.

"We have decided," said Max. "It is best probably if we leave here this evening. The children would like to get on the train again." He glanced at them. "Have you seen the Boys so we can work it all out?"

Avram swallowed heavily. "I am not sure they will be joining us," he said slowly. He wanted to say more, but somehow, the words just wouldn't come. He looked away from Max's eyes.

"Is that so?" said Selena, apparently completely unconcerned.

"Huh. Well, we have to get tickets," said Max with a little frown. "We need to get this organized."

Avram turned back to look at him. "Yes, I get that, Max," he snapped.

Max started at his reaction, his eyes going wide. "Okay, okay," he said.

Avram bit his lip and shook his head. "Whatever you need to do, Max," he said. "I need to do something of my own."

"I see. Well, whatever you need to do, we should meet somewhere in time. The train leaves the station at 17:40. It is another overnight trip. We get to Budapest at 08:50 in the morning. If you see Joe and Marcus you can tell them. I will get the tickets and let us meet at the station. We would like to go around, see a few things. Is that okay?"

"Yes, yes, it's fine," Avram said, only half paying attention to Max's organization. He was watching the children. They, in turn, were watching him back.

Breath

Barely having taken more than two sips of his coffee, Avram pushed his chair back and stood. Again came the urge to say something, and once more, the words died on his lips. Samantha was looking at him, her eyes slightly narrowed, her lips set in a thin line.

"Okay, look, I have to go," said Avram, turning away from her.

"Fine," said Max. "If it is as you say, then I will not get the tickets for the Boys. They can look after themselves."

Avram stumbled from the breakfast room, out through the lobby and straight out onto the street. He looked up at the clear sky as soon as he was outside, pulling in a deep breath of air and exhaling slowly. The closer he was to the children, the harder it was. He looked up and down the street, wondering what he was going to do, what it was that he needed. The burden of belief was sitting heavily upon him. No one would believe him. No one.

Vaguely, from having seen the pamphlets on local guides that Selena had been waving about, he knew the direction of the old Jewish Quarter from their hotel and he turned in that direction. If he could not find solace in a young religion, perhaps he had to seek something older, not that he was sure that any form of faith would hold an answer now. Blindly, he wandered streets, following instinct as much as anything else, seeking something, he knew not what. As he moved through the roads and alleyways, he found a mix of eras, of legacy communist concrete towers of apartment buildings interspersed with older, more traditional buildings. There seemed to be no logic to the placement, it was all jumbled together. Brick, stone, concrete, he would see all within a few paces and then move on. It became evident when his entered the Jewish section. The older buildings were architecturally different; there were decorations and designs consistent with the culture. He wandered aimlessly through those narrow streets, waiting, perhaps for something to strike him, for some sort of answer to appear from out of those narrow streets, but there was nothing.

At last, he turned a corner and standing there, before him sat a large patterned brick building. Diamond lozenges of darker brick set in lighter faced the front, changing to striped patterns at the side. Ornate windows sat high in the building's front, four round windows joining to one central one and crossed by circular arches of more brickwork. Out front, stood a large iron menorah, forged, dark gray-black, pointing to the sky. He stopped dead in his tracks. He read the sign. This was the Choral Temple. He stood there considering for a few moments. Perhaps here ...

Inside, rows of dark wooden bench seats clustered in rows either side. A scuffed red carpet ran down between them, but above, the ceilings, the walls were patterned in gold, blue red of the brickwork beneath coming through, ornate designs mirroring the shape of the windows he had seen outside. No one was here. He stood, feeling the space, feeling the emptiness and drinking in the years. It was places like this that drew him, had always drawn him. He wasn't sure whether it was the accumulation of age, or something else; when people came to a place regularly for years to spill out the contents of their souls, it left a lasting impression. Was it possible for people's energies to be absorbed by brickwork, by stone, by mortar? He turned slowly round, feeling the atmosphere as he looked up at the ceiling. Somehow, here, he felt shielded, cocooned away from the outside events. He took a deep breath and looked back to the temple's front, stood there for a few moments biting his lower lip and then shook his head and turned once more. This was nothing more than the familiarity of an old place that came with such a visit, and the comfort he was feeling was the familiar, nothing more. With a sigh, he walked back outside again. The only place he was going to find a real answer was within himself.

He left, roughly knowing the direction he was heading in, down Strada Baia de Fier, past old parked cars, low stone three-story buildings and chipped and crumbling plasterwork exposing naked bricks beneath. A construction site, more cars and a narrow street led him further to a double-laned main road and across towards the Old

Town proper. All around, advertizing hoardings displayed a combination of the local language and English, as if the city had somehow partially lost its identity.

Back in the pedestrian area, he started to regain his bearing; a certain familiarity grew with narrow paved streets, archways, old doors and window shutters and then, there, was the street upon which sat their hotel. He wandered up to the café where they had met the previous evening and sat. After ordering a coffee, sipping at it slowly, he considered his other options, and then, he had an idea. The old guy in the antique shop had seemed to know more than he had let on, or was it just merely a cultivated impression he wanted to give the tourists. He took one last sip at his coffee, got up, and not waiting for the waiter to come and collect his payment, he walked inside and settled up at the counter. He wasn't completely sure he could find the little shop again—it had been night; places looked different—but generally, Avram's sense of direction was pretty good. Right now, he was prepared to try just about anything.

After a few false starts, he managed to locate the tiny glass-fronted shop, but the interior was dim. He glanced at his watch. It was nearly midday. Perhaps it was only open to catch the afternoon and evening tourist trade. He pressed his face up against the glass, immediately fogging it with his breath, but if there was anyone inside, there was no sign. He stepped back, looking over the front and then the door. Beside the door sat a small bell, barely noticeable unless you were looking at it. Avram stepped forward again and pressed it, once, twice and then a third time before stepping back, looking up at the windows above the shop and then back into the shop itself. He was just about to step forward and press the bell again when there was a hint of motion from the shadowed doorway inside that led into the back room. The shopkeeper, the man from the previous evening emerged a moment later, a woollen cardigan wrapped around his shoulders despite the day's warmth. He peered out through the glass door, reached up unlocked something at the top, then eased the door open a sliver. He clearly recognised Avram.

"What you want?" asked the man. "No refund, no return," he said.

"No, no, it's not that," said Avram, holding out his hands in a placating gesture.

"What then? I am closed. Can you not see this?"

"Yes, I'm sorry, I just thought that ..."

The little man studied him for a moment, and then seemed to change his mind. He pulled the door wide enough for Avram to pass inside.

"So ..."

"I just thought ... I thought last night that you knew something, that you understood a little of ..." Avram didn't quite know what to say next.

The shopkeeper nodded slowly, a look of almost compassion on his wrinkled features, his dark intelligent eyes knowing.

"You have some trouble," he said. "That was why you wanted the cross, no?"

Avram nodded.

"Yes," said the shopkeeper. "Last night I could see this in your face. The look I have seen before. But you took what you wanted. Why do you come back?"

"Because ..." Avram wasn't really sure why he had returned. Desperation? "Because it didn't work," he said finally.

"What does this mean—didn't work?"

Avram suddenly felt uncomfortable with what he was saying. How much of the old man's reaction was his own imagination? He swallowed.

"Have you ever heard of Shedim?"

The shopkeeper frowned and pulled back, then shook his head. "I do not know this Shedim."

"But you sold me the cross. You knew why I wanted it. I could see that you knew."

The old man's expression became knowing again. "This is Bucharest. This is Romania. This is the home of the strigoi, the moroi, that which you call the vampire. Of course I know why you want this."

The mocking words of Lilith came to him then.

"Vampires are nothing," said Avram. "You should fear the Shedim. That's what you should fear." He said the last through closed teeth, turned on his heel and yanked the door open and stepped out onto the street, his shoulders heaving. He was not going to find any help here, nor anywhere else. He glanced back at the shop, saw the old man still standing there, watching him with a narrow-eyed look of confusion.

Avram didn't know what he had been thinking. He strode rapidly away from the shop and back towards the hotel. He needed to get his things, check out, meet Max and Selena at the station and get away from this city. He knew that Marcus and Joe would not be joining them, not any more. He wouldn't find the answers he needed in this town. Sure, it was a place filled with legends and folklore, but they were legends that he did not need. He didn't know what he needed any more.

Then a thought came to him. Why didn't he just leave—grab his stuff, find some passage home and get away from this nightmare? He stopped in his tracks. That was it. Forget about Max and Selena and the children. Forget about the grand adventure and everything that had happened. He just needed to get away from it all, from all of them. He took a deep breath. Why not?

Something cold slipped like tendrils through his head, closed and tightened; the sensation slipped down further, blossoming in his chest, then squeezing like fingers. He gave an involuntary cry and then doubled over. A warm breeze blew, somewhere touching his cheeks with warmth, ruffled his hair and flapped around the bottom of his trousers, tugged at his shirt.

"You are with us now," came the words, whispering, echoing through his thoughts.

He stood back upright, his breath coming in shallow gasps as the cold and pain dissipated from his chest.

"With us."

He glanced around the street, but there was no one. No one to whisper, no one to see, no one to protect him. The warm wind was gone. He took a deep shuddering breath. She was with him and he with her. There was nothing else he could do.

He closed his eyes and then opened them again.

He had to get back to the hotel. It was only a few minutes back there to get collect his things. Then he needed to meet Max and Selena at the station. There were places they all had to be.

NINETEEN

Shew'd him her comeliness, (yea) so that he of her beauty
possess'd him,
Bashful she was not, (but) ravish'd the soul of him, loosing her
mantle,

—The Epic of Gilgamesh

At the station, Avram sat on the floor, his leather bag lying beside him, waiting for what he didn't understand. People moved all around him, mere cyphers, objects in motion, barely registering on his consciousness. The echoes and scents of humanity cannoned off the vaulted ceiling and swirled around him, but he merely stared down at the ground between his feet. He was lost, and he didn't know why or what he'd done to cause it. He sat like that for more than an hour, playing with his sluggish thoughts and memories, trying to find something that could help him break through.

"Avram, what are you doing sitting down there?" It was Selena's voice.

"Yeah, come on, guy. That's not right."

Avram slowly lifted his eyes to meet theirs.

"Just waiting," he mumbled. "Waiting for you I guess." He got to his feet, dusting off his trousers, looking vaguely around at the station interior, not looking for or at anything in particular.

Max and Selena both had large pieces of luggage with them, certainly not the ones they'd arrived with, large black coffer style suitcases on wheels. The children had their own, smaller variants. He looked down at his own meagre version and reached for it.

"Where have you been?" he asked.

"Oh, we saw a couple of things," said Max.

"And then we went shopping," added Selena.

"Yes, I can see that."

"Well, you know, we needed clothes and things. We could hardly continue the way we were." She was completely unapologetic about it. She looked at Avram's bag. "Maybe you can find something at our next stop. Not now, of course."

"No, not now," said Avram with a sigh. "Have you got the tickets, Max? Do you know where we are?"

"Sure." He turned without waiting, heading off towards one of the platforms. Avram bit his lip briefly and then followed. He avoided even looking at the children. He didn't want to look at them. In fact he didn't want to look at any child.

"Did you see Marcus and Joe?" asked Max over his shoulder.

"No," he responded. "No. I didn't see Marcus and Joe."

Selena stopped walking. "Maybe we should wait for them, Max."

"No," Avram told her. "I don't think that's a good idea. I don't think they'll be coming. I'm pretty sure."

Of course he could be wrong, and everything could be nothing other than a bizarre fantasy, some sort of aberration inside his head, but deep within, he knew better. It could be days or even weeks before the Boys were discovered missing. The hotel would be first when they didn't check out, didn't settle up the bill, but then they'd probably just think that the couple had skipped out. They were travelling, weren't due home for weeks yet, and then, who knew how long before they were missed even there.

"Well, I think that's most inconsiderate," said Selena and continued walking. "They could at least have said something. After all, Max bought them tickets too."

"I said that wasn't a good idea," said Avram. "Perhaps he can cash them in at the other end."

Max waved his hand behind him dismissively. "It doesn't matter. They didn't cost too much anyway."

The fact that neither of them asked if Joe and Marcus were okay, why they might not be coming wasn't lost on him. What he wasn't sure of was whether that was just Max and Selena being Max and Selena, or something else far more sinister.

Max led them to their train, wandered along the carriages comparing numbers with the tickets held in his left hand and then stopped at the end of one of them about halfway along. Of course, it was first class.

"This is it," he said. "We should get on board." He handed

Avram a ticket, turned, pulled open the door and then shoved the other tickets into his pocket before hefting his luggage on to the train and then turning to do the same with Selena's and the children's in turn. He stood at the top of the stairs, leaned out of the doorway and looked up and down the platform.

"So, definitely no Joe and Marcus. Well, too bad."

He disappeared inside and started maneuvering the luggage down the carriage and towards their reserved compartments. Selena stepped up into the carriage, slid past the children's luggage and then turned inside, the children following suit a moment later. Avram looked down at his ticket, then at his bag, then back up at the carriage. He didn't have a choice either. He glanced up and down the platform, but there was no one there to help. There was no choice. Reluctantly, he climbed aboard.

Working his way down the carriage, he found his compartment. The Greens were getting settled in their own. He passed theirs first, and then another empty one before coming to his own. Of course there would be an empty one between himself and the Greens. An empty compartment that should have been filled by Marcus and Joe, wherever they were now, whatever was left of them. In some ways, he was relieved to have that buffer between himself and the children, despite the circumstance of its vacancy. He dumped his bag and then made his way back up to the Green's compartment and stuck his head through the door.

"Budapest and then where, Max? Have you thought that far ahead?"

Max looked up. "Oh sure. We can make our choices about how long, but it's pretty easy from there. I looked it all up. From Budapest we go to Zurich via Vienna. Maybe it's a pity, but we don't actually stop in Vienna. It's better I think to go straight to Zurich."

Avram leaned on the door frame simply watching as Max enthusiastically recounted his plans.

"So, it is about twelve hours from Budapest to Zurich. The train leaves in the evening and then gets there first thing in the morning. We," he said pointing to Selena and himself," of course have been to Vienna before. It's very pretty, but it's pretty boring too. I don't know, something about the people maybe. Anyway, we've never been to Zurich. And then, from Zurich it's not far to Paris. Only a few hours. We can choose when we go. There are lots of trains."

Avram merely nodded. He thought that Zurich, from what he had heard about it, might suit Selena and Max just fine. Well, under normal circumstances that was, and now, who could say? It might still suit them just fine too.

"And in Paris," Max continued blithely, "We can hook up with the travel company and sort out this mess. Everything should have died down a little by then. They will be probably happy to see us."

Selena gave a little grunt and an affirming nod as if what Max was saying was perfectly natural.

"Fine," said Avram, pulling back from the doorway. "Sounds fine, Max. Listen, I'm feeling pretty tired, maybe a little bit upset about the other two. I don't think I'm going to be very good company, so I think I'll leave you to it. I'll see you at the other end."

Samantha slowly turned her head and met his eyes. Quickly, he turned away and withdrew down the corridor, away from their compartment, away from her gaze. He couldn't deal with that now, not with the knowledge he was carrying inside. He still couldn't quite understand why Max and Selena seemed okay, well as much as they ever did. They were in the company of that pair almost constantly. It could only mean that their presence was convenient to Samantha and Alfred, or whatever it was they had become. Really, he should have realized it before. It was a natural thing for children to be travelling with their parents. Why would they not keep them around? And more than that, keep them in a state of virtual ignorance. With everything he had felt, everything that had happened he had to believe that that could not be too hard for them, or at least, if not for them, definitely not for Lilith herself. He retreated into his compartment and sealed the door firmly behind him.

The train drew out through the suburbs which quickly gave way to countryside, farms, rustic villages, fields and always off in the distance, the looming presence of mountains. After a while, the succession of passing countryside with the gentle rocking of the train itself lulled him into a state where he was simply staring out the window, barely registering what he saw. The light faded slowly as they travelled further. Eventually, the internal lights in the train filled the compartment, and he got up to look around and see if he could find a way of turning them off. He had no hunger, no thirst, and as he sat there in the gloom, a foreign land whisking away outside the window, he felt wrapped away from the world. He got up once to relieve himself, walking unsteadily down the corridor until he found the facilities and then made his way back to the cabin and sealed himself away. After a while, he started to doze. Once or twice, he started awake, and then decided that if he was going to sleep, he'd better do so without risking a stiff neck, so he reclined fully, his head towards the doorway so he'd still have a view of the sky outside. Sleep—he'd had little enough over the last few days. He just needed to find a place of darkness, a black cave of unconsciousness where he could withdraw from it all and get a hold of himself. He shut his eyes and concentrated on the back and forth motion of the carriage, the sound of metal on the tracks and nothing else. At least there was that escape. Eventually, he began to drift.

"Why do you fight me, Avram?"

Her voice cut through the veils and he opened his eyes to darkness. Light from outside illuminated the compartment's interior with a milky glow. Out there, the moon was up and full. She sat opposite, her hands crossed in her lap, her long dark hair framing her pale features with dark wings. Her eyes were clear, dark, staring at him across the shadowed space.

"Why do you fight me?"

"I-I do not," he said hesitantly. Once more, his heart beat strongly in his chest, his palms felt slick, cold. He tried to work some moisture into the dryness of his mouth.

"Foolish man," she said. "I can feel you."

"I-I just want it to stop. Can't you leave me alone? Why?"

She gave a short laugh. "It is too late for that, Avram Davis. Have you not come to realize yet? I am with you and you are with me. Wherever you are, so I am there."

He crossed his arms across his chest in a futile gesture of protection as the import of her meaning hit him. Wherever he was, so was she. It made some sort of icy sense, and the feeling of powerlessness washed over him. Even though he understood it, there was always the doubt.

"What are you saying? Why can't you just leave me?"

She smiled sweetly and stood, looking down at him. "We are one Avram Davis. We are joined. I am with you and you are with me."

He shook his head, trying to sit up. "It cannot be. I've done nothing."

"Oh, but you have ..."

She took a step towards him, gave a slight frown. "What is it, Avram? Why do you struggle? Perhaps you need to be rewarded. Perhaps I have taken you too much for granted. You mere mortals have needs. Perhaps the knowledge is not enough."

She reached towards him with one small hand and he shrank away from the touch. He thought to cry out then, but found himself unable to utter a cry, suddenly unable to move. At that moment as he was frozen in place, the child started to transform. Shadow grew, coalescing from the air around her into a pool of darkness. Within that darkness, eyes, darker than the rest, but somehow strangely illuminated, regarded him.

"Now, Avram," she said, a hand and arm formed out of dry darkness stroking his face, running her fingers through his hair. "I can make you feel as you have never felt before. Remember, I have had centuries...."

Her fingers ran across his chest, lingered, traced across his belly. He felt her breath, warm against his neck, the sound of it whispering gently in his ear. He felt the taste of arid sands, the breath of the desert flowing against his skin.

"Let me show you, Avram," she said. "Let me provide you with what you deserve. You are mine. You must not fight me, you must struggle no more."

He felt cold lips against his skin. She drew back, her face close to his now, in front of him, looking into his eyes and he felt himself falling, drifting, plummeting into those depths and washed away. Her hands were upon him, undoing his clothing, never breaking the gaze.

"Let me show you the pleasure of ages," she said as she moved her lips to his throat. His breathing became shallow, panting, despite himself. He tried to fight against the sensations, willing himself to feel nothing, not to react. He tried to struggle, to push her away, but his limbs were stuck, immobile. Nothing would obey.

And then, he simply could not think any more as she swept him away.

There was light when he finally awoke. He struggled to open his eyes. The gentle rocking of the train went on. He felt drained, exhausted, aching. He moved his head, and winced as a pain stabbed through the side of his neck. He lifted one hand and felt gingerly at an area of tenderness on his skin.

She had been here with him. He remembered.

He looked down at his rumpled clothing, at the disarray, at open buttons and fasteners, at more, a deep damp stain upon his trousers, and he grimaced in revulsion. The memories were coming back, the darkness, her touch, her lips, her breath. The taste of the desert in the darkness, within him and around him. He had shared her breath.

He swallowed at the thoughts and looked desperately around. He couldn't be seen like this. As he struggled with ridding his thoughts of the images that kept swimming up, of the disgust and shame he was feeling, his thoughts were racing. He reached up to the bag stowed in the rack above his head, pulled it down and dragged out the spare pair of trousers he had there. He fumbled with his buttons doing up his shirt, pulled his trousers shut. He stood and then, opening the compartment door, ducked his head out into the corridor and looked in both directions, but there was nobody there. His heart racing, he stepped into the corridor and quickly made his way towards the bathroom, the fresh trousers wrapped in front of him, hiding the tell-tale patch. With a quick sigh of relief, he sealed the bathroom door and proceeded to change. He checked himself in the mirror, running his fingers through his hair, and then tilted his head to the side, inspecting the angry purple bruise upon the left side of his neck. Gingerly, he probed at it with his fingertips and winced.

He was not imagining things. He was not dreaming this. There was no doubt any more, not a shred.

He turned on the water in the basin and cupping his hand, splashed his face. He took the pair of trousers he had been just wearing, and putting them under the stream, hastily rubbed the fabric together, trying to wash out as much as he could, and then he bundled them into a ball. It would do for now, but it was going to be nothing more than temporary.

Checking himself in the mirror once more, he took a deep breath, and then cautiously opened the door. There was still no sign of life, and he strode quickly back to his compartment, slipped inside and closed the door. The trousers, he bundled into the valise and sealed it shut, and then finally he sat, breathing deeply.

Already, the city's outskirts were becoming more crowded outside the window as they drew closer to their destination. Soon they would be at Budapest's Keleti Station and then … and then, he had no idea

TWENTY

After this, take the Needle, or other convenient instrument of
the Art…and pierce the bat in the vein

–The Key of Soloman

Budapest's main station was similar to every other major station he had been in, except bearing those legacy Eastern European touches that he had come to expect. Avram checked his clothing one more time before clambering down from the train to join the others waiting for him on the platform. Right now, he had no other plans than allowing himself to be swept along by circumstance, hoping that somewhere within he would find the clue to his escape and the end to all this. There had to be an answer somewhere, and if it wasn't here in Budapest, then it might be in their next stop, or the one after that. In the meantime, he had felt the pain of resistance and he wasn't particularly eager to experience it again any time soon.

Max and Selena were scanning the station, looking for the way out, as usual, a little impatient as they waited for him to join. Avram glanced up, again finding a high arched roof, similar, but not the same as their previous stop, the sounds echoing in the vast space, distorted across multiple surfaces.

"So, where to?" he asked them.

"We thought about two places, decent hotels for a change," said Max. "That last one was okay, I guess, but it wasn't wonderful."

Selena pursed her lips in unspoken agreement.

"Maybe the Kempinski. That looked pretty good," he continued. "Or then there is the Hilton, up in the Castle District."

"I like the sound of the second one," said Selena. "There is something romantic about it."

"What about you?" Max asked him.

Avram rubbed the back of his neck. "I don't really care," he said. "Or more to the point, I don't really have an opinion. You seem to have done your research, Max."

"Sure. It's always better to be prepared," he said. "So, let's find our way out of here. We will go to the Kempinski. It is on this side of the river, on the Pest side rather than Buda."

He immediately turned and strode off down the platform,

luggage in tow, taking the lead as he always did. With yet another wash of resignation, Avram hefted his bag and followed on behind, watching as Selena pouted with her disappointment at Max's decision. The station itself was somehow less chaotic, more ordered and modern-feeling than the one they had left in Bucharest, and the architecture was definitely more Bohemian rather than communist. Eventually, they located a taxi that could take them all and they bundled in with their luggage, and gave the driver his instructions. Avram turned to watch the station gradually shrinking behind them.

They pulled up at the Kempinski Hotel Corvinus, a vast and impressive modern affair. Surely much more in keeping with what the Greens were used to, Avram thought. They waited as Max bounded inside, only to return a few moments later, looking put out. He stuck his head back in the cab.

"No room. They are sold out. Some conference or something. We should have booked in advance, but we probably wouldn't have had any chance anyway, the girl said. So, I guess we go to the Hilton."

He looked at each of their faces as if seeking confirmation, though it was already pretty clear that he had made up his mind already. A slight smile curved across Selena's lips. It seemed that she was going to get her way after all.

Their cab pulled out from the hotel entrance and into the traffic. Avram watched the buildings as they neared the river, the ornate spires of the parliament building, and across the water on the other side, the castle itself perched atop a large hill and looking out over the rest of the city. As they moved through the cluttered buildings and streets, his interchange with Max was playing through his head. You seem to have done your research, Max. Sure. It's always better to be prepared. He didn't know what was wrong with himself. He always did his research, always sought out the literature and the descriptions in preparation, studying the places and what he was planning to do there. The passion for history was one of the things that drove him. He looked up at the castle, the stone walls, the impressive windowed front, the central domed tower, the columns arrayed across the front—not a traditional castle as you might think about it—but a castle nonetheless. If he had thought to do some research, he might have known. Perhaps when they finally got settled in the hotel, whether the one they were heading to now, or some other, he would have a chance. But it would not be Budapest he was researching. He had other things on his mind.

They crossed a broad metal bridge, and then started climbing towards the castle itself, winding up the hill and onto streets that became cobbled, the taxi's wheels thrumming on the uneven stone. They passed the castle itself, and moved into a series of tightly clustered buildings, pulling up in front of the flat white front of the hotel. Again Max leapt out, dashed inside and then reappeared a moment later, waving for them to join him. He leaned in, paid the driver and then moved around to help with their luggage. Avram stepped out of the cab, looked up examining the renovated front and then followed the others inside. He had decided; he had many things to do here. He needed to take Selena's lead and shop, to supplement what remained of his meagre wardrobe, and then, he had to find somewhere he could do his research. In a city with a history like that of Budapest, there was bound to be repositories, archives, libraries, somewhere where he could get some hints about the current situation and perhaps, just perhaps, some clue to engineering his escape. In the meantime, he had to make sure that he appeared to be submitting. If he let on to the children particularly that he had any sort of plan, he was sure it would not end well.

"Let me just understand," he whispered to himself as they entered the hotel lobby. "Then we will see." Feeling the resolve was like a weight had lifted from him.

Max was already at the reception desk, dealing with the check-in procedure, and Avram wandered up to a free spot to the side, handing over his own documents. He looked over at Max.

"How many nights?"

"I think two. That's what I said. There's a lot to see here. Tonight, tomorrow night. If we decide to leave earlier, then we can. The next train doesn't leave until about seven-thirty in the evening, but just in case, that should give us enough time."

That suited Avram just fine. He glanced down at Samantha and Alfred, but, for once, the children's attention was elsewhere. He turned back and made his own arrangements. Maybe, indeed, it would give them enough time … well, at least give him enough time to do what he needed to. Finally, he was starting to feel an actual shred of hope, however slim it might be.

The hotel clerk handed over his key and Avram turned, seeking out the elevators. He was on the fourth floor, river view. He would come down later, once he was settled, get a map, perhaps find somewhere to buy some fresh clothes, maybe find a guidebook and work out what he was going to do.

"Avram, wait," Max called from behind him. He stopped, feeling his shoulders tense and slowly turned.

"Where are you?"

"What? Oh, I'm on the fourth."

"Ah, we are on the third."

Frankly, that suited Avram just fine.

"Maybe when you get settled we can do something?" said Max.

The children were watching him now.

"Look, I'll tell you what," said Avram. He didn't think that Alfred and Samantha could actually tell what he was thinking. "Let me get settled, work out what I'm going to do. Why don't you call my room if you come up with any plans? We can decide then."

"Okay, sounds fine," said Max and turned back to deal with the last of his check-in procedure.

Avram turned away and walked quickly towards the elevators before they might have a chance to catch up.

Breath

Inside, the room was basically decked out in pale creams or white. A single window looked out over the Danube with a view of the parliament building opposite and the bridges. Just below, sat a large round stone dome, stairs leading up inside it, ancient buildings clustered around. He dumped his bag on the bed, and then looked around for any information that might be around the desk, pamphlets, guides. He found a hotel information booklet, sat down at the desk and started reading. The hotel itself apparently boasted the Baroque façade of a 16th century Jesuit College and a 13th century Dominican Churchyard. Normally, he might be interested by such things, and if he had not already known better, that deeply Christian heritage may have given him some comfort, but for now, they were merely interesting facts. He flicked through the guide, looking for local attractions, seeing what else was around.

There was plenty to see, galleries, museums, cafés, restaurants all in profusion, but nothing he was seeking specifically. He stood, crossed to the window and stared out, watching the river sliding past. First things first, he could do something about his clothes. He turned away from the window, crossed to the bed and opened his bag. He stepped over to the wardrobe, sought out the usual plastic bag they had for laundry plus the list that went with it, laid the latter out on the desk and one by one, pulled the clothes from his bag, counting, including the wadded-up pair of trousers that lay inside. As he scrabbled around inside the bag, checking if there was anything else, a stray sock or something, he felt a small hard shape inside one of the inner pockets. With a frown, he probed at it with his fingers, feeling the shape and then opened up the pocket, withdrew the thing and held it up to see what it was. He'd seen the object before, he knew it and yet …

The small amulet dangled from his fingers suspended by a simply braided cord. It was worn in places, almost frayed. It looked old. He peered at the stone, lying in a very simple metal setting, dark, hints of blue running through it, but in no particular place, almost as if the colors were flowing together, dark upon darkness. He took hold of the stone itself, and turned it first one way, then the other, and then, not really trusting his eyes, moved over to the window to see it better in the light. Still, the colors seemed to blur and shift. The blue was shot through with flashes of violet and green. He ran his thumb over the surface of the stone. It looked smooth, but there, with the gentle touch of the end of his thumb, there were striations, lines, perhaps something engraved or etched upon the surface, impossible to see because of the way the stone seemed to absorb the light, suck it into the blackness and stir it within its own depths. He rubbed his thumb over the surface, back and forth and as he did so, he felt something clearing in his head. Where there had been a sense of thickness, of sluggish inactivity, a gentle buzz pushed the slowness aside. He jerked his head back in surprise, and then slowly, gently, placed the object down on the windowsill. As he severed the contact, the gentle humming slowly faded. Now that he thought about it, it was less of a buzz and more of a hum, a chorus of low voices, holding a uniform note, gently rising and falling, just below the level of hearing as if deep within a cave or a chamber far below ground. With the image came the feeling of darkness, the spark of fire and a touch of warm wind, though like reminiscence than actually felt. Avram took a step back from the window, still looking down at the necklace lying there.

There had to be a reason he had this. There had to be a reason why he couldn't remember how it had come into his possession. But there was something teasing at his thoughts….

He left it where it lay. It was just yet another mystery that he needed time to figure out. First, though, he could equip himself so that he could at least feel some level of comfort while he sought out what he was after. He shoved the clothes into the laundry bag, finished filling out the list and then placed that inside the bag as well. Only then did he turn back to the window and retrieve the necklace. Immediately he noticed the humming growing in the back of his head as he came into contact with the stone. He was just about ready to believe anything by now, and he wasn't about to question the strangeness of the sensation. It was yet another thing that just was, something he had to accept. Turning, he moved over to the wardrobe, found the hotel safe and placed the object inside and then locked it away. For the moment, it too would keep. It wasn't going anywhere in a hurry, and neither, frankly, was he. As he sealed it away, the sensation faded entirely. He turned, collected the laundry bag, gave the room one more scan, including a final glance at the view out the window, made sure he had his key-card and left the room, closing the door firmly behind him.

He deposited the laundry at the concierge's desk and asked for directions to a store where he might pick up some clothes, and where he might also acquire a guidebook in English. The latter was easy enough—there were several tourist shops in the castle district—but for clothes, unless he was looking for designer boutiques, he would need to venture further afield. He asked the concierge to write down the address, after expressing his preference for a department store rather than individual shops or boutiques, but in response received a brief laugh.

"Go to Westend Shopping Center. Everything is there. It is right next to Central Station. You do not need an address. The taxi driver will know it. It will be easy for you to get back too, being right at the station. There will be plenty of cabs."

He also took the trouble to exchange some cash at the outrageous rates charged by the hotel, but at the moment, he wasn't feeling very fussy about it.

Avram thanked the concierge, and armed with his directions left the hotel. First he sought out one of the many tourist shops within a mere few steps of the hotel entrance and after browsing through a couple, finally settled on a guidebook and paid. He then wandered back to the hotel, got into a taxi, gave the driver the directions he'd been given, and settled back for the ride, barely pausing before opening the guidebook and starting to flick through the pages. As the taxi wound down from the castle district, over the bumping cobbled streets and down to the river, he paid little attention to the passing buildings and streets, absorbed within the pages he held now within his hands.

"Mister," said the driver, dragging Avram back to awareness. "Mister, Westend Shopping." They had arrived.

Just as the concierge had told him, it was a modern department store complex, and after about two hours of wandering around, acquiring some trousers, shirts, other essentials, he returned to the front of Central Station, located the taxi queue and headed back to the hotel, laden with bags, his precious guidebook shoved inside one of them. On the return journey, he paid more attention to the city, looking for landmarks, points of direction he could follow, watching the passing streets, the grand buildings, the people walking by, and the position of the bridges in relation to the rest of the city. He was going to need to find his way around if he was to accomplish what he intended.

With every further step in his newfound quest, he was regaining his confidence. As soon as they arrived back at the hotel, Avram paid the driver, grabbed his bags and made his way back up to his room. He dumped the shopping bags unceremoniously on the bed, dug around in them for a moment or two, dragged out the guidebook and immediately too it to sit at the desk, turning to the pages he had spotted earlier. There was a whole section detailing the city libraries, but there was one in particular that caught his eye. The University Library with its ornately tiled tower and its impressive stacks gave him hope. The guidebook said that it was frequented mainly by academics and scholars—just the sort of place that might hold what he was looking for. The fact that it also held many antiquities amongst its collection gave him further optimism. He looked up the address and cross referenced it with the map in the back of the book. It looked easy enough to get to, straight over one of the main bridges and into the city center itself.

Breath

He nodded to himself and shut the guidebook again after staring at the picture for a few more seconds. It was only then that he noticed the red message light blinking on the desk phone. It took him a few tries to navigate the menu, but he was eventually able to access the message, for there was in fact something there rather than just simple a pre-recorded welcome and instructions on how to use the phone. Of course, it was Max.

"Avram, hello. I guess you are out somewhere. Selena has decided we need to visit one of the special baths here. You know, Budapest is pretty famous for them. We plan to go in the morning. I don't know when you are getting back, but maybe call us, or if not— we might be going out—you can meet us in the lobby in the morning about 10:30. Bye."

Avram replaced the receiver and sat there staring at the phone. He glanced at his watch. It was about 12:30 now. He wasn't sure what time the library closed, but it should give him enough time this afternoon. He wouldn't mind seeing one of these baths despite everything. Getting rid of some of the journey's stink at a deeper level might be something nice, washing himself in therapeutic waters. It couldn't hurt. And once his research was complete, or at least underway, it would give him a further chance to observe, armed with some more knowledge.

He thought that he should join them. Rationally, with all that had been happening, it didn't really make sense, but inside he knew it was something he needed to do. Perhaps he would find further answers there as well.

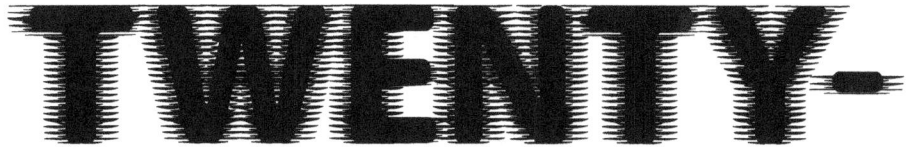

She spawned monster-serpents, [Sharp of] tooth, and merciless of fang; With poison instead of] blood she filled [their] bodies.

—Enuma Elish Tablet 1

Breath

A short taxi ride back over the other side of the river took him to the library. The University Library stood there, looking just like it had in the pictures, yellow fronted stone topped by an ornate tiled dome, an ornate, cross patterned, diamond design picked out in elaborate tile work, a completely renovated building with a fountain standing on the street outside. He shoved his hand into his pocket, feeling the hardness of the little pendant within the handkerchief he had wrapped it in before leaving to come here. He'd remembered it just as he was about to leave, pulled it out from the safe and after wrapping it, pushed it into his pocket. Well, now he would see. Maybe here he would get some answers.

Inside, the library boasted tall shelves, an upper gallery level, polished wooden floors and ornate ceilings. A tall portrait sat overlooking the room, someone from a bygone age. On the balcony level, ladders sat beside the shelves allowing access to the upper levels. Several desks both standing and conventional filled the space and several people sat around with open books or piles of paper at desks, or browsed the extensive array of books. Avram stood there for a moment or two, drinking in the atmosphere, then spotting the main desk crossed and spoke to the man sitting there. The librarian, for so he was, had limited English, but he managed to direct Avram to the catalogue and gave him rudimentary instructions on how to use it, then withdrew to his position behind the desk.

It did not take Avram long to locate the first set of things he was looking for, and he spent some minutes collecting a stack of books and transporting them to one of the standing tables. A few were in English, but not all, and he started to doubt if perhaps this excursion was going to be of any use at all. His one word, 'Lilith' was leading him into a maze of historical treatises in a variety of languages. He probably wouldn't be able to puzzle through a fraction of what now lay stacked before him. There were one or two, however, that looked like they might be promising—one in particular. He ran his hand back and forth over the topmost cover, considering. Was this little more than a fool's errand?

Taking a deep breath, and then giving a frustrated sigh, he dug around in his pocket, withdrew and then carefully unwrapped the mysterious necklace, and placed it down on the table top next to the stack of books. He then proceeded to open one of the first ones that looked like they might be closest to what he needed. He spent the next few minutes scanning page after page of text with a jumble of ancient myths and legends. He came across a passage referring directly to Lilith. He had not been mistaken at all. She was here. He leaned over the page, reading the words that filled him with a sudden chill.

Yet she escaped the curse of death which overtook Adam, since they had parted long before the Fall. Lilith and Namaah not only strangle infants, but also seduce dreaming men, any of whom, sleeping alone, may become their victim. B. Shabat 151b.

Just as he had become her victim, bound to her in ways that he didn't yet understand. Avram swallowed. It was far too familiar. And there, the strangulation, depriving her victims of breath. It could be interpreted that way. He leaned back from the page and stared blankly in front of him across the desks at the stack of books on the opposite wall. Images of the train, of the hotel, others floated up in his thoughts. Taking another deep breath, he turned back to the page.

"Excuse me …"

Avram turned from the page to see a man standing nearby, a green jacket, graying hair swept back and a hawk's beak of a nose, small round glasses perched upon his face.

Avram pointed to himself in query.

"Yes, I am sorry. Excuse me again. It seemed evident to me that you are not from here, and I could not help noticing what you were reading."

The man's English was perfect, though accented with a strange sing-song lilt to the words.

Avram nodded in response. "Yes, right," he said. "Why, are you interested in these books?"

The man stepped forward. "Do excuse my intrusion. I am Professor Szeni, of course retired now, but yes, this is one of my lifelong passions. I end up spending much time here, so I know most of the regulars by sight. You do not seem to be one of the regulars."

"Avram. Avram Davis. No, I am just visiting."

"Is there a particular reason you are interested in these texts yourself?"

Avram started to reach for the amulet and then thought better of it. The Professor's gaze watched his hand, turned to meet his eyes and then turned back to the amulet.

"May I see?" he asked.

Avram hesitated and then thought better of it. "I guess so," he said.

The Professor reached for it, cupped it in his palm, allowing the cord to drape over the top of his hand.

"Hmm, interesting," he said. "This looks quite old. One would almost say original. Where did you acquire it?" He placed it down gently on the desk again, beside the stack of books.

"Oh, not here. Somewhere else."

The Professor nodded, seemingly unfazed by Avram's vague answer.

"So tell me, if you don't mind, what are you looking for? Perhaps I can help."

"Lilith," said Avram. "I am trying to find out about …" He waved his hand at the pile of books. "The problem is that a lot of this stuff is not in English."

"Yes, of course," said the Professor. "Then, naturally I can assist. You are touching on one of my favorite subjects. It is a passion. One that has been with me for years."

Avram looked around the library, but the few other occupants had their attention either in books or on papers in front of them, clearly uninterested in Avram or in his new companion.

"Okaaay," said Avram, not really understanding why this man, this complete stranger may be compelled to offer him assistance. He was not about to throw away the opportunity though. "So, then, what can you tell me about Lilith?"

The Professor cleared his throat, lifted his gaze to the ceiling and then turned back to look at Avram, as if putting his thoughts together before commencing a lecture.

"Well, Lilith actually, as a concept, or a being goes back many, many centuries. She existed in several forms long before any of the Judeo-Christian mythos. The word 'Lilith' comes from the Babylonian/ Assyrian word Lilitû, a wind spirit or a demon, but she appears earlier as 'Lillake' on a tablet from Ur in the Gilgamesh epic. She is very, very old. Not hundreds, but more like thousands if you were to count years."

The Professor peered into Avram's face, making sure that what he was saying was being absorbed.

"She took several forms, and when you get into the later tradition, she had various roles. There is, of course, the most known variation, where she was Adam's first wife, but in several of the traditions, some of the more obscure ones, she actually seduced God and spent some time as his consort."

Avram frowned and shook his head. "Really?"

"Oh yes," said the Professor, clearly warming to his subject. "And, of course, Lilith's children are called lilim."

"She has children?"

"Oh yes indeed. Children form a significant part of the story. In fact, there seems to be some evolution of the myth, and as with all myths, there is some basis in fact. The 4th C Greek commentator Hieronymus identified her with Lamia, who was a Libyan queen deserted by Zeus. Hera had robbed her children, and so she took revenge by robbing others of theirs."

"So, are they hers, or not?"

"Well, that is not clear, see here, this text?" He stretched across, flipped a couple of pages of the book Avram had been looking at and drew his finger down the lines and then stopped at the passage he was seeking. "It became embedded in many of the traditions. This extract is from the Targum Yerushalmi and the blessing from Numbers vi. 26 is rendered as 'The Lord bless thee in all thy doings and preserve thee from the Lilim!' Lilith's children are a thing to be feared, that much is certain. Whether they are hers or not, does not matter in the end. They are also a thing to be afraid of and like Lilith herself, they are capable of stealing the lives of men."

"And women?"

"Well, well, yes I suppose so. Of course these ancient texts are very biased in their depiction of men and women. Women are always the harlots, men the just and brave who need to overcome their evil ways." He shrugged. "You need to be able to interpret. It is like everything in history. All of it is contextual. You need to place it in the circumstance and the contemporary beliefs within which it grew. Just as there may be an origin in truth somewhere, you need to step back, trace the path and then see what surrounds it. That way you can get a better understanding, and sometimes even the reading will divulge the real truth behind it. Unless you understand the patterns of belief that surround the creation of the concept itself, then you cannot truly understand the concept or its construction. All of these totemic archetypes are constructions after all, formed by belief and informed by what lies behind them."

The Professor rocked back and forth on his heels, his hands clasped behind his back, apparently tasting the wisdom of his own words. After a moment, he looked back at Avram.

"And is there anything to guard against her, and against these Lilim?" Avram asked.

"Well," the Professor said slowly. "It was an ancient tradition. There would be writing on walls, sacred names, sometimes special rituals and chants and often …" He reached over and lifted the amulet. "… there would be talismans carved with special symbols, special names. Not unlike this one." He turned it slowly in front of his face, peering at it, rubbing his thumb over the surface gently and then turning it first one way and then the other in the light. He held it out in front of him closer to the light, and leaned forward to inspect it closely.

"Hmmm," he said. "It would appear that these markings …" he traced his finger over the surface again, "are deliberate. There are curves and they are joined together. It is too regular to be just scratched. Unfortunately, it is far too difficult to see, but I would suggest that this is writing."

He looked at it for a few moments more and then placed it carefully back on the desk and patted it thoughtfully. "I think perhaps you might want to look after this. You never know when—how do you say—it might come in handy."

He cleared his throat again, looked up. The librarian was looking over their way, obviously having noticed their continued conversation. The Professor lifted one hand in the librarian's direction, and the latter saw who exactly it was, nodded in recognition and turned back to whatever he had been doing before.

"Wait a moment," said the Professor, then dug into the stack of books that Avram had in front of him. He pulled one out from near the bottom of the pile, and laid it open on the desk. He ran his finger down first the table of contents, and then turned to the back, searching through the index of plates.

"Ah yes, I thought so." Flipping rapidly through the pages, he found a black and white photograph of a round stone, markings clearly inscribed on its surface. "See here. This is not dissimilar. These markings on the stone spell out the names of angels. These are heavenly beings, not as we might think of angels today. They are more like spirit warriors, generals in a fight against evil. They battle against demons and their names are powerful, or so it was thought. This is why they were used in a talismanic fashion."

Avram leaned over. The pictured stone had certain similarities to that of the necklace, not quite the same, but yes, he could see the resemblance. He straightened again and turned back to the Professor. He was thinking hard. He couldn't lose the opportunity to learn as much as he could. Not now. And this strange man was clearly immersed in his subject.

"Is there anything else you can tell me about her?"

"Well ..." The Professor paused, stroked his chin, considering. "Many of the accounts are the same. It doesn't matter whether they are Assyrian, Sumerian, Babylonian, or even the later Jewish traditions. You have to remember, the legends were born from a desert setting, so they are filled with elements that come from that landscape; scorpions, jackals, wind."

"Wind," said Avram, latching on to the word.

"Yes, of course. The wind across the arid lands. As I mentioned before, the wind spirit was one of her guises. The hot breath of the desert."

Breath, thought Avram. The hot breath of the desert. He had felt her breath, felt the stirring of warm breezes around him.

"And of course," the Professor continued. "As with any desert people, water plays an important part of the story. Water is a life-giving element. There is one particular part of the tale where you can see this." He riffled through a few pages and then stopped at a particular passage. "See here? Lilith's flight to the Red Sea recalls the ancient Hebrew view that water attracts demons."

Avram looked down at the words, thinking.

"Well, there she is," said the Professor. "That is Lilith. I do not know if that gives you what you want. There are many more texts, many more different renderings of the tale, but you get the impression here. Lilith is not a very nice being in the end. She has, as you might say, an axe to grind. She is all about revenge. Perhaps that is enough to help you, at least a little bit."

"Yes," said Avram. "Yes. And you? Do you believe any of it? Do you think any of it could be real?" he said, turning to face him.

The Professor took a long time to answer, and when he did, the words came slowly, thoughtfully. "Belief is a curious thing," he said. "Belief often has its basis in fact." His gaze drifted to the necklace where it lay on the desk as he spoke. Avram turned to follow his gaze. He reached for the pendant, rewrapped it in the handkerchief and placed it carefully back into his pocket, making sure it was pressed right down inside, the Professor peering curiously at his actions all the while.

"Listen," said Avram. "I want to thank you. You've helped me a lot."

Avram had what he needed now, or at least enough. The Professor was watching him, seemingly waiting for something.

"It was my pleasure," he said.

"So, I guess I should really be going now," Avram said.

The Professor nodded in understanding. "You take care then," he said. "You take very good care."

Avram merely nodded in reply. As he left the Professor standing there, with the stack of books and headed towards the entrance, his hand was thrust deep into his pocket, fingers curled around the carefully wrapped object sitting there. He could sense the Professor watching him all the way out.

Later that night, in his hotel room, Avram prepared himself for bed, having spent a solitary dinner mulling over the things that he had learned. He was starting to develop a strategy, and with it came the threads of hope. Perhaps the sense of vague optimism was misplaced, but as he pulled the covers over himself, he didn't think so. Gradually, he drifted off to sleep, the carefully wrapped handkerchief clutched within his hands in the center of his chest. For the first time in days, he slept deeply, undisturbed and dreamless and awoke to the early morning light, feeling refreshed, and something else—almost a feeling of liberation.

TWENTY-TWO

"... snakes in her hands and with a scorpion between her legs"

−Die Dämonen

Avram showered, and feeling more alive than he had in days, called downstairs and ordered an in-room breakfast. After it arrived, he took his time, relishing each bite and watching the city out of the window. He sipped from juice and then coffee. He tracked a couple of birds flying past the window, watching as they angled their wings to catch the breeze, thinking about how effortlessly they rode upon the wind. He wondered in turn what other creatures might also transport themselves using similar means, riding the air to get from place to place, and with the thought, his appetite suddenly disappeared. He stared out of the window at the empty sky, his insides gone cold. Suddenly, he was less convinced that his choice even to partake of breakfast had been a good one.

Pushing the small wheeled table out of his way, he stood, dropping his napkin atop the remains of his food. After yesterday's discoveries, he had some suspicions, or better, more suspicions and he wanted to try a little experiment. He searched around the desk, found the hotel's information booklet, was about to call room to room, and then realized, he didn't actually know which room the Greens were in. Instead, he called reception and asked to be connected. If they were planning to meet, then hopefully they had not gone out anywhere yet. He looked at his watch. There was still half an hour before the suggested meeting time, so they should still be there, making ready. The phone answered on the second ring.

"Yes?"

"Max, it's Avram."

"Ah, we were starting to wonder what had happened to you. Several times, Samantha asked where you were."

Did she? Avram thought.

"Oh, you know. I was out and about. Did some shopping. Thought I'd take your lead."

"Very good," said Max.

"Listen, are you still planning on going to the baths?"

212

"Sure."

"Okay good. Can you tell me which ones? I know there are several. We're going to need two cabs anyway probably and I've just got another thing I want to take care of. If you like, I can meet you there."

Hopefully, Max wouldn't find it too suspicious, and he shouldn't. Avram was often wont to go off and do things on his own. And, he really did want to see them at the baths. That whole water thing that the Professor had spoken about …

"Yes, sure," Max said. Inside, Avram felt a touch of relief. "We decided on the Rudas baths. They look pretty cool and not as public as some of the others. They change one day to another, one day men, one day women, but today it is both."

"Sounds good. I can look up the address."

"Oh, and one more thing," Max added. "On days when both sexes are there, bathing suits are compulsory."

"Ah, good thing you told me," said Avram. Now he really did have something to do. He could probably pick something up at one of the nearby shops. Not that he would have even thought about it. Shared naked bathing was not generally on his agenda, not with friends and not with complete strangers.

"Avram?"

"Yes, sorry. I was thinking."

"So we will see you there?"

"Yes, you can count on it."

"Okay, bye," said Max and rung off.

Avram hung up and stared down at the phone for a couple of seconds before turning to the guidebook and flipping through the pages. It didn't take him long to locate the entry he sought.

The Rudas baths were built in the 1560s and situated at the foot of the Gellert Hills. They consisted of one main room with an octagon-shaped bath in the center surrounded by four thermal baths of varying temperatures. Local advice was to encourage guests to dip from the hottest bath to the coldest bath for the best therapeutic experience. The main room sat under a traditional Turkish bath-style domed roof featuring an array of small circular windows that allow sunlight to filter onto the main bathing area. Looking at the picture, he could see why the Greens thought it was a good choice, but there was something about the look, or at least in the guidebook picture, something reminiscent of somewhere else he had been, and recently. He'd know better once he got there. The stone arches, the pools of water, they conjured images of a dark and damp place in another city, now far away. He noted the address down on a piece of hotel stationary, but really, it was right at the bottom of the set of hills upon which the castle from which the district derived its name was perched.

There were some further historical notes in the description. The baths were used by Sokollu Mustafa Pasha, the Ottoman ruler between 1566 and 1578. Apparently, that was inscribed in Hungarian in the baths, on a stone on tope the Juve spring, which was believed by locals to have a rejuvenating effect. Avram thought about that for a moment. Like some ancient historically sanctioned graffiti—"Mustafa Pasha was here, 1566." The briefest smile came to him. Was it the purported rejuvenating properties that attracted the Greens to the place, or was it simply that it looked interesting? He had no real way of knowing. The other item that was of note was that the waters themselves, apart from being full of an array of minerals, were slightly radioactive. That latter, gave him pause for a moment, but then he dismissed it; what more could a little radiation do that was worse than what was already happening to him? He shut the book and stared out the window, and then, making sure he had some cash with him, left on his errand.

As he'd suspected, Budapest being, after all, a spa city, there was an array of bathing gear available within the local boutique shops. He wandered from store to store, shuffling through racked items with his fingers and feeling that there was nothing that suited. Call it personal modesty, or a simple nod to taste, but he refused to wear any of the Speedo-type bathing briefs on offer. Finally, he settled on a more restrained set of boxer-style bathing shorts, loose enough to conceal the most prominent of sins. The only drawback was that they were patterned with pink hibiscus flowers. Considering the rest of the merchandise on offer, they would have to do.

Having made his acquisition, Avram returned to the hotel, donned the bathing trunks and then redressed, finally opening the safe, withdrawing the carefully wrapped bundle that lay inside and placing it carefully in the depths of his trouser pocket. He glanced once more around the hotel room, almost clinical in its whiteness, and then satisfied that he could actually do no more to prepare—he considered taking the guidebook with him, but then decided there was no point— he left the room and pulled the door securely shut behind him. Once outside the hotel, he turned left and started wandering down the cobbled street, past the hulking box-like building and statuary that sat overlooking the city and down towards his appointment and the experiment that awaited him.

It took him only fifteen minutes to walk down the hill and approach the complex that sat, stretched almost like a military barracks beside the river and close to the end of one of the major bridges spanning the water that divided the city into its two halves. He knew that the baths had several sections, but he presumed that Max and Selena would have headed for the pictured octagonal bath room that had been there from the very beginning. After negotiating the entrance, he headed inside, removed the outer layers of his clothing and placed them into one of the lockers, including the item he had brought with him. The smell of mineralized water was all around him and the noises from the larger rectangular pool, apparently already well-populated, echoed through the rooms. Taking his towel and robe, he sought out the pool room where he thought he would find the Greens, his feet slapping on bare stone floor. Despite his resolve, the nervousness, not quite fear, but more uncertainty, rose in his chest and dried his mouth. He had no idea what he was doing, not really, but at least he had to try … something.

The octagonal bath was not hard to find, and when he reached it, he stood just outside the stone arches for a few moments, simply observing. There were not many people in the pool, one or two possibly locals and of course, easily spottable, the Greens. They hadn't noticed him yet, so he had the chance to take in the setting. The Ottoman style was evident in the stonework, blocks of lighter and darker stone in the archways that surrounded the pool and in the walls. A herringbone pattern tiled platform ran around the entirety of the pool itself. The pool's floor was also tiled, concentric darker russet and pale bands, octagonal circles that moved in to a central point, drawing the eye like a hypnotist's wheel. Above the pool sat a stone dome, several small round holes opening to the sky above and sending shafts of light downwards. The interior was dim, but nothing like the underground cistern that he remembered, and though the atmosphere was thick with the smell of minerals, the scent of moss and wet stone was absent too.

When Selena spotted him, she gave him a little wave. They were lounging over the other side of the pool, Max with his arms draped backwards, stretched out flat and extended against the stone lip, Selena bobbing gently in place beside him. On either side, sat Sam and Alf, not fully in the pool, their legs half immersed in water. Steeling himself, Avram stepped into the pool room proper, found a stone bench, where he dropped his robe and towel and then gingerly entered the water and sweeping his arms slowly back and forth at the water's surface beside him, approached his waiting companions. As he crossed the pool, Samantha and Alfred turned their attention from staring blankly at the opposite wall to Avram himself. Even though he avoided meeting their gaze directly, he could feel their eyes on him.

"Hi there," said Avram unnecessarily unable to think of anything else to say.

"Hi," said Selena. Max just nodded.

"Well, I made it," Avram said. "You were right; it's pretty nice this."

"Yes, not a bad choice," said Max.

As he stood there in the water in front of them, slightly crouched, Avram looked both of them over, looking at their pale skin. Max showed a visible difference in the skin of his arms, neck and face, more deeply tanned than the rest of his body, his pale hairs showing up in contrast in those places that had seen the sun. Selena wore a one-piece bathing suit, vivid green. He noticed, but looked quickly away as he saw what appeared to be a purplish mark poking out from beneath the suit on her left breast. Almost unconsciously, his hand rose to his neck, touching the skin there. He turned back to look at Max again, but right now, there didn't seem to be any apparent discoloration on any of the skin on display. It had to be there; possibly on his body somewhere currently concealed below the waterline. He glanced back at Selena, struggling to keep his breathing even, his demeanour as normal as possible. No, there was definitely evidence there. She was watching him curiously and he turned his body away, wading slowly over to another side of the pool where he would not have to position himself next to either of the children. Once there, he adopted a posture similar to Max, lowering himself further into the therapeutic waters and leaning back with his arms draped over the pool's edge.

An old couple appeared in the entrance then, and Avram watched them as they entered the pool slowly, bobbing around and holding each other's arms, and then simultaneously dunking their heads below the water. They repeated this three times, and then moved back and forth across the width of the pool before finally choosing a position opposite him and bobbing slowly up and down. Not a word passed between them. He turned his attention back towards the Greens. Max had his eyes closed, his head back. Selena was watching him, taking handfuls of the water and splashing them over her shoulders and neck. Samantha and Alfred, however, simply sat there unmoving, their legs in the water, their gazes fixed on Avram himself. He looked away, swallowing back the chill that rose inside him in response to their attention.

He was not getting anything new here. His suspicions about Selena had been partially confirmed, and he could only presume that the tell-tale discoloration that he had noticed had been inflicted by one of the children. Briefly, he wondered which one, or was it both? The old couple were still across the other side, immersed to their necks in the water. He watched them for a few seconds as he thought. If it was as he suspected, the children were nothing more than Lilith's tools. Attempting to do something about them would be a futile act, and even if he were to find some way to deal with them, he had no real idea how far Max and Selena were influenced. He glanced over at Samantha. Her clear blue gaze was still fixed on him. He could feel that look, touching him inside somehow and he clenched his jaw in response. He looked away and up at the shafts of sunlight lancing down from the domed stone ceiling. Avram had two choices: he could use his best efforts to do something about it or he could escape from it completely, or at least try.

The old couple were leaving the pool, and Avram waited the few moments it took for them to depart, then pushed himself up from the wall and stood. He waded over to the Greens, stood in front of their small group and cleared his throat.

"I'm sorry, guys," he said. "I've come to a decision."

Max looked up at him, half-interestedly. "Oh yes, Avram. And what's that?"

"I'm going to leave you. I've had enough of this, everything that's happening. I just need to get away. You can go on on your own."

Max said nothing, Selena said nothing, just staring at him impassively. The children continued watching his face without moving. Nothing else was said.

He was just about to turn away, convinced that he had conveyed his decision, that that was it when Max finally spoke again.

"Do you think that's a good idea, Avram?" He said it quietly, and there was a hint of something else in the words that chilled Avram.

A faint stirring in the air touched feather-light, warm on his damp skin. It gusted, blowing warmth, then faded, grew and then faded, like warm breath all over his exposed flesh. As one, the Greens, Max, Selena, and the children, turned their faces slowly towards one side of the pool. Avram shifted to follow their gaze in turn.

There, beside one of the columns encircling the pool, she stood, one hand upon the stone pillar, her dark eyes drilling across the intervening space, right into him. Cold fingers closed within his chest, pressing, increasing the pain that suddenly flowered within him. Still her eyes pinned him, seeming to grow larger in his sight. He staggered back, splashing through the water as the pain increased, spreading up from his chest and into his head. He couldn't breathe, could not suck in enough air, and he gasped, falling heavily back against the stone wall.

"You should be wise, Avram," said Selena.
Still struggling to gain breath, he turned his face to look at her, panting.

As suddenly as it had come, the pain dissipated. He looked back over to the other side of the pool, but of the small girl, there was no sign. She was simply gone. He scrabbled at the tiled edge of the pool, his hands slipping off the stones and then finally gained purchase, steadying himself. For several seconds he could do little more than stand there, hunched, swallowing large gulps of the mineral-filled air.

As soon as he felt that he could breathe properly again and his heart stopped pounding, he turned, waded across the pool and stepped haltingly out. It seemed he did not have a choice after all. His legs trembling, he left the octagonal pool room, leaving the Greens where they sat.

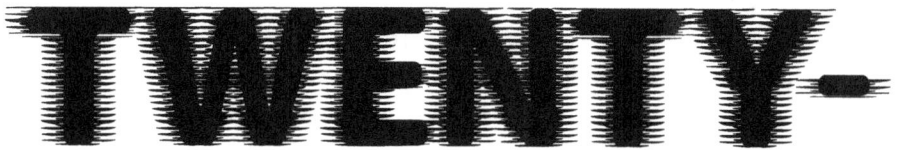

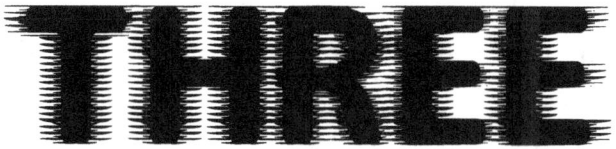

And her mouth is smoother than oil:
But her end is bitter as wormwood,
Sharp as a two edged sword,
Her feet go down to death.

—The Proverbs

Breath

Back in the locker room, Avram dressed slowly, still reeling from the cold, the wash of pain, and ultimately, the shock of her appearance by the poolside. At least now he had his confirmation. He struggled with his buttons, his hands trembling, and then with his trousers. After several attempts, he managed to get himself halfway presentable, and then stood in front of the mirror, ran his fingers through damp hair and simply looked back at himself. There were no real answers to be found there in his reflection, and even though he knew it, he stood there, immobile for a few minutes, just staring. He was along for the ride, until he found some way to escape. Unfortunately, he knew within himself, that simple escape was just not enough. He had to do something about it. He'd had some vague, naïve hope that perhaps he'd be able to call on Max and Selena, but now he knew for certain that there would be little chance of that. Somewhere on Max's body sat a mark, unseen, but there all the same. He tilted his head to one side, leaning in to look more closely at his neck. His own, personal disfigurement was fading, but still there. He probed at it gently with his fingertips. There was no pain, no discomfort, apart from the awareness of its presence, and now, more than ever, it troubled him, causing an involuntary curl of his lip. He would not, could not succumb to her. And now, it wasn't merely about himself. He knew that. It was time he grew himself a spine.

Someone walked into the locker room and he turned away from the mirror, feeling awkward. At least he had his shaking under control, enough so that he could face the world. Pushing a hand into his trouser pocket, he felt for the object secreted there and gave a satisfied grunt. He still had one more thing to explore before this little episode was done. Looking as he left to check if there was any sign of the Greens, he went out front, crossing the road to stand by the river and kill the time, letting the flowing water soothe him while he waited for them to emerge. It was nearly midday and the sun threw slivers of light from the water's surface, sparkling little diamonds in his vision. Next to him, the cars hummed, roared and clattered past, the occasional truck belching the scent of diesel. He turned back to watch the front of the bathhouse. Everything just appeared so normal. It was as if nothing had happened. A couple, and then a family group emerged from inside. Avram tensed, and then immediately relaxed; they were clearly locals. He turned back to watching the river, one eye on the front doors of the bathhouse in case anyone else came out.

Eventually, his patience was rewarded and first Max, then Selena and the children emerged from the baths. Avram waited for a break in traffic then dashed back across the road to stop a little way up from the entrance, ready to intercept them. Max spotted him first and raised and hand in greeting, as if simply nothing at all had happened inside the pool room. As far as he could see, both of them, Max and Selena, looked as normal as they ever did. Avram chewed at his bottom lip as he waited for them to approach.

"Ah, there you are, Avram," said Selena. "We wondered where you had disappeared to. You left us so suddenly. Is everything all right?"

"Yes, fine," he answered, willing for the moment to play along with the charade, if charade it was. It could be that both really had no memory of the events that had unfolded inside.

"So …," said Max.

Avram glanced down at the children's faces. They were watching him curiously.

"So, what now, Max?" he asked.

"I think back to the hotel. I don't think there's too much more we want to do here. We need to get on our way again. We don't want to leave getting to Paris too late. The travel company will have written us off. We can get back to the hotel, check out … maybe ask for a late checkout, take a couple of hours to get ourselves together, head to the station and I am sure we can find somewhere to grab a bite to eat, kill some time before we have to get on the train."

"   You said Zurich, right?"

"Yes, Zurich and then it's a short hop, only about four hours to Paris, so it should not be too difficult. We can take the chance to look around the place where all that money is and then head on our way."

"And in Paris, the plan is ...."

"We want to go and see some dead people," Selena said and laughed, looking quite amused with herself.

Although it was said lightly, the words filled Avram with a new chill.

"What do you mean?" He almost hesitated to ask.

Again Selena laughed. "Why, Père Lachaise, of course. That great Parisian cemetery. We have never been. You know, there are so many famous people there. Oscar Wilde, Piaf, de Balzac, Max Ernst, others. So many. We really have never been. I must see it."

"And, of course, we can sort out where we go from there and how we manage it with the travel company. Also some compensation, I think, for our things," added Max.

Selena's explanation had suppressed the chill that had grown within him, but the apparent normalcy of their conversation was troubling him. It really did seem as if they had no memory at all of what had happened. He looked to each of their faces, but they were merely looking at him interestedly, waiting for his response.

"Okay," said Avram. "That makes some sort of sense. Paris is such a great city."

While he was talking, he manoeuvred his hand inside his pocket without trying to make it too obvious. Using the ends of his fingers, he probed inside the small bundle made up of the handkerchief and what it contained. With a bit of dextrous movement, he was able to push his finger inside so that the very tip was in contact with the necklace contained therein. The effect was immediate, not with Max, not with Selena, but the children. Samantha got a sudden startled look, her eyes going wide, and she took two quick steps backward, away from him.

Alfred too looked suddenly panicked, looking at his sister and then all around as if seeking something that wasn't there. Avram withdrew his hand. After a couple of moments, the children seemed to relax a little but Samantha was looking at him now, an expression of … something he didn't quite recognise on her so-young features.

"Well," said Max. "I guess we could stand around here all day. Shall we head back to the hotel?"

Avram glanced around quickly, nervously expecting the sudden appearance of one other figure, but of her, there was no sign. He breathed a sigh of relief. He tracked a couple of cars as they rumbled past, and then another truck.

"Yes, let's go," he said and turned towards the castle and the hill that would take them back to the hotel.

As he started walking, keeping pace with the Greens, he felt a grim sense of satisfaction and he had his teeth clamped tight, his lips pressed together tightly. There was a feeling of resolve now growing inside him. His experiment had been a success, as far as it went, and now he had some sort of a direction, ill-formed yet, but there all the same. He barely paid attention to Selena's chatter as they walked. She was talking about this and that, what they were going to do in Zurich, what they might do in Paris. Max, walking beside her, took it all in stoically. All the way up the hill and beyond, Avram could feel Samantha's gaze drilling into his back, or perhaps he was just imagining it, but it made his shoulders tighten all the same.

Back at the hotel, he waited while Max negotiated their late checkout, and returned to their group, announcing his success and then planning to meet back in the lobby at about 2:30. It would give Avram enough time to pack, think and properly consider his options. He had no real plan yet, just the shred of an idea, and he was uncertain about where it was going to take him. He wished he still had the local Professor to consult with, but there was going to be little chance of that now.

Breath

Once back in his room, he carefully withdrew the small bundle from his pocket, and placing it carefully on the bed, unwrapped the necklace. Again, he was struck by the shifting colors within the stone's depths, and he picked the whole thing up by its cord and transported it over to the window so that he could look at it under more direct and natural light. There was no defined pattern; the colors just came and went. He ran his thumb over the stone again, feeling the markings that were etched upon the surface, but no matter which way he looked at the thing, he still couldn't see what they were. He thought about trying to transcribe them on paper, feeling them with his fingertips like brail, but then had another idea. Crossing back over to the desk, he tore off a thin sheet of paper from the hotel message pad, took the nearby pencil, and then rubbed it across the surface, but without any result than a gray smudged oval. The lines, whatever was there, were too shallow to leave any sort of recognisable impression. Had they been made that way, or had they been worn smooth with age? There was no way of knowing. He transported the necklace back to the bed and carefully rewrapped it in the handkerchief. Pulling his valise onto the bed and opening it, he just as carefully slipped the bundle into the inner zippered pocket and sealed it shut, then one by one, located his clothes, his toiletries, and packed them inside the bag as well. With his acquisition of new clothes the bag was almost full and that gave him a little extra comfort. It would be hard to locate the pendant simply by accident; it would need to be a deliberate effort. That possibility, however, could not be discounted, and he promised himself to keep the luggage close by and observable during every part of their forthcoming journey, or failing that, to have his tiny precious cargo with him and securely on his person.

He still had about an hour to kill before he needed to go down, and he spent the time reading through the Budapest guidebook, looking at all the things and places he might have liked to visit should the circumstances have been normal. It was disappointing—so much that he was going to miss. Maybe, one day, he'd have a chance to come back and make up for it, but at the moment, he had no certainty about where he'd end up, not even any certainty that he'd still be alive to take the opportunity. Even if he was, unless there was a significant reversal of fortune, it would be years before he'd be able to afford a trip like this one. Or rather, a trip such as this one was meant to be.

Checkout was unproblematic, and he joined with the Greens at the agreed time, baggage in hand. They were standing around with their own new improved versions waiting for him.

"So where to?" he asked, again looking for any sign that they were aware of what had happened at the baths.

"Well," said Max. "We go out from Keleti again. We're sure to find somewhere around there. Maybe we can dump our luggage at the station."

Avram eyed their large wheeled cases dubiously, but he considered; it didn't have to be in a locker. There was no doubt a left luggage station or something there. Although, he'd certainly be much more comfortable if he could stow his own within a properly sealed container with a lock. A pity they wouldn't be leaving from Central Station. As he already knew, there were plenty of venues in that general vicinity. He smiled wryly to himself. If this went on he'd be turning into a leading authority on the world's greatest stations.

"Of course, we still have to get our tickets," said Max. "I can't imagine that will be a problem."

Max's comment brought Avram back to the present. "Well, let's hope not," he said.

"We'll be fine," said Selena.

"All right then, let's do it."

Max, as usual, headed first towards the hotel's exit and arranged with the doorman to call a suitable cab, waving him away when he offered to assist with the luggage. A few moments later, and their taxi, a small minibus arrived, and Max beckoned impatiently at them to get on board. Luggage bundled into the back and all safely on board, they left the hotel behind, heading for the next station, the next train and the next set of potential torments that Avram would have to face, or so he thought.

On the way, he took note of the fact that Samantha and Alfred appeared to be reacting to him normally. No, that was wrong, he realized. They were not reacting normally. Still there was that impassive staring, the lack of animation, the fixed gaze. More correctly, he thought, they were just not reacting to him right now. He turned his attention back out the cab window, watching the city stumble past.

#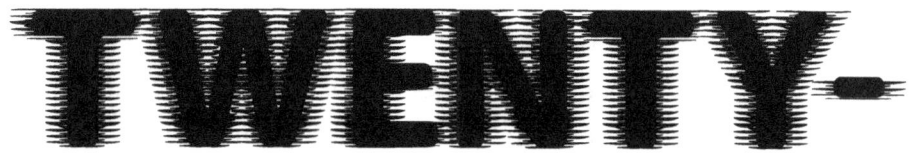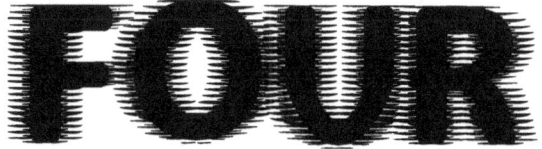

I am a fierce spirit of myriad names and many shapes.

—Testament of Solomon

Breath

As with the standard set of major stations, there were slim pickings to be had in the general area. For some reason, stations as a whole tended to attract the itinerant and the down and out, those on the grift. The buildings too were dilapidated, in many cases, in need of repair, but it looked like any renovation was a long way off. Standard, four to five stories in the Bohemian style, they showed vestiges of their past glory, when Budapest had been a center of commerce and culture before the regime took over and changed all that. Now, there were only memories of the opulence that used to exist.

They pulled up in front of the station, wheeled their luggage inside and looked for somewhere they could store it as they wandered round. Baggage deposited, Max told them to go and wait for him outside. He'd only be a few minutes sorting out the tickets, and then they could see what was in the vicinity, somewhere they could sit for a couple of hours, have a proper lunch and kill the time before they would have to head back and board their train. Avram wandered out to the front of the station, a little apart from Selena and the children and stood there looking at the passing people, a construction area off to one side—something to do with the station itself, rather than any attempt at improving the surrounds—and at the faded bleakness that lay all around. He was not feeling entirely comfortable without his bag in his hand, but it was as it was, and it would only be for a couple of hours. He doubted anyone would be breaking into the locker and rummaging inside.

He was casually observing the passers-by, avoiding looking at Samantha and Alfred, consciously, when a child walked past, turned as he passed by, fixing Avram's face, continuing to hold the look as he walked behind and into the station. Avram looked over his shoulder, following him with his gaze. The boy was watching him still, looking back over his own shoulder as he walked, and then he was gone. Avram turned back to look at the street in front, a sense of unease working in the pit of his stomach. Perhaps it had only been coincidence and he was reading too much into it. Merely a local child interested in the obvious stranger standing out in front of the station…that had to be it. But then, there had been those other children in Bucharest, that whole episode inside the People's Palace. The picture of their expressionless faces washed up in his head. The passing child's face had held nothing too, blank, conveying emptiness above everything else. He swallowed and grimaced.

Max appeared a couple of minutes later waving a sheaf of papers in one hand.

"All done," he said. "I booked us couchettes, so we can sit or we can sleep. It's only eleven hours. When we get to Zurich, it will be 7:30 so we can find somewhere to have breakfast and then work out what we will do for the day."

Avram stepped back over to join them. "And now?"

"Well, I don't know," said Max. "There's bound to be somewhere around here that makes its living off passing travellers, no? Let's have a wander around and see."

They did precisely that, Max in the lead, strolling for a few blocks along streets lined with stone buildings, mainly in mustard yellow or cream, graying with the patina of age and showing cracks or flaking surfaces. Low-end convenience stores popped up here and there, painted in lurid colors, green with orange, or faded pink. Eventually, they stumbled upon a small restaurant serving local fare, and peering in through the windows, they could see a few patrons inside, several of them looking like locals. That was generally a reasonable indicator. They entered, to the rich smell of food and local spices, and the noise of conversations in the local language. The owner of the establishment welcomed them in with a broad smile and directed them to a bench table right by the window. A few moments later, and he was back with plastic covered menu cards, the listed items in several languages. So, it appeared he was well enough prepared for the local tourist trade. Looking at him, though, Avram suspected that it was likely to be a process of choose and point to order from the menu. The patron left them for a few minutes to make up their minds after taking their drink order. Max ordered beer, and Selena wine, soft drinks for the children. Avram decided to take Max's lead and also ordered a beer. He scanned the menu feeling not overly hungry, but he supposed he should eat. The last few times he had been together with the family, even though food had been ordered, neither Samantha nor Alfred had done more than merely pick at their meals. He glanced at them, but both of them had their attention turned away, watching out the window, their menus sitting in front of them, ignored. Avram knew from his reading of the guidebook, that lunch was the main meal of the day here, and he scanned the menu. There, in line with Hungarian tradition was a selection of soups, and a number of pancake type meals that would normally serve as mains. He decided on a soup and then something called Hortobágyi palacsinta, with an English translation telling him that it was a "savories pankake with veal." When their host returned with their drinks, fussed around placing them in the right places and then took their orders, he seemed to approve of Avram's choices.

Little conversation passed between them as they concentrated on the food. Avram ate slowly, observing the children as he did so, but trying not to be noticed doing so. It wasn't hard; Max and Selena appeared absorbed and oblivious, and for most of the time Sam and Alf sat, their attention firmly fixed on the outside. At one point, a young girl walked past outside and stopped. Both children followed her with their gaze, and then she suddenly halted. She turned to face the window. Alf, who was seated beside the glass lifted one hand and placed it palm flat against the window. Outside, the young girl lifted her own hand, placed it on the outside of the window, in the same spot as Alf's as if they were touching each other through the glass. Then she turned and walked away. Alf and Sam watched her as she moved down the street and then both turned back to watching the street right outside.

"Did you see that?" said Avram, unable to stop himself.

"What?" said Selena, with a slight frown.

"There was a girl outside and …" His voice trailed off. It was pointless. "Nothing," he said. "No, nothing."

Selena gave a little shake of her head, glanced at Max and then turned her attention back to her food. Avram poked at the remainder of his 'pankakes' with his fork. He went back to mute sidelong observation, waiting for a repeat of the incident, but none came. Even though he was gathering information, evidence of what he suspected, he was coming no closer to a solution, and all he was left with was a vague fear of the more that was yet to come. He glanced down at his watch. The time was passing too slowly. He just wanted to get out of this city now, move on to somewhere else, somewhere that might offer him some hope, because he was convinced now that he was not going to find it here.

They took their time over dessert and coffee. Their host plied them with a small glass of pálinka "on the house" with their coffees and Avram appreciated the astringent aromatic burn in his throat as he swallowed. In some way, it reminded him he really was still alive despite everything.

At last, Max settled up the account and they rose from the table. They still had about an hour before the train was due to leave, but it would take at least twenty minutes to wander slowly back to the station and they still had to retrieve their collective luggage. Avram felt full, and the touch of alcohol, though small, had been enough to induce a sense of pleasant numbness in the back of his head. There were all sorts of oblivion, he thought. As soon as they left the restaurant, he stood for a moment looking up and down the street. What sort of oblivion, exactly, awaited him, he shuddered to consider.

"Avram?" said Selena.

"Yes, sorry. I was just thinking." He turned to follow them.

Gradually, they worked their way back to Keleti, taking their time even though in actuality, there was very little to see. Once more, as they turned the corner and headed down another street, they passed a small child, a boy this time. As he neared, he looked at first Samantha, and then at Alfred, holding their gaze for an instant. He seemed to ignore Max and Selena completely, and then his eyes locked on Avram who was trailing a little behind. He held that gaze, and though he wanted to, Avram found himself unable to look away, to break that contact. He was suddenly filled with a sense of dread. The boy passed him, looked back, continued watching him as he walked steadily away down the street. Avram stopped dead in his track, turning to watch the disappearing child. And then he was around the corner and gone.

"Avram!" It was Selena again. Already they were several yards further on. He turned back and quickened his pace to catch up.

How many more of them were there? They had been in this city not even two full days and already the blight had spread more than he could have expected. That's what it was—a blight, a disease, a pestilence, and if he understood what the girl called Lilith had conveyed to him, then he, Avram was the vector. It was funny, he could not associate the name directly with the child. It was 'the girl called Lilith' not just 'Lilith.' Was that some way for him to cope with everything she represented, to remove himself by placing an extra step between the way she thought of her and her actual presence? He had always had difficulty directly confronting the true harshness of his reality, wanting to distance himself. Somehow, he suspected now, that no simple mental trick was going to protect him from his fate. If he was going to do anything, he needed to act directly rather than at a remove.

Keleti Station loomed before them across a wide traverse of streets. He followed as the Greens led the way and towards the place where they had left their luggage. As soon as he had picked up his bag, he felt an easing of his current tension. There, within, was something that at least offered him some protection, or the knowledge of it. The normal station noises, the colorful shop-fronts, the scents and sounds of humanity washed him in a sense of normality, and he hefted his bag, gripping on to its solidity and weight within his hand. He watched the people passing by. At the moment, at least, and he was thankful for that, there were no more children, nothing else to undermine the brief sense of concrete reality that was now with him.

"Okay, all done. Shall we find the train?" said Max. He looked at his watch. "It's probably in by now."

Avram nodded. "Yes, let's go." Right now, he really could think of no better action.

They found the train without trouble, located their carriage and climbed aboard with their luggage. As Max and family stowed their luggage and entered the compartment, a six-berth couchette, Avram hesitated at the doorway. He hadn't had any thought that he would be travelling in a shared compartment with them. The prospect of spending the eleven-hour journey, overnight and in the darkness, especially with the children, filled him with a new dread. He swallowed several times, standing there, unable to force himself to move inside. And what if they would have another visitor in the night, a particular visitor?

"Come on, Avram. What are you waiting for, standing there like a statue? Come on in. There's plenty of room." Max was looking at him, his lips pressed together on the verge of annoyance. "We don't smell do we?"

No, they didn't smell. It was something far worse.

Taking yet another swallow, he stepped fully into the compartment, placed his bag down on one of the seats and withdrew his Budapest guidebook. He then stowed his bag on the overhead rack and sat, reaching for the printed itinerary that lay on the seat opposite, looking at where the train would take them and avoiding looking at any of the compartment's other occupants. As he traced their route with his finger, he could feel his hand trembling.

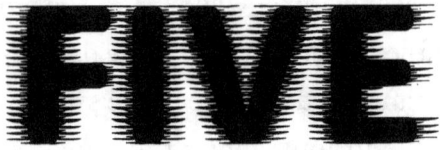

You should not cut the throat of that which has already had its throat cut.

–Sumerian Proverb

Despite his worst fears, Avram spent the night undisturbed apart from the constant feeling of being observed within the darkness. It kept sleep a distant thing well beyond his grasp. He could not see them in the darkness, but he sensed that they were watching. He wondered if they even slept any more. Eventually, he did sleep, but it was black and full of threatening darkness that he could not give any shape to, interspersed with the sensation of large flapping wings and heated air.

It was already light when he finally awoke.

"Ah, Avram, you are finally with us," said Selena as he struggled to consciousness and to sit up.

"You missed Vienna during the night," said Max.
Any other time that might have disappointed him. He merely nodded.

"Excuse me," he said. "I just want to freshen up." He wanted to do more than that, but he wasn't exactly going to inform them what he was about. Suddenly remembering, he looked up at his valise. He was hardly going to leave it here in the compartment with them. He reached up and dragged it down. He could make a show of rooting around inside for his toiletries, but he thought that it would be just as natural to take the whole thing with him.

"Which way is the bathroom? Do you know?" he asked.

Max looked up and gestured down towards one end of the carriage. Avram nodded, slid the compartment door open, and clutching his valise in front of him, walked down the corridor in the direction Max had indicated, adjusting his steps to compensate for the train's rocking.

Firmly locked in behind the bathroom door, he placed the bag down on the toilet seat, opened it and then felt carefully down the side, checking that his little package was in place. The small nub of round hardness was still there, solid beneath his probing figures, and he felt the wash of relief. Next, he turned to the mirror, tilting his head first one way then the other, checking the skin at his neck. There was no sign of any fresh marking. The fading purple of the existing blemish was there, but now only barely visible. Again, he felt the relief fill him. Only then did he find his toiletries, splash water on his face a couple of times in succession, lean forward and examine his face in the mirror. The cold water brought him back to a more conscious state. He ran dampness back through his hair and then applied a brush. A section of hair on the side that he'd been sleeping out stuck out stubbornly and he splashed more water on it and brushed it into place, repeating the process until it acquiesced.

He at least looked human again.

Was he even human anymore? He wondered. No, he had to be.

As a last thought he splashed some cologne on his face and reached inside his shirt to apply some deodorant. He looked a little crumpled, but it would do. He sealed his bag again, unlocked the door and headed back to their compartment.

"Ah, good," said Max at his return. "We'll be there in about twenty minutes."

Avram looked at his watch. Max was right. He had lost any real conception of what time it was. Rather than stowing the bag again, he placed it securely between his feet after retaking his seat. Selena was watching the passing scenery out the window, Max doing the same. The children just sat there watching him. Avram decided to follow Max and Selena's lead and turned to look out of the window too, watching the green fields, the recognisably Swiss houses they passed, and then slowly, the outer edges of suburban growth. It was all noticeably different from the place they had left just yesterday evening. Just a few hours by train and it could be worlds away. There was an impression of cleanness about everything they were passing.

The train pulled into the station and together, they left the compartment, worked their way down the corridor and then stepped down to the platform. Again, the station felt cleaner than the one they had left. The platform stretched beneath a high roof, higher than the

Keleti and with the real feeling of air and space. At the platform's end, there was the usual selection of small shops and eateries, but they were more discrete, almost tucked away, unlike the riot of colors and smells that had been Bucharest. The platform end led them to the main entrance area of the station proper, again, high-ceilinged clean, polished floors and a large poster suspended from the roof at one end, advertizing an art exhibition.

"I'm going to get tickets now," said Max, "for this evening. We can get to Paris tonight. Can you take my case, Avram? Find the storage place and put it in for me? I'll meet you back here and we can decide how we'll spend the day."

"Sure," said Avram.

"Thanks," said Max, handing over the luggage and heading off towards the main ticket area. Together with Selena and the children, holding his valise with one hand and wheeling Max's large baggage behind him with the other, Avram walked towards a series of signs that seemed as if they might offer a left luggage service. Once again, he deposited his luggage and Max's as well, feeling a sense of the repetitive. Was he going to end up spending the rest of his life visiting baggage storage services and putting in bags for a few hours then taking them out again? He took the luggage tickets, deposited them in his wallet, and then making sure Selena and the children were all done, turned back to where they were supposed to meet Max.

"All set," said Max as they walked up. "Let's go."

He led the way out to the station's front entrance. Just outside, there was a large tram stop, people waiting all along the length. Avram could see even from his first brief impression that they conveyed a sense of prosperity, of well-to-do-ness that had been visibly absent in their last port of call. He looked around himself, suddenly realizing that the children were not with them.

"Max," he said. "Samantha and Alfred."

"What?" said Max.

"We seem to have lost them."

"They are not lost," said Selena. "They've just got something to do."

Avram stared at her. What could they possibly have to do? Whatever it was, it could be nothing good. And how was it that Max and Selena both seemed unaffected by their sudden absence. He looked around, back into the station proper and up and down the street, but they were clearly gone.

"You're just going to leave them on their own?" he asked.

"They can look after themselves," said Max.

And of that, Avram had no doubt. What that might entail, he didn't really want to think about.

"Okay," said Max. "Let's get going. I'd like to see the lake. I think it's down this way," he said pointing out past the tram stop and into a nearby side street.

"Oh yes, me too," said Selena. "Maybe there'll be some nice shops along the way."

Biting his tongue, Avram followed Max's lead, trailing along behind as he crossed the street and headed in the direction he had indicated. What choice did he have?

They entered tree-lined streets, everything in good repair, tramlines running up and down between boutiques stores and upmarket shop fronts. Well-dressed people wandered past, and they crossed stone bridges walked between ornate stone buildings. Gradually they moved further into the city, tracking the river's flow down towards the lake. There was something impressive about the city's upkeep, but it left Avram with a sense of something artificial, pristine, almost antiseptic. After about twenty minutes of walking, the lake itself hove into view, the clear crystal waters sparkling in the sunlight. Across from the lakeshore sat an open space, currently filled with what looked like some sort of flea market. At the sight, Selena oohed enthusiastically.

"Oh, yes. Let's go look, Max."

"Sure," he said. "Maybe we can find something. Avram?"

Avram shook his head. "No, you go on. I think I'm going to go and sit by the water for a while. I have some things to think about." He could see well-maintained park areas by the water's edge, benches, and rows of neatly trimmed chestnut trees providing shade. And frankly, right now, he couldn't think of anything worse than tagging along with Selena as she poked around market stalls, pretending a sense of normalcy that simply didn't exist. The problem with Switzerland and with Zurich in particular, was that people had way too much money. He had seen it in the streets, in the people who walked by, in the cars that passed. He could understand why normally it would appeal to Max and Selena, but the "normally" wasn't a part of the equation right now. He wasn't sure whether to both of them, Selena and Max, things were nothing more than standard, but regardless, he refused to take part in the charade. They had already dismissed the sudden absence of their children, and that in itself was simply not right. All the same, there had to be a reason that motivated them to come here, and he wondered what it might be.

"Okay, Avram, whatever you feel like doing," said Max. He looked at his watch. "We've got about four hours before we need to be back at the station. Our train leaves at 1:34. I can tell you for sure, it will leave right on time. Perhaps we should meet back at the station."

"Yes," he said. "That would suit me fine." He knew better now than to offer anything else. The memory of the pain resulting from any intended resistance was still sharp.

Max nodded, took Selena's hand and headed off into the market, leaving Avram standing there staring after them. He let them go, and then turned, heading for the lakeshore and the small park that sat across the other side of the road. Waiting for a passing tram to roll by, he negotiated the road running along the lake's shore, and then stood in front of the small, slightly raised park that sat opposite. It was less of a park than a paved area, with its neatly trimmed double row of chestnuts, their tops a little unnaturally manicured like perverse arboreal poodles. He took the few steps up to the paved platform and crossed to stand in front of the statue, raised on a plinth and greening with the patina of age. Behind it, the water threw reflections from the windows of grand houses set all around the lake's shore. Boats sat moored or plied the waters. He looked up at the statue after reading the inscribed name: "Ganymed." It depicted a naked youth, reaching down to an eagle.

Avram knew the Ganymede legend of old. Zeus, being attracted by the comely youth Ganymede, had transformed himself to an eagle to steal the boy and take him back to Olympus to serve. Avram studied the statue with a wry expression. Wasn't that the same as what was happening to him? Some winged, or at least a flying creature had stolen him away to serve. So, it wasn't a god, or not that he understood, and Avram didn't think of himself as particularly comely, but the principle was the same. The essence of the thing was what was driving everything happening to him at the moment. He shook his head, and in so doing, noticed a nearby bench—an ideal spot to sit and watch the water on a fine summer's day. It would be the sort of thing he would do if he were your standard tourist, watch the lake, the passing boat traffic, the couples and families out for a promenade along the waterside.

He moved over to sit, his hands crossed in his lap and simply stared out at the water, breathing slowly, deeply, trying to come to grips with his circumstance.

"Hello," said a young voice beside him.

He looked to the side to see a young boy seated on the end of the bench not far from him. The chillness of falling grew in his chest. He hadn't heard the boy arrive, even if he had appeared from somewhere. He looked around seeing if he could spot the child's parents, but there was no one else around. The frigid fingers within him grew stronger, making it hard to breathe.

The boy, who had been watching him, now turned to face the water.

"We do love it so much," he said in English. "It reminds us of what we missed. Water is precious," he said matter-of-factly.

Avram had no words, he could do nothing more than stare.

"It is precious, like breath," said the child. "It is a thing of life."

Turning his gaze back to Avram, he sat looking for a few seconds, his eyes boring through, right into the depths of Avram's being. Then he turned away again, looked almost longingly at the water, and then stood, and simply walked away. A few moments later he was gone, with nothing left behind to say he had even been there, apart from the pounding in Avram's chest.

There was no doubt that the child had been one of them. Avram watched the place where the child had been last visible for several minutes, desperately trying to get his breathing and heart-rate under control. How had this plague spread here so quickly? They had been in the city not more than a couple of hours by now. Perhaps that explained Samantha and Alfred's disappearance. What had the Greens said, that the children had something to do? Right now, he had a reasonable suspicion what that might have been. But then, why Zurich? Again, perhaps it was something about what Max had said, the place where they kept all that money. Was there something more purposeful about their visit? If they had the ability to control, which they clearly did, then there could easily be another reason for them being here. Power, control … money made the world go round, or so they said.

Avram stood and walked over to the railing that stood in front of the water, staring down into the crystal depths, but there was nothing, nothing at all there that was going to provide him with any kind of answer. He turned away from the water, and back to the city itself.

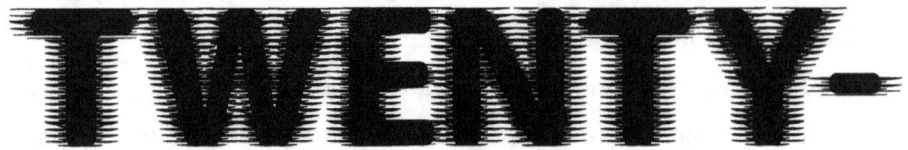

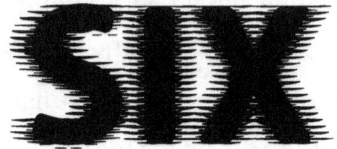

In three ways they resemble men: They eat and drink like men, they beget and increase like men, and like men they die.

–The Talmud

243

For a long time, he wandered aimlessly, randomly heading up streets and seeing where they might take him. There was no specific direction or purpose in mind, just a way to walk through his thoughts, see if something was lurking in the back of his head that might suggest a solution to his current state. More than once he passed a child, once a girl and another boy. He passed others, of course, but these particular children filled him with the sense of foreboding he was coming to expect. As they approached they fixed their gaze upon his face, holding contact with an import of knowledge that simply left him cold, right until they passed and then beyond. He drew them to him. They knew who he was.

They knew what he was. Something he didn't even know himself any more. Avram Davis, what had you become?

The city did nothing to change his initial impression. It was pretty in its way, but he simply could not divorce himself from the sense of surreal artificiality, a sense that echoed his own current state of existence. And in the meantime, he had to find something to distract him. If every moment was spent dwelling upon it, then there would be no chance for his subconscious to work on the problem, lead him to a new path. He felt hopeless, helpless. He passed a bookstore, then a men's clothing store, and had second thoughts and turned back. The trip to Paris would be just over four hours by TGV. He couldn't bear the thought of sharing a carriage for four straight hours staring across at the children with them staring back at him in turn. It was unlikely that he'd be able to escape into sleep, not that he really wanted to do that either. The bookstore might just provide something to keep him distracted during the journey, though whether he'd be actually able to read was another question.

For a little while, he simply browsed the shelves becoming more frustrated as he realized that most of the texts were in German. Languages had never actually been his strong point. Finally, he located a section where he found a limited selection of English novels, but most of them were the standard populist crime novels and a few romance, one or two thrillers and a couple of historicals. There was nothing there that attracted him. He moved to another section and found some travel guidebooks, but it too was a very limited selection. One or two were in English. Thankfully, there was one about Paris. He levered it out of the shelf and carried it over to pay. At least it was something. He left the store with the small paper-wrapped package clutched in one hand, stood for a moment looking up and down the street, unsure which direction he should head. At the moment, his internal compass seemed to be failing him. This one tree-lined street looked like many of the others he had travelled and there was no significant landmark to point him in the right direction. Perhaps, instead, he ought to have purchased a guidebook to Zurich instead.

Avram turned in a random direction and simply started walking. Zurich was not large. In fact, from what he had seen so far, it was a tiny city, almost a town. He had to reach somewhere soon that would tell him where exactly he was. He passed a couple of chain hotels, thought about asking for directions inside, and then decided against it. He peered up at street signs, turned a corner into something called Stockerstrasse and continued walking. Within a couple of minutes, the shimmer of bright water told him he was almost to something he would recognise. He came out by the lake and across the road sat parkland, a narrow strip, but this time with grass and trees instead of simple paving. Now, he knew roughly where he was. If he could only find the Ganymede statue then he could retrace his steps from the morning. Access to the park was blocked, directly across by a wall of low shrubs and trees, but further along was a set of traffic lights and a crossing that led to an entrance. He turned in that direction, waited for the lights to change and then quickly crossed. The neatly tended enclosure ran right by the water's edge, contained lawns and various monuments, a fountain. Now that he was past the concealing barrier of trees that now, instead, blocked the road, he could see all along the shore to what looked like a jetty he remembered from before with a large white pleasure boat drawn up beside it. Just beyond, he thought, he would see the Ganymede statue, and then it would be an easy trip back past the flea market, into the city following the river then up to the Hauptbahnhof. He was just about to set off in that direction when a voice stopped him dead in his tracks.

"Uncle Avram, we have been waiting for you."

He spun, turning to look at Samantha and Alfred standing hand in hand and looking up at him. He glanced around nervously, but there was no one to help him. Nor, thankfully, was there any sign of the other one, the one he truly dreaded to see.

"It's time to go back," said Alfred.

"Back to the station," said Samantha.

"Let us take you," they said together. Still their faces remained impassive.

He knew already what resistance would result in. He closed his eyes and took a deep breath, and then slowly opened them again. The children were still there. Still holding hands, they were looking out at the lake, longingly. They turned back to face him and stepped forward, one on each side of him as if guarding against him escaping. He suddenly felt like a prisoner being escorted to a cell. At least they did not reach for his hands.

"Come on. Let's go," said Samantha.

They walked unhurriedly along the rest of the park area and then turned into the city proper. Avram clutched his book to his chest, merely walking with them, not saying anything. They passed the flea market and he looked back over his shoulder at the Ganymede statue, now silhouetted against the lake's shining surface. Following the route that Avram, Max and Selena had taken in the morning, they walked further into the city, tracing the river until they came to the stone bridge and turned left. As they crossed the bridge, a child approached them from the other direction, looked from Samantha's face to Alfred's and as he passed, turned his head to maintain the contact. Alfred watched the passing boy back over his shoulder. How many more of them were there? There had to be an end to it. There had to be, but if there was a way, he did not yet know it.

It did not take them long to reach the main station. The children walked him casually inside. There, in the center of the main entrance hall stood Selena and Max. They already had Selena and the children's luggage with them.

"Ah good, you found the children," said Selena as if it were the most normal thing in the world.

"Well, rather they found me," said Avram wryly.

"Good, good," said Max. "I think you have my luggage, Avram."

"Yes, yes. Of course," he said, reaching for his wallet and leaving parents and children both standing where they were, relieved to do so. He headed for the luggage storage and then retrieved his and Max's bags. Slowly, he wheeled Max's luggage back to the group after placing his book into his own bag, feeling surreptitiously for his hidden object as he did so, making sure it was still there. It was, and the knowledge have him some little sense of security, whether misplaced or not.

As soon as he re-joined the group, Max took possession of his own case and immediately headed off in the direction of the platforms.

"This way," he said.

With a heavy sigh, Avram trailed along behind, his bag in hand and a sense of helplessness walking along with him.

As they scanned the boards to locate their platform, Max turned to him.

"You bought something," he said conversationally.

"Yes, sure. Just a guidebook. Paris guidebook."

"Ah," said Max. "Selena and I, we know Paris quite well. You don't have any real need for a guidebook. We can tell you where to go, what to do."

Avram looked at him for a moment or two. He was sure they could, but it wasn't in the way that Max was meaning. He looked away again.

"I like to be prepared," he said, looking up at the indicator board.

Another train, another station, another destination. Was this going to go on like this forever? Paris, and then what? Yet another city? More opportunities to spread this plague of children? He looked down at the ground, at his feet, awash in his helplessness.

"Come," said Max. It was more a command than anything else and Avram looked up. From what he could see, it was just Max being Max, already striding down the platform ends heading towards where their train sat, Selena and the children in tow. With another sigh, Avram turned to follow, quickening his pace to catch up.

They found their platform, the sleek long, shovel-nosed train already sitting there all blue and silver and white. Max located their carriage—1st Class of course—and they climbed aboard. Inside the tall well upholstered seats sat in groups of four, a table in between each set. At one end of the carriage, sat a luggage storage area, and the Greens bundled their cases into place and then headed further down the carriage length, Max checking their tickets as he went, finally stopping when he reached a group of four seats down the other end. He looked back up and waved Avram forward.

"You're down here too," he called down the length of the carriage, pointing to some seats across the aisle from them. Rather than stowing his bag, Avram carried it the length of the carriage in front of him and then placed it on the table.

"Which seat?" he asked.

"That one, over there by the window."

At least there was that much. He had two advantages now. Not only was he facing in their direction of travel and he would have enough to see out the window to keep him occupied, but no longer was he forced to sit in a compartment opposite the children, having their constant stare worming beneath his skin.

He pulled out his guidebook from inside the valise, unwrapped it and placed it down on the table in front of his seat, and then sealed the bag again before lifting it into the overhead luggage shelf. He turned to look at Max and Selena, avoiding the children's faces and leaned back to perch on the end of the table.

"So, Paris," he said. "What do we do when we get there?"

"Apart from seeing some dead people?" said Selena and laughed. She waved her fingers in front of her face and said in a childlike voice, "I see dead people." She laughed again.

"No, I didn't mean that," said Avram, not particularly amused.

"What, hotel?" said Max.

Avram nodded.

"That's already been taken care of."

"What do you mean?"

"Well, I phoned ahead. Did not want there to be any slipups. I know where we are staying. All sorted out." He sat back looking smug.

"Well, maybe you'd like to tell me?"

Max shook his head. "Call it a surprise. It is something very nice. I'm sure you'll like it."

Avram remained unconvinced, but he wasn't going to argue. He slid into to take up his seat and spent a couple of minutes simply staring out the window. The carriage gave a little lurch and an announcement came over the speaker system and then was repeated in two other languages, English being one of them. Standard stuff; welcome on board, route, duration, arrival time, available facilities. Avram listened with half an ear, watching instead the station slide past him out the window.

It didn't take them long the clear the outskirts of Zurich, and they were soon back in countryside, green fields and distant mountains looming, snow-capped still even at this time of year. He turned back to the guidebook and started riffling through the pages. He found the entry for the cemetery that Selena seemed so fascinated with. After reading just a short bit, he could understand why. It was the sort of place that he'd be interested in visiting any time, but certainly if the circumstances were normal.

He leaned his head back and closed his eyes, allowing the train's rocking to soothe him, bring him to a state of calmness. He had not actually seen the girl for a while. The child, Lilith. There, he had given the name substance. He'd seen enough evidence of her though. Just not the girl herself. Why was that? Did she only appear when he was on the verge of offering an active resistance? He wondered.

He half opened his eyes, looking sidelong at the children, Samantha and Alfred, but for once, they were not observing him. They sat looking directly at each other across the table, their parents in place by the window, watching the passing scenery. There was no expression on the children's faces. They looked blank. And then, as he was watching, Samantha turned her head and looked directly at him, her expression unchanging.

Quickly, he turned his head away, leaned his forehead on the window, feeling the cool glass and watching the rails whip past below, allowing himself to be drawn into the clatter of the wheels and the rocking of the carriage, just attempting to let himself drift.

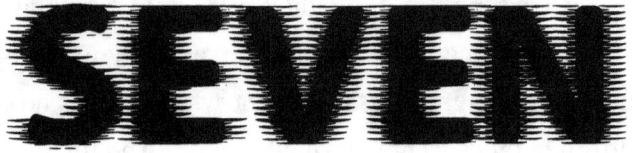

I marvelled at her appearance, for I beheld all her body to be in darkness.

—Testament of Solomon

As they entered the outskirts of Paris, Avram started to realize how truly vast the city was. The suburbia seemed to go on and on for ever. Throughout the journey, he had spent time dipping in and out of his guidebook, but it had given no real indication of the scale of the place. There were houses, apartment buildings, trees, and then in the distance, the dome of Sacre Coeur set atop a hill surveying the spread of the city, its white stone painted pastel through the city's urban haze. He turned to the map at the rear of the guidebook, tracing their progress noting as they neared the great river upon which the city sat, and as they streamed past the vast Bois de Vincennes of to the right. They clattered across the bridge into an expanding network of rail tracks, signals and bridges, drawing them ever closer to their final terminus, the Gare de Lyon. As they slowed, pulling into the station, there were trains and people everywhere. There was a vastness of scale and population that had been missing in Zurich. This was Paris. Everything had to be grander. At least he expected it to be so. He threw out a hand to steady himself as the train lurched to a final stop.

"So, here we are," said Max, slapping his hands down on the table surface. "Paris. Everybody out."

Already they were standing, leaving their seats and heading up the aisle towards their luggage.

"Wait, Max," said Avram.

He turned, a look of query on his face.

"You know where we are going?"

"Of course." He turned away again and continued up towards the carriage end.

Avram took his guidebook, retrieved his valise and followed. Down on the platform, the noises echoed from the glass roof, the sound of people, so many people. Avram wondered if it was always this crowded, and then he had another thought.

So many people …

He could see why they wanted to be in Paris; it was a major

population center. So many opportunities for them to … feed. Was there another word for it? He didn't think so. Hesitating, he paused and then quickly followed them up to the platform entrance. All around, the sounds of humanity bombarded him, blurring into one vast noise as they echoed from the surrounding walls and roof.

"Max, wait. Where to now?"

Max turned and looking as if he was impressed with his own cleverness spoke. "So, there are three ways we can get there. A few stops on the RER, but then there is a very long walk inside the stations. We could catch the Metro, but then we would have to change and with the luggage …" He shrugged. "I think we will catch a taxi."

Selena patted him on the arm.

So, here they were, yet another station, city, taxi, hotel. But this was Paris. Avram had always wanted to visit Paris. He shook the thought away. How could he be so … mundane … about it all?

"Come on," said Max. "This way."

He led them out to the front of the station, weaving in and out around groups of people, avoiding a man pushing a large metal trolley, and then out onto the street where a line of cabs stood waiting. Here too, there were people and cars everywhere. The area was throbbing with life. They located a cab of appropriate size and heaved the luggage into the back, then clambered aboard. The driver looked at Max, a query on his stubbled face.

"Hotel Plaza Athénée, Avenue Montaigne," said Max, again looking pleased with himself.

Even Avram had heard of the Plaza Athénée. It looked like whatever might happen in Paris, it was destined to divest him of whatever remaining funds he might have. In the end, perhaps that wouldn't matter, he thought wryly.

The taxi driver nodded and pulled out from the station, entering a chaotic flow of cars and traffic and then turning into another street where there were even more cars and apparent confusion. On every side, the streets and pavements swarmed with people, a mix of black, white and everything in between. Clothing of multiple colors, scatterings of rubbish on the street, everything spoke of a vast and diverse collection of people, living, vibrant, moving about their lives.

After winding through the Paris streets, both cobbled and not, between ornate buildings and some in need of repair, they moved into the area around the Louvre and beyond. All around, Avram could see famous landmarks, things he only knew from pictures, the statues, the river, the spires, the nouveau entrances to the Metro stations. In every direction were parts of a setting he had only dreamed of, and here he was now, unable to take a part of it or appreciate it properly. He felt the resentment build inside.

They pulled up in front of the hotel, and Avram could only be impressed by the grandeur. Red awnings stretched out over the street and all above were floors and floors of little curved balconies, window boxes full of flowers. Liveried doormen stood on either side of the entrance, and as Max and Selena exited the cab, they rushed forward to assist with the luggage. Within moments they were inside a marbled lobby all chandeliers and floral arrangements. Avram stood inside just looking; the place was way out of his league.

"And tonight?" asked Max, stepping up to Avram, his own registration routine already done.

"I think I just want to spend some time alone," he said.

"Not dinner?"

No, I'll be fine. I'll just order something in."

"Well, if you're sure," he said. "We plan to head out about 9:00. You can meet up with us again then. Down here? We'll catch the Metro out there. Have to change once, but it's not too far. This is Paris after all. What do you do in Paris apart from eat, and of course shop?"

Avram merely nodded in response. He knew he wouldn't have a choice.

He went through check in procedures with a sense of unreality and then was shown to his room without properly registering what was going on. Left alone, he looked around the room itself. Out the window, he could see the Tour Eiffel, silhouetted against the later afternoon sky, thrusting up above the wrought iron of his own little balcony, the floor to ceiling windows open to the view. He dropped his bag on the bed and simply sat, not knowing what he was supposed to do. Instead of unpacking, he pulled out his guidebook again and read in detail about the cemetery they were supposed to be visiting in the morning. The place was vast—44 hectares and 70,000 tombs. When Selena said she was going to visit dead people, she hadn't been kidding. They were already too late today; the place closed at 6:00. He shut the book and placed it flat on the bed.

Slowly, Avram unpacked, at the very end, seeking out the necklace, unwrapping it and holding it, his fingers wrapped around it. Having it there, in contact with his palm gave him some sense of comfort. He didn't know why. He pulled his closed hand closer, pressing it against the very center of his chest and breathed in and out several times. He felt the calm washing through him. He sat there at the end of the bed, reluctant to let go of what he held.

Briefly, he thought about the children, about what they would be doing tonight. It could be that they would accompany their parents to dinner, but then, after that? Would they be out and about, roaming the streets seeking more to add to their group? Even if they were, there was very little that Avram could do about it. He looked back out the window, watching the slowly darkening sky. He looped the cord around his fingers, threading it in and out between them.

After a while, he did just as he had said and ordered something from room service, something that would cost him an arm and a leg, but not an entire mortgage as some of the dishes cost. When it eventually arrived, he ate his burger slowly, picking at the fries and barely tasting a single bite. He left the tray outside the room, then locked himself away. Eventually, he slept, the necklace clutched between his hands held firmly right in the center of his chest.

Having spent an undisturbed night, Avram arose, carefully placed the necklace in the safe, looking at it longingly for a few moments before closing the door and keying in the code, waiting as the safe door whirred and finally signified that it was locked. He showered, dressed, still barely believing as he stood in the middle of the luxurious bathroom that he was even in this place. Feeling that he at least looked halfway presentable, he made his way down to the lobby to meet the others. They were there waiting for him when he arrived.

A short walk up to Franklin D. Roosevelt, right there on the Avenue des Champs-Élysées and they descended to the Metro station. The platform and the connecting set of passageway were full of tourists and Avram and the others were barely out of place. They boarded the train, Line 9 and after a few stops, arrived at Republique where they changed again to Line 3 which would take them right to Père Lachaise. Three more stops and they were there. They emerged from the station and wandered down to stand in front of the stone entrance, a square gate with twin constructions on either side, with words and carvings. Pausing for a moment just to look at them, as a group they entered the cemetery proper.

Tree-lined cobbled pathways led off into the distance in each direction within the high stone walls, and on every side stood graves, mausoleums, statues, stretching as far as the eye could see. Just inside the gate was a large map, showing sections, lettered and with a key to notable gravesites. Avram stepped up to it, scanned the listings. They were all here, the great and good of literature, theatre, art, music. There were several he thought he'd like to see: Proust, Wilde, even Jim Morrison, he thought. He turned to Max and Selena.

"What now?" he said.

"Well, we intend to wander around, look at some of the special sites. It's up to you I guess. You can come with us, or …"

"That's fine," said Avram. "I guess I'll be okay on my own."

256

"So, shall we meet up?"

"No, that's okay," said Avram. "I can find my way back to the hotel, I think."

Selena narrowed her eyes for an instant, but then the look faded.

He glanced at the children, but they were staring off into the graveyard itself, seemingly fixed on something. There was a look of almost expectation on their faces. Avram watched them all as they departed, heading off towards the left, feeling relieved as they disappeared from view. Avram chose a direction, heading a completely different way from that which the Greens had taken.

As he wandered through the shadow-dappled pathways, some of them more cared-for than others, up and down steps, the smell of vegetation and old stone and earth all around him, he felt a growing sense of unease. Grave after grave, monument after monument passed by him, the stone faded, chipped in places, the marks of lichen and old moss patterning the stonework with darkened blotches. Blank eyes stared at him, or past him, an angel with half a face. He stepped up to one tomb, and there, behind an iron gate sat a picture of a small child, rendered in stained glass, surrounded in deep blue. He stepped back from the doorway with a chill. All around him were the legacy of death, a thousand sightless eyes tracking his progress. He swallowed back the sense of unease and kept walking. Though it was late morning, the sun beating down, the overhanging branches and thick trunks filled the pathways with shadowed gloom.

The paths seemed to go on and on forever. He climbed up steps and descended, passing graves long forgotten, visited by no one in particular. And he was struck with a sense of sadness, the reality that was mortality, nothing left but crumbling bones encased within crumbling and broken stone. Was this all we had to look forward to?

Eventually, more by accident than design, he came upon the tomb of Oscar Wilde. Done in pinkish granite in an Egyptian style deco sphinx, there was already a crowd gathered. He stood watching them as a couple of young girls leaned forward and placed their lips upon the stone. He stepped closer. All over the monument's stone surface, there were lipstick marks. He shook his head and turned away. He considered briefly how such rituals might come into being. There was no logic to them. Nor was there any sense of what they might actually achieve. He wandered away again, pausing at one grave, then another, reading the writing engraved on stones, or leaning closer to puzzle out that which had faded with the passage of time.

He kept remembering that look on Samantha and Alfred's faces. Something was special about this place. No, that was wrong, he corrected himself. There was something special about this place, but it was more than that. There was something about it that was important to Samantha and Alfred. All of them, Max, Selena, even himself, they were here for a reason.

Without realizing it, he had already spent a couple of hours here. He glanced at his watch surprised and then turned around and around where he stood, trying to get a sense of direction. The place was so vast that it was easy for him to lose himself among the paths and alleyway. He turned in the direction that he thought the entrance might lie, digging in his pocket for the metro tickets that max had handed over to him.

He needed to get back to the hotel. He needed to prepare for what was going to come, and by now, he was almost certain that something was going to come. He remembered the People's Palace in Bucharest, the events that had taken place there, the collection of children. Somehow, she seemed to be drawn to places with a history of death, and here, he thought, here had a grand history. Setting his jaw with a new resolve, he picked up his pace. He would be ready this time. He didn't care about the Louvre, about the Eiffel Tower, about anything else now, though they might be there on offer. He simply needed to be prepared and the knowledge was burning inside him.

TWENTY-EIGHT

A raven, the bird that helpeth gods,
In my right hand I hold;
A hawk, to flutter in thine evil face,
In my left hand I thrust forward.

-Babylonian Tablet

Back at the hotel, he knew what he needed to do.

He needed to remember.

Whatever had happened to him in the meantime was still lost within a fog, a fog full of holes and absences. He crossed to the safe, opened it and withdrew the necklace. Clutching it within his hands, he sat at the end of the bed, his thumbs stroking the stone's surface, willing himself to replay the events of the last several days. It was difficult; so much had happened that it was like one confused blur of images and events, not to mention the seemingly deliberate gaps in his memory.

He thought back through Zurich and before, back to Budapest, turning the recollections first one way and then the other, trying to give them shape and form. He went back further, Bucharest, Istanbul, the ship, reliving the events in reverse. He strained, driving sharpness through his thoughts, and all the while keeping his hands firmly closed around the necklace. It had to be the key, he was convinced of it. He thought back further to that first city where this had all started, back to Tel Aviv, back to those old stone walls and the harbour, the accumulation of history and the ages. There had been a particular building, a lost stop before they….

Since that time back in the city of Tel Aviv, he had been struggling with the memories, trying to rip away at the tissue thin veils that obscured his recollections. But now, here with the stone in his hand, came clarity, a clearing of his perceptions and his mind. He pushed at it, willing himself to replay the scene, that first encounter, the exact place and time when he had first acquired the necklace.

He played the memory back in his head, the stone tower extending down into the depths of the earth, the young girl, his first encounter.

And then, suddenly it was so clear.

"No," said the girl. "Please take this off." She indicated the small pendant around her neck.

"I don't understand. Can't you do it?"

"I'm not allowed. I cannot wear it in there." She gestured at the darkened hole that seemed to swallow light.

She couldn't do it! Avram savored the memory. That was important. She couldn't do it.

Avram shook his head and reached for the necklace. This child was becoming more and more strange. He sighed. Whatever he had to do to get this over with now. He didn't want to offend the child. It was as if the weight of ages contained in the chamber stilled any protest. He lifted the thin cord past her hair and over her head, letting the tiny stone dangle between his outstretched hands.

"Haaaah," the child said with a gentle exhalation of breath.

The last he could see, vivid as if it had just occurred. He lifted the necklace and looked at it, examining it. He lifted the stone and ran his thumb over the surface.

Breath. Everything was about breath. He could hear that exhalation, the touch of wind upon his skin.

And then? And then he had been lost. His awareness of where he was and what had happened, vague.

He remembered seeing the necklace lying on the bare stone floor, stooping to scoop it up and then absent-mindedly shoving it into his pocket. It had been with him ever since.

Very, very carefully, he took the stone, placed it back in his pocket. His sense of certainty was starting to grow, along with his determination. The Professor in Budapest, the clues, all of them had been there. Avram had just been unable to grasp them, whether it was because of her and the influence she exerted or something else.

All he had to do now was wait.

Even though there was nothing else to do, the tension he was feeling inside kept him alert, expectant as he sat, waiting for what he believed was inevitable.

He was not surprised when the slight tapping came at his door.

It was almost 11:00. Had so much time passed?

Avram stood and placed the necklace cautiously into his pocket, careful to remove his hand before crossing to the door, severing contact. He opened the door a crack and looked out to see Samantha there looking up at him. She was wearing a white dress, one that he knew now that he'd seen before.

"It is time to come, Uncle Avram," she said.

Avram bit his lip and simply nodded, stepping out into the hallway and shutting the door behind him. Samantha reached up and took his hand within her own, leading him gently but insistently down the corridor and towards the elevators. He struggled to keep his breathing, the pounding of his heart under control. He struggled too with the urge to thrust the child's hand away from his own. He had to play this out now. He had no other choice. Whatever meaning their apparent ritual had, he needed to be there, right in the midst. It was the only way he could be sure of gaining the access to her, to try to put a stop to this once and for all.

Samantha led him out through the lobby, on to the street, and up towards the Metro station that they had taken earlier in the day. Of Max, Selena and Alfred, there was no sign. Samantha and he were clearly alone. Briefly, he wondered what had happened to them. Within a couple of minutes they were at the Metro, and they descended, and she drew him along to the very same platform where they had caught the train before. So far, it looked like Avram's suspicions were correct. Simply waiting to see what happened next, he allowed himself to be led onto the train, and not even bothering to sit, he grabbed one of the hanging straps and stood there as the train whirred along through stop after stop. Again they changed line, boarded the next train and when they reached the stop, exited. Samantha drew him out through the station barriers and up to the street itself. This late, there was little sign of life. The streets were quiet, a vast contrast to how they had been, full or tourists and visitors, simply thronged with people. The streets themselves were slick with evening damp as she led him along away from the station and towards the cemetery's gates. There was simply no one around, no one, and Avram felt the trepidation rising inside him.

The familiar gates stood open, revealing darkness and shadows behind, dim pathways leading off into further darkness. There was no reason for the gates to be open, and yet they were. Swallowing back his fear, Avram allowed himself to be led forward and inside the cemetery grounds proper, into the darkness and shadow. All around him, vague shapes clustered, the whiteness of stone bleeding through the dark to give smudged forms and hints of movement where there was none. Samantha continued walking forward, Avram's hand held firmly within her own small fingers, uttering not a word. On every side, there was the rustle of leaves, and other, unidentifiable sounds stirring unseen between the graves. Still she led him further into the cemetery's depths.

The child turned up a pathway, and though it was difficult to see, Avram felt the ground rising, twigs and leaves crackling underfoot atop an uneven surface. His eyes strained to pierce the gloom, but all he could see was vague impressions. After what seemed an eternity, Samantha led him to a more open area atop the rise, free of trees. Lines of gravestones stretched out in front of him to either side. Here, out from beneath the trees, moonlight illuminated some of the more polished stonework, sending a pale light across the space.

There, right in the middle of the space, stood four figures, clearly defined in the moonlight. He knew those shapes. Samantha continued to draw him forward. There was a space in the center clear of graves and in the middle of it stood Max to one side and Selena on the other. They stared off into the darkness blankly, their expressions emotionless, their eyes wide. Between them stood Alfred, decked out in a dark suit, and beside him, one step forward, stood the girl child Lilith, dressed in just the same way as when he'd first seen her. Come to think of it, he had never seen her dressed in any other way. Avram shook his hand free and took a step towards her, leaving Samantha behind him, his heart in his throat.

"Welcome, Avram," said the girl in front of him. Lilith he had to keep reminding himself. She was no girl. She was no child, and she never had been.

She spread her arms wide in an expansive gesture. From every side of the square open space, from behind trees and gravestones and tombs stepped children, moving in towards the center with slow step. All of the girls were dressed in identical white dresses, all of the boys in the same dark suits.

Avram swallowed and took another step forwards, his mind racing, trying desperately not to think. Who knew if she could read what was going on inside his head?

All around, the children grew closer.

"You have done well," she said. "You, Avram Davis and these, my children. Soon, you will travel from this place to another and spread our blessing further."

She slowly lowered her arms and fixed him with her gaze. He felt the numbness spreading through him.

He took another step towards her.

Lilith looked to either side of her, scanning the children approaching on every side, and then at Max and Selena.

"These ones will travel far overseas. You, Avram will continue on your path to the next great city, and in so doing, you will take me with you as you have. Gently, gently, the cattle will become mine."

Struggling, Avram took another step, forcing his limbs to obey him.

Around him, the children started a low moan, like a wind through branches, seeming to fill the entire space with sound.

Despite the difficulty of moving now, he summoned up the effort of will required to move his head. The black suited boys and the girls in their white dresses were all around, so many of them, so many more than there had been in Bucharest. All of them, their eyes glowed faintly with an inner light, and all around him, their voices swelled and faded as one in a low moan like the sound of the wind.

Lilith raised her arms and he turned to face her. She beckoned him forward. Step by reluctant step, his feet feeling leaden, he grew closer.

"Come, let me embrace you Avram Davis. Come and feel my breath."

His heart was pounding in his ears, his chest filled with cold, despite the warmth of the air that seemed to stir around him, breathing on his skin and through his hair like a desert wind.

He knew what he had to do. He hoped beyond hope that he was right. He judged he was close enough now. He was virtually right in front of her. She wanted him there and that was all that he needed. Summoning every last vestige of his will, he lowered his hand into his pocket, made contact with the necklace and drew it forth.

Lilith's eyes went wide and then immediately narrowed. Her mouth opened wide and she breathed out a long hissing breath, her teeth evident in the pale light, her lips drawn back in anger. There was nothing in that face left that belonged to a child. This was Lilith and Avram knew, he knew then that he was lost.

He felt the cold pain blossoming in his chest, in his belly. His limbs felt encased in ice. He could not move. He cried out, once, a strangled yell and then again. The pressure, the agony drilled through him, tearing at his being. He summoned his concentration, what remained of his will, drawing from the pendant everything he could, trying desperately to hold on to nothing more than himself. He could not fail. He must not fail.

The air battered at him then, whipping all around his body and he staggered back. The sound of the children's voices grew all around him. Fighting with everything he had he forced himself forward, one step, then another. She screamed at him, the sound of her voice attempting to drive him back again.

Summoning the last shreds of what remained of his volition, the remaining vestiges of his strength, Avram threw himself forward, the necklace held before him at arm's length, and then with every effort he could muster, he thrust it over her head, letting it drop from his near lifeless hands as he staggered to the ground.

She cried out then, a deep howling protest coming from deep within her. She looked down at the object around her neck, touching it, her face screwing up in anguish, and then, in the next instant, she began losing substance, becoming paler, her form turning to dark wisps, being blown apart on the breeze and dissipating into the moonlit sky above them. The last to go where her eyes, staring into him in accusation.

"What the hell?" It was Max's voice and Avram turned to look at him.

Avram still had his arms stretched before him, supporting him on the cold ground, and gradually, hesitantly, he drew them back and sat, then slowly pushed himself to his feet.

"What the hell?" said Max again. "Where the hell are we? What is this?"

All around them, children were looking around aimlessly, blankly and in confusion and one by one starting to drift away. Towards the back of the square, a little girl started to cry. Across the other side, a boy began to wail.

"Mama," said Samantha and ran to Selena's side, clutching at her clothes.

"Yes, baby, I'm here," said Selena, stroking the back of her hair with one hand.

Slowly, slowly, Avram looked around, searching, not quite knowing what he was looking for, but looking all the same.

There was nothing left to do here, nothing left to see.

He turned away from the Greens, and carefully, he started to pick his way between the gravestone and towards a path that would lead him away from this place. Out and away from here forever.

Breath

"Avram?" said Max. "Avram, what the hell is … where are you going? These children. We need to do something. Avram?"

Avram simply lifted one hand, and then kept walking hesitantly away from what had just happened. What became of all these children now was the last thing on his mind. He'd done enough. He'd saved them hadn't he?

TWENTY-NINE

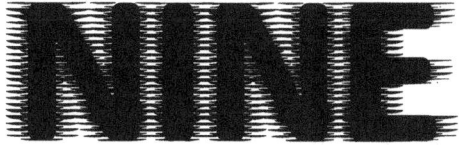

Free me now from the burden of living, for it is terrible to be brought back from the dead.

—16th C German Folk Tale.

Breath

It was over, or at least it was over for now. Avram had to believe that he had accomplished what he had set out to do when he ventured out for the cemetery. Lilith had been sent back to where she had come from. She was gone, banished to some place of darkness from whence she came, from where Avram himself had been instrumental in freeing her. At least she was gone until she found some other unwitting soul to unleash her upon the world again along with the Shedim that came with her, the Lilim, her children, or at least he hoped so. He had no way of knowing, but he had seen what he had seen.

And now, what was there for him? He didn't know. He really didn't know.

He entered the metro station not even knowing if the last train had already left. There, on the platform, he was relieved to see the last train was still five minutes away. He stood there just staring at the opposite platform, numb, until the whir, clank, and hiss of the approaching train shook him out of his fugue. He clambered aboard, vaguely registering the number of stops he needed to pass before he would reach his destination. It was but ten stations to Opera where he would need to get off. It should only take him about fifteen minutes, and then he would need to walk.

Avram wound his way back through the streets of Paris to his hotel, still in a semi daze. He found his room and collapsed into his bed, fading almost immediately to a troubled and restless sleep. He awoke still troubled, wondering what he was really going to do. Over the past few days, he had lost several of his friends, never to be seen again. Aggie, he could imagine, would never want anything to do with him ever. And Max and Selena, the children? He really didn't want to see them again either. Perhaps it was cold, unfeeling, but it was much about self-preservation as anything else. To relive the experiences of the last few days would be too much. They too, had been his friends; but he would never be able to forget what they had become and he would spend the rest of his life seeking signs that it had truly been purged. In the interim, Lilith had taken his will, his freedom and she had robbed him of whatever remained of the shreds of his life. She was gone now, but so was everything else, everything Avram had been trying to hold on to and ultimately rebuild. He had at least a life, whether there was anything to look forward to or not. He had repaired the damage that he had been responsible for back in that faraway city, or at least he hoped he had. Perhaps all those children would go back to whatever lives they had been living and grow and mature as normal.

In the meantime, he could go back, try to reconstruct the remaining fragments of his life.

And if she ever came back, if some poor soul released her again … what then? Would he still be bound to her? Would she seek him out? He recalled that last look of accusation and he thought again about how the Professor back in Budapest had described her. She had existed for centuries. She was sure to be patient.

He simply didn't dare to think about that.

Not now.

Not ever again.

He didn't even spare a thought for the small amulet that had tumbled from the dissipating shreds that had for a while been the corporeal form of Lilith. It now lay forgotten on a lichen covered gravestone in the middle of a vast cemetery that he had gratefully left behind, and simply waited.

About the Author

Jackson Creed writes generally dark fiction that has had outings in a few venues to date. He lives somewhere in the wilds of Europe and rarely ventures out of his cave. This is his first novel.